I0600942

Feeding Frenzy

Loon Lake Magic, Volume 1

Maaja Wentz

Published by Loon Lake, 2018.

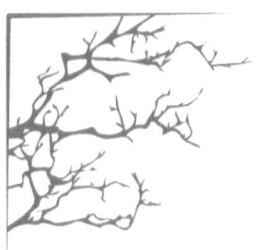

AWAKENING

S he searched the body carefully, cleaned it, spelled it with wards, and sealed it in what was supposed be his eternal tomb. She used a backhoe to bury him under the Great Ash, below the subsoil where nothing lived.

By charm or chance, she overlooked the spore he had hidden in his ear.

At this depth, the ground didn't freeze but water went where it liked, dissolving minerals, and wearing down stone. It took years for the first crack to split his cement prison. Greedy, hair-like shoots converged on this weak point, forcing the concrete aside thread by thread. The Entity emerged over weeks and months, an expanding mass of unnatural shoots that only knew *up*.

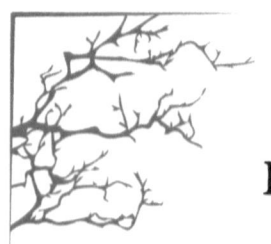

LEAF PENDANT

Tonya chopped carrots like it meant revenge. She should have been hap-py. Accepted into University of Toronto, she could finally leave Loon Lake behind—except her parents had other plans.

The doorbell rang. High heels clicked across tiled floor with a familiar rhythm that made Tonya smile.

"Hello this place!" Her aunt's voice rang out.

Tonya let the knife drop to the cutting board and dashed to the front hall.

She saw dark circles under her aunt's eyes, which contrasted with her snowy hair. "How are you?" asked Tonya.

"Is she expecting me?"

Tonya shook her head. "This is an emergency."

Aunt Helen squared her shoulders, grown angular in recent months. "Tell me."

Tonya led her to the living room. "My registration slot starts tomorrow at 2:00. I have until then to convince them I should go to Toronto."

"That's between you and your parents." Helen crossed her arms, exactly like Mom did. In childhood pictures, before Aunt Helen's hair suddenly went white, the Lennox sisters looked like twins.

"Talk to them. Even Dad thinks I should stay here when U of T has twice as much of everything. They know I want to study in Toronto."

"Why don't you?"

"They're paying."

"Loon Lake is cheaper, but it can't just be the money."

"Agreed, but they won't budge. It's like they're terrified of Toronto. Talk to them? I know you can persuade them." Tonya didn't say charm them, but her unspoken plea hung in the air.

Her aunt sighed. "I should go."

"Stay for dinner. I need you to back me up."

"If Barbara says okay."

"Help me finish cooking and she'll have to."

In the kitchen, Tonya put on an indie playlist and chopped to the beat while her aunt peeled potatoes.

The music stopped.

Tonya's mother stared at them from the kitchen doorway. "Helen?"

Aunt Helen offered Mom a small smile. "Sorry to barge in on you. Tonya invited me."

"How's your health?" Her mother approached Helen cautiously.

"Fine." It was a polite lie.

"How's the store?"

"Still living the dream." Helen's pale face looked drawn opposed to her sister's apple cheeks. In contrast to Aunt Helen's tidy ponytail, Mom let her dark hair flow over her shoulders. Tonya wondered if they had ever done anything the same. Her mother was the good girl. She detested magic and spent her time baking for community events. Aunt Helen defied her anti-magic Pure family, until the mayor exiled her when she was a few years older than Tonya.

Mom rolled up her sleeves. "You'd better stay. Tonya's making orange chicken."

The three women peeled and chopped silently until Aunt Helen bundled the peelings onto her cutting board and walked to the green bin.

The lid raised itself as Helen tipped the waste in.

Her mother's jaw dropped. "What are you doing?"

The bin lid quivered under her aunt's spell then dropped with a slam.

"Nobody can see us here. Don't make a fuss."

"Not in my house. There will be no magic in this house!"

Aunt Helene shrugged.

"You're not even sorry! Leave."

"You're looking good, Barbara. Say hi to Jim for me." As she left the kitchen, Aunt Helen told Tonya to "have fun at school."

Tonya walked her to the door.

On the stoop, Aunt Helen paused. "It's time you had this." She slipped a golden pendant, shaped like a leaf, into Tonya's hand.

Tonya held the necklace under the porch light. "It's beautiful. Is it antique?"

"Yep, a real family heirloom. Promise you'll wear it?"

"Of course. I love it!" Tonya gave her a hug.

Aunt Helen held on a little too long. "Don't worry. University won't be like high school."

"I wish you could stay."

"It doesn't matter."

"Stay."

"Oh, Tonya. You're better off without me."

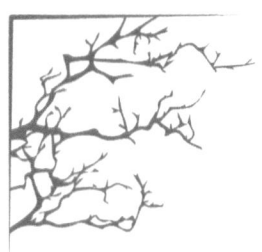

PRIYA

Tonya lined up outside the Loon Lake University registrar's office. Courses had already started, and she had been trying for weeks to get out of a third-year physics class and into the first-year English class she was supposed to be taking. How did these screw-ups happen? Torn between defying her parents and attending University of Toronto, or relenting and going to Loon Lake, she had waited until the last moment and chosen her courses in a rush. She was so flustered she had clicked the wrong selection and now the course she wanted was full.

It wasn't a long lineup, but it was moving so slowly she would need a haircut soon. Breakfast was hours ago. Tonya's stomach grumbled for lunch. She shouldn't even be here except the computer system had mysteriously rejected her password and wouldn't allow a reset.

She had tried phoning and email but couldn't get a reply from anybody. When things got this messed up, Aunt Helen always said, "face-to-face is best."

Aunt Helen's preference for face-to-face wasn't completely innocent. As a child, Tonya's parents had kept her aunt's powers secret. It wasn't until the summer Tonya went to work in her aunt's Herbal Healing Shop that the clients told her everything. One lady credited Aunt Helen with changing her life in grade six. A mean girl bullied her every day so one night, Aunt Helen had charmed the neighborhood dogs to howl under the bully's window and keep her awake all night. The next morning at school, when she threatened to keep doing it, the bully promised to reform.

Too bad Tonya's family were Purists, the strictest of Loon Lake's magic factions. Like the Trads, they kept magic from outsiders, but they also forbade its study. It was a rule her aunt chose to ignore.

Aunt Helen could have charmed Tonya up to the front of the line. Tonya sighed. After their aborted dinner, her aunt hadn't answered texts or calls.

Mom admitted she was seeing specialists but would say no more. Ever since Aunt Helen insisted on kissing her and giving her that pendant, Tonya suspected the worst.

Ahead of Tonya, a girl with shiny black hair streaked with purple raised her hands over her head and posed, as if she just finished a gymnastics routine. Next, she put her hands on her hips and thrust back her shoulders like a comic book hero. When the girl started conducting an invisible orchestra, Tonya couldn't help but ask, "What are you doing?"

The girl turned, revealing a pretty, brown, heart-shaped face, nestled in a mane of black and purple curls. "I'm claiming my power. You must see this Ted Talk." She held her phone out to Tonya. "Women lose marks in school and fail in business because they get meek around assertive men."

"Hmm," Tonya wasn't that interested in the video, but she was fascinated by a girl who wasn't embarrassed to do crazy things in public.

"I'm Tonya."

"Priya." She reached out and shook Tonya's hand like they were grown-ups which, Tonya supposed, they were.

"What are you in for?"

"Huh?"

Priya grinned. "What are you studying?"

"English and History."

"Whose history?"

"Local history." There was a three hundred-year-old schism between the founding families of Loon Lake. History class would be an excuse to visit City Hall's archives and read about the feuding, in the words of the individuals who started it.

"That sounds absolutely fascinating." Priya chuckled.

Tonya didn't blame her. To an outsider, the history of Loon Lake must sound yawn-worthy.

The line snailed forward. "So, what should I take instead?"

"Take Feminist Theory in Popular Culture, with me." On her phone, she showed Tonya the course description.

"That's a second-year course."

"I'm a quick study. I just have to convince the registrar." She smiled.

Tonya caught herself envying Priya's perfect teeth and striking looks. Her clothes were straight out of a Gothic novel, all black chiffon and Victorian lace. Definitely not department store stuff. If university was going to be a new beginning, Tonya wanted interesting friends like her, people who didn't remember her eating lunch alone in the high school library.

The line moved, and it was Tonya's turn, but Priya was taking different subjects. Their paths might not cross again for weeks.

"Wait, after this, do you want to go for lunch?"

Priya flashed her perfect teeth. "Thought you'd never ask."

"How about Mackenzie Cafeteria?"

"Sure."

Loon Lake University grouped students according to their passions and vocations. Students interested in native studies and the environment were housed in one college. Future leaders and politically active students lived in another. Nursing students shared space with students interested in science and agriculture.

"What's your major?" Tonya asked Priya as she walked her bike along the path back to the dorms.

"Fine arts."

"So, you're at Mackenzie too."

"Top floor," said Priya.

"I'm on the third."

Tonya left her bike on the rack outside and entered the main floor cafeteria, watching for her roommate, Lynette. With lecture halls on the second floor, and their dorm room on the third, she was always running into her. With her cool new friend in tow, Lynette was the last person she wanted to see.

As they lined up with their trays, Tonya checked for messages from her parents or Aunt Helen. Both numbers went straight to voicemail. That was unusual for Dad but not for Aunt Helen. For good measure she sent them each a text. *Why weren't they responding*?

The line moved forward, and she handed the cashier her meal plan card. After lunch she would try again.

"One thing about Mackenzie," said Priya as they sat at a table, "if I sleep in, I can go downstairs and catch my first lecture in my PJs."

"No tromping through snow." Tonya knew too well what to expect from winter in the region. It was one of the reasons she had wanted to study in Toronto. At least her parents had insisted she stay on campus.

"So, tell me about Loon Lake, local girl." Priya smiled encouragingly.

"It's a pretty little city."

"Picturesque. What else?"

"The Village of Loon Lake is hundreds of years old."

"Any original buildings still around? I'd love to take some pictures," said Priya.

"The new part of town is much nicer. Have you visited the farmer's market?"

"Who wants to photograph vegetables? I want to visit Loon Lake Cemetery. The city website says there are tombstones 300 years old."

"What's so great about that?" Tonya didn't like the way Priya's eyes lit up when she said cemetery. There were good reasons to keep outsiders from getting too interested in that place. "Anything else you want to see?"

"There's this tall log cabin on Kenny Road. I saw it when I drove in from Toronto."

"That would be my aunt's Herbal Healing Shop."

"We could visit both."

"It's just a boring store."

"With interesting architecture."

"If you like log cabins we should go to the Ice House. They used to cut blocks of ice out of the lake in the winter and store them in sawdust all summer. It's more authentic than the store."

Priya took a bite of her veggie lasagna before she answered. "I should warn you, when somebody tells me not to do something, that's exactly what I want to do."

"Then let's hit the cemetery, right after lunch."

"No way!" Priya laughed. "I have class. In fact," she checked her phone, "I'm almost late. What's your number?"

Priya stayed long enough to add Tonya's contact info before rushing to class. The moment Priya headed for the staircase at the opposite end of the building, Tonya called her Dad.

No answer. Not good.

With the weird way her family wouldn't discuss Aunt Helen's illness, Tonya feared her Mom was protecting her from something she considered worse than disease—magic.

Between classes, Tonya called Loon Lake Hospital, but Aunt Helen hadn't been admitted. Tonya rode her bike west through campus and cut through the cemetery, coming out through a small break in the tall, wrought iron fence opposite the shop. She crossed the small field between cemetery and store only to find the closed sign posted. Tonya knocked but nobody answered. She tried phoning, but her aunt's mailbox was full. It seemed Tonya wasn't the only one who couldn't reach Aunt Helen.

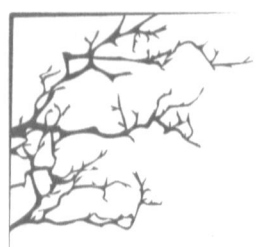

TEAM SPIRIT

Tonya shivered as she lined up at the high board for her chance to try out. The Diving Team was supposed to be an escape from stress, but it wasn't turning out that way. Instead of concentrating on preparing for her dive, all she could think about was family. A couple of days ago, she had received an email from her aunt saying everything was fine. At least she was alive, but since then she hadn't responded to texts or email.

Ahead of her, divers in their Tyr and Speedo suits looked slim and twice as muscular as Tonya. She took a deep breath and tried to visualize herself spinning perfect somersaults above the trampoline. She loved the weightless feeling of bouncing high into the air, and had spent the summer practicing. Varsity represented a new, athletic life for her, something she'd never had before. Could she belong here? Ahead of her, girls with perfect, tanned bodies executed dive after dive. Her turn was coming, much too fast.

When a short, hard-bodied girl cut in ahead of her it was a relief, until the girl smirked back in Tonya's face.

"You? In a swimsuit? Try not to belly flop, Freak."

Tonya placed her hands over her stomach. It was Marta, Donna Ashton's daughter. Donna and her beef-shouldered brothers thought the Trads foolish for concealing magic from the Mundanes, but Marta was worse. She called Pures like Tonya freaks for denying their supernatural abilities.

With bullies like Marta, offense was the best defense. "How do I know you're not going to cheat?"

"I don't need magic to beat you, Freak." Marta climbed to the top of the board and stepped gracefully to the edge.

Tonya watched Marta execute two and a half reverse somersaults with two and a half twists in pike position. Perfectly, of course. Tonya's best dive was two somersaults with a twist. Would that be good enough to make the team? She wiped her palms on the front of her swimsuit. If she failed, Marta would tell every Mod in town.

Legs trembling, she mounted the ten-meter ladder. At the top, she tried not to look down. Somehow, practicing her spins on the trampoline never gave her the same vertigo standing on the platform did. It was a long way down and Marta's stupid comments had activated a chorus of internal doubts.

She couldn't do it, not with everyone staring at her. The pool below seemed to move to the left while the diving platform felt like it tilted beneath her feet. Her toes tensed on the emery board surface of the platform, and she fought the urge to retreat. Tonya couldn't look down. Were the chlorine fumes making her dizzy?

Unwilling to face the drop, she turned her back to the pool and launched into unrehearsed reverse somersaults. She spun two, three times, then stretched out to enter the water, catching it at a harsh angle that sent her off to the side. She touched bottom meters from the center.

When she surfaced, Tonya imagined all eyes on her as she performed a slow front crawl to the ladder. Head down, she got out and crossed the deck to retrieve her swim bag, too rattled to make a second attempt. On her way to the change room, one person applauded behind her.

"Nice try! Good job."

Tonya recognized Marta's voice but didn't look back.

In the showers, Tonya stretched out her shoulders under the hot spray. She toweled off and retreated to the side of the change room farthest from the girls wearing Varsity swimsuits. Clearly, she would not be joining them. Once dressed, she grabbed her bag and went to the bathroom mirror to brush her hair.

She was about to leave when she heard retching coming from the toilets behind her. She hoped the girl inside was okay. Tonya looked under the stall door and saw a pair of knees on the floor. Somebody was throwing up. Maybe somebody even more nervous about the tryouts than she was.

"Are you alright?"

"I'm fine!" The voice was sharp and harsh.

"Can I help?"

"No."

The heaving resumed. Tonya stood between the sink and stalls of the cramped bathroom. What was the etiquette for a situation like this? Should she walk away? What if the girl passed out?

"Do you want me to call someone to drive you home?" Tonya was head-down, fumbling in her bag for her phone, when the bathroom stall door flew open, knocking her back. She staggered and grabbed the sink for balance. When she opened her eyes, a slightly green face glared at her. Marta.

"Seriously, can I help?"

"What made you think you can dive?" Marta pushed past Tonya and went back to the change room where the rest of the team was dressing.

Tonya had to walk past them to reach the exit. As she followed Marta, the other girls went quiet.

Marta turned on her. "If you can't dive, why did you come out?"

"At least I tried."

"Why? You can barely swim. I mean, look at you." Marta was staring at Tonya's plump belly.

"Screw yourself." Tonya loved swimming and she wasn't going to let Marta ruin it for her.

"You dive like my granny."

"I'm a lifeguard. I can save your granny."

The girls murmured.

Marta laughed. "Lifeguards. You're so proud you can do two lengths of the pool, towing a rubber dummy." She looked around at her teammates. Some smiled, but others stared at Marta, which gave Tonya courage.

"Take care of that tummy now, Marta. Wouldn't want you to miss your next practice." Tonya rushed for the door, but Marta stepped into her way. Tonya tried to step left, then right, but Marta blocked the doorway like an enraged imp, her chin jutted up at Tonya.

"My stomach is fine. Don't spread rumors."

"Why, are you pregnant?"

Marta's eyes widened, then her face relaxed. "Don't worry about me, worry about you." The corners of her mouth curved upwards as she stepped back to let Tonya go.

Outside the Athletic Center, chilly October wind whipped wet hair into Tonya's face. She hoped nobody noticed her hands were still trembling as she hoisted her bag onto her shoulder. At the edge of the road, guys from the team were waiting for the girls. She recognized Shin immediately from team photos in the foyer. The tallest in every picture, he usually had his arm around Marta. Tonya thought of telling him Marta was sick, and about the weird way she'd gone after Tonya for noticing, but why? Maybe it didn't mean anything, except that he had terrible taste in girlfriends.

She wished she had come by bike, so she could leave. Tonya took a deep breath and let it out slowly. Priya would get here soon. The move into residence had been so rushed in September that Priya was helping her collect her last boxes.

Tonya's house was in the new part of town, on the opposite side of Loon Lake as the university. Her parents had put it up for sale the same day Tonya moved into residence. It was weird, and she tried not to feel hurt about it, but it still stung. First, her parents wouldn't let her go to school out of town "for her own protection," and now they had left town themselves? They said it was because Aunt Helen would be in and out of hospital for tests in Toronto, and they wanted to get a condo nearby. It would make sense, if they didn't hate the big city.

Tonya couldn't imagine Aunt Helen abandoning the Herbal Healing Shop. This illness was serious, no matter how many times her mother downplayed it. Tonya wanted to see for herself, but every time she emailed, asking to visit her aunt in Toronto, her parents refused to tell her which hospital she was in. "You're safer close to home," they replied. "Aunt Helen will get better and then she'll visit you."

If her parents weren't so blind, she would be going to U of T and be able to see Aunt Helen any time she liked.

The sound of a car horn startled her out of her reverie. Tonya dashed to her friend's rusty Toyota and got in.

"Sorry I'm late. Baby didn't want to start." Priya patted the old car's dashboard. "Aren't you cold?"

"Like a wet cat."

"How was the tryout?"

"A lot like high school."

"Boring, stupid, and full of pimples?'

"You must have gone to a *good* high school."

"Uh oh. Somebody needs to escape the past, fast." She cranked the radio and opened the windows as they pulled onto the highway. "Let's speed dry it outta your hair."

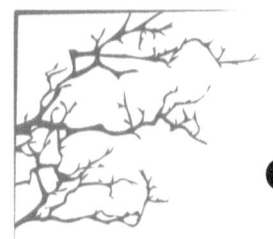

CONSPIRATORS

Donna sat at the kitchen table with her brother, Marvin, who was doing their accounts on a laptop.

"He won by a landslide, again." Marvin pushed silver specs up on his nose. He was tall and broad-shouldered in a white polo, accessorized by a pencil over his ear.

Donna shrugged. "People like Mayor Thornton. He never does anything." From her bag, she extracted a mirror, and a crimson lipstick which she applied precisely. "Things will change when we're in charge." She shut the mirror with a snap.

"Between his Trad cronies and gray power, the Mundanes might as well be running the town." Marvin ran a hand through his brush cut, knocking the pencil to the kitchen floor. "He's approved another nursing home. Doesn't he understand what that does to us?"

"Our day's coming."

A man strode in, Paul Bunyan with a cell phone. He waved it at his siblings. "Have you seen the election results?"

"Where have you been?" Donna stood, hands on hips. "Marvin's been redoing our projections for hours."

Junior slammed his brother's laptop shut. "You can't fix this with accounting. Time to think big."

"Please, expand our little minds." Donna rolled her eyes at Marvin who reopened his computer and resumed typing.

"Len's coming." Junior glared at Marta. "Play nice."

Without lifting his eyes from his spreadsheet, Marvin said, "You can't trust him."

"At least he doesn't sit on his ass while the Trads run things." Junior dropped into a chair next to his brother, his comic book muscles straining to escape his red checked shirt. "He's a Mod, and he's got Waldock."

"You're a genius! Why didn't I think of asking for Waldock's help? Oh wait, maybe because he's dead." Marvin shook his head.

Junior stood to face Donna. "What about you? Will you help Len?"

"That depends on what he's offering."

"Waldock, in total control."

"I'll believe that when I see it," she said.

"But he needs your support . . ."

Donna palm-blocked Junior and returned to helping Marvin with the accounts.

When Junior tried to object, she turned her back on him. Pouting, he went to stand behind the kitchen counter and started drumming his hands on the marble surface. Next, he picked up a pair of spoons and drummed louder. Marvin kept typing. Junior walked over and tried to catch his brother's eye. Marvin didn't look up. Donna smirked but kept her eyes on the laptop as well. Junior cleared his throat to no avail, then pulled out his phone and started playing a game.

There was a knock at the door and it swung open. A chill breeze reached the kitchen. Limping steps sounded in the hall which Donna strode to intercept.

"This is a pleasant surprise." She brought Len into the open-concept living room adjacent to the kitchen.

"You mean because I'm not dead?" Len lowered himself into a leather chair. His knees wound up higher than his waist, the drape of his loose pants clinging to his skeletal leg. Cancerous growths marred his white-stubbled chin. Against a black leather jacket, his face looked ghostly.

"Can I get you a drink?" asked Donna.

"Ginger ale."

"Sorry. Coffee?"

"My stomach can't take the hard stuff anymore. Tea."

Donna looked up at Junior, standing behind the counter. "You making the tea?"

Junior shook his head.

She strode into the kitchen. "Then shoo!"

Len appeared to shrink as Junior sat next to him on the couch.

"Why are you here?" Marvin hadn't moved from the kitchen table. "We're busy."

Len sighed. "Jack knew things would end in a showdown. As Helen got weaker, she couldn't control him, but the hag wouldn't admit defeat. When she realized she was dying, she was desperate to kill him first."

Junior caressed the knuckles of his left fist. "She won."

"No, we have. I know how to eliminate her, once and for all." The lids drooped over Len's rheumy eyes. "But my strength is failing too."

Marvin's chair scraped as he got to his feet. "I don't understand. You want to kill Helen for revenge?"

"Better. Jack expected her to kill him, so he made a backup plan."

"Which obviously didn't work," said Marvin.

"A plan to bring himself back." Len showed his teeth.

"That's Waldock for you, too tough to take death lying down." Junior knocked his fists together.

Donna crossed her arms. "You're lying."

"He figured out a way to manipulate gravedigger fungus."

Junior quirked his head. "What?"

"An underground fungus that grows into the neural pathways of the dead."

"The nurr—huh?"

"Junior's taken a lot of headshots," said Donna. "Let me translate." She turned to Junior.

"You know, those gray mushrooms that sometimes come up in graveyards."

Junior made a face. "I hate those things, whispering at you and creeping you out."

"To protect burial sites," said Len.

"I don't see the connection," said Donna. "They're harmless—and rare."

"Tell me about it."

Junior shrugged shoulders like mountains in an earthquake. "So, Gravediggers make people hear creepy voices in cemeteries. That's not exactly a weapon."

When Len showed his teeth this time it was almost a smile. "That was before Jack Waldock."

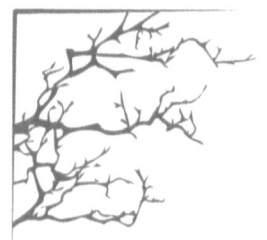

HOME?

Priya drove Tonya away from the Athletic Center. "So, where to?"

"Stay on Lakeshore and keep going west." Wind from Priya's window tossed damp hair into her eyes.

Loon Lake City stood on the northern shore, directly across the lake from campus. Like a pig in a python, Loon River widened into the lake on the western end and shrunk back down to river size to the east.

"How far is it?" asked Priya.

"Imagine Loon Lake is in four quadrants, with the x and y-axes meeting in the center of the lake. My parents live almost straight up the y-axes. I'll tell you when to turn north."

Looking at it that way, campus filled the southeastern and most of the southwestern quadrant, with the cemetery to the west, and Aunt Helen's shop just west of that. Riding her bike through campus from east to west, sometimes Tonya took the southern drive, which passed between the Athletic center lakeside, and the arena to the south. Next, she would pass between the various science buildings, below the stadium and the library, continuing off campus to Kenny Road.

Most of the time, however, she took the northern drive along the lakeshore which passed between the lake and the Rowing Clubhouse, the DNA lab, Environmental Sciences Buildings, and the college residences. It was cooler along the lakeshore and gave her a view across the water to downtown.

Downtown, which wasn't huge, had started to develop along the northern shore of the lake a hundred years ago, then continued north with the construction of the city's first concrete-and-glass buildings in the 1940s.

Lakeshore Drive North followed the north shore, which was flanked by city parks, the farmer's market grounds, and out toward the east and west limits, lakefront estates.

As if anticipating a need for quarantine, Loon Lake hospital was built on cheap land northeast of city limits.

Priya continued west through campus, passing the residences.

As they exited campus and entered the tiny, three-hundred-year-old Village of Loon Lake, Tonya's scalp tingled with a change like air pressure. At university, she was an anonymous student, but to the Old Families of Loon Lake, she would always be her aunt's niece.

"Turn right."

Priya cut north on Kenny Road, and drove between the cemetery on the southwest shore of Loon Lake and Tonya's aunt's store to their west.

"My parents live on David, just north of downtown."

Priya drove them north over River Bridge, then turned east onto David, slowing as they reached Tonya's childhood home. Maple leaves covered the lawn, but her father wasn't out raking them.

Priya pulled into the driveway.

"Hey! The porch swing is gone. Wait here." Tonya got out and went to the front door.

The porch was crowded with liquor boxes labelled "Tonya," in her Aunt Helen's wavering hand. She had packed Tonya's stuff and left it in front of the house. *Why?*

She tried the front door, but her key didn't fit.

Picking up a box, Tonya walked back to the car. "I can't believe this. They changed the locks without warning me."

"Your parents moved out already?" Priya got out and opened the hatchback.

"Looks like." So Priya wouldn't see her face flush, she went back to the porch. Her hands trembled as she called Dad's mobile.

It went straight to voicemail. Mom didn't carry a phone. Without optimism, she left him another message and grabbed a box.

When she returned, Priya had the back seats folded down. Tonya slipped the box in and, together, they went for more. She could hardly look Priya in the eye for fear she would tear up. Something was wrong. Her parents had been acting weird, ever since they had talked her out of U of T. If they wanted her to stay here for safety, why had they left so fast? It was a question that preoccupied her until they loaded the last box.

"Well?" Priya stood behind the car, drumming her fingers on the glass. "Are you going to tell me why you haven't said a word since we started moving boxes?"

"I never thought my parents would leave this place. I should say goodbye to it." Tonya would miss the plant-filled kitchen and her bedroom with its second-story view. "It would be easy to go around the back and get in through the kitchen window. The lock's broken."

"But you won't."

"Of course not."

Priya crossed her arms but didn't say anything. *Was she disappointed?*

Since Tonya met Priya, they'd eaten dozens of meals together in the Mackenzie College cafeteria, but she still wasn't sure what it meant when Priya frowned like that. Tonya slotted the last box into the back.

The motor was running when she got in beside Priya who said, "Come to the pub tonight?"

"I don't know . . ."

Priya batted her eyelashes. "They have nachos."

"I can have nachos anywhere." Eating always made her feel better, but she didn't share Priya's enthusiasm for Hub Pub food. Besides, she should stay in her room and call Dad.

"You have to come with me and meet Duck."

"Duck?"

"Well, Drake, but not Drake the Hip Hop star. He's runs the Digital Ninjas."

Tonya frowned. "I hate clubs."

"How long have we known each other?"

"A month?"

"In that time, have I ever steered you wrong?"

"No . . ." How could she explain to cool, artistic Priya that Digital Ninjas sounded uber geeky? She sighed. Geeky but fun. Maybe it was time to stop thinking about what other people thought of her and do what she liked.

"C'mon. You two will be perfect for each other."

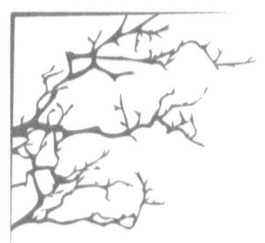

EMPANADAS

Roberto Alvarez sat in the Hub Pub, hands wrapped around a glass of Canadian draft, bummed at the prospect of falling leaves and too many science labs. Back home October meant spring, and the coming prospect of long summer afternoons on Lima's beaches. Loon Lake was wet, windy, and already colder than midwinter back home. He missed watching hang gliders catching thermals off the cliffs in Miraflores. He missed daily blue skies and driving past surfers along the beach-hugging Costa Verde highway. He missed dancing with girls who knew how to salsa. Most of all he missed Barranco bars like Ayahuasca which, unlike this moose's armpit, had atmosphere and fresh tropical cocktails. He hadn't found a Pisco Sour since he'd left Peru, let alone his favorite mixed drink, Maracuya (passion fruit). Plus, the Canadians kept carding him everywhere he went. The drinking age was nineteen here, and he knew he looked older. It was starting to feel like harassment.

A dark-haired couple came in, the guy, unusually tall. People's heads turned, and the hubbub dipped. Who were they? Back home Roberto belonged among the well-connected, the private-schooled, the kids whose families ran things. In this shabby little Canadian town, a couple who turned heads was the closest thing to *his* people. He waved at a waitress, intending to buy them a round but, of course, she ignored him. Everything was self-serve here. Leaving his beer at the booth to save his seat, he pressed his way through the crowd. Up ahead, the chalkboard behind the bar advertised "Cuba Libres." *Well "Viva la revolucion!"* He smiled to himself. At last, something worth drinking in this place. He swam against the tide of students until he washed up beside the intriguing couple at the bar.

"I'm Roberto." He smiled at the girl. "I'm new." Usually, this was all it took. Canadian girls loved his accent. Jocks gravitated toward a fellow athlete.

"I'm Shin." The guy waved, Canadian style, rather than shaking hands. "This is Marta."

The girl stared. "Do I know you?"

"Not yet, but you two seem cool. Can I buy you a round?"

"Are you some kind of diving groupie?" Marta asked.

"I surf." Roberto wasn't sure what she meant by "groupie."

Marta crossed her arms in front of her chest.

"Have you ever been to Lima?"

She shook her head, setting dark, shiny hair in motion. She was beautiful. Perfect skin, naturally ruddy lips . . . too bad she was frowning.

She looked him up and down like he was a beggar. "*So* nice to meet you but we're heading up to the dining room." She towed Shin away through the liquid crowd. Neither spared him a backward glance.

Feeling lonelier, and stupid as well, Roberto cast off against the current. Back at the booth, his lonely glass had been cleared away and four lumberjacks had taken his place. Tossed on this sea of blondes and pale, northern faces, the crashing waves of English chatter were starting to wear on his ears. Time to go back to his dorm and Skype his friends in Lima, that is, the ones who weren't already out partying on a Thursday night.

It wasn't fair. When Madre heard rumors that an obscure Canadian city exuded a powerful magical aura, Roberto's wishes stopped counting. She had to discover why there was so much power in Loon Lake, and how much she could get for the family.

There was no intel available overseas, so his parents registered him for university and told Roberto to integrate with the locals. His goal was to secretly locate the source of magical energy.

"Make us proud," said Papí. "Take some of that power for yourself."

"You'll triumph like a Conquistador in El Dorado," said Madre.

"Or suffer like a convict in Australia!" He tried to object, but they refused to listen. Madre would do anything to gather more power and Papí, well, he always agreed with "the Flower of his Soul." Roberto suspected he was scared of her.

Roberto found an empty stool at a tiny table and ordered a draft. At least Canadian beer was good.

The seven-hour flight to Toronto had given Roberto time to reflect. It was one year out of his life. Worth the sacrifice, if this place held the kind of power Madre suspected. As the plane touched down in Toronto, he had resolved to make the best of banishment. So, he found a cute blonde to distract him from his loneliness. What else could he do?

Too bad Lynette wasn't here to keep him company tonight. His stomach growled. Roberto had a sudden craving for *empanadas*, even though he'd eaten a big dinner at the cafeteria. Chicken and olive *empanadas*, broken open and spritzed inside with lime juice. Mmm. He closed his eyes and remembered the pastry from his favorite bakery in Miraflores. Peruvian food . . . What he wouldn't give for a plate of *ceviche* right now, or potatoes in yellow sauce the way the cook did them. Yeah, *Papas a la Huancaína—that* was what he craved most of all. Hunger stabbed his stomach. He took a gulp of beer, but it didn't help.

Could this aching hunger be a curse? His *abuela*, Madre's madre, would know, and her sisters, his *tías*, would know how to counteract it. Without his powerful family, Roberto felt more alone than ever, and hungrier. Homesickness was steering his imagination toward strange conclusions, but the hunger gnawing at his insides felt too intense to be natural. Desperate to eat anything, Roberto exited the bar and inhaled crisp fall air. He had to find a restaurant, a bakery, a street vendor. He was so desperate, right now he'd even settle for crappy North American drive-through.

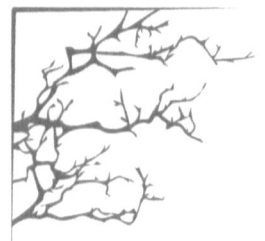

LYNETTE

The following afternoon, Priya took the elevator down to Tonya's floor. The wall pulsed with Top 40 beats coming from her friend's room. Priya knocked, then hammered the door until a salon-fresh blonde opened up.

"I'm here for Tonya."

"What?"

Priya shouted over some kind of autotuned Michael Jackson clone.

"Tonya!"

"Check the library."

Tonya's roommate did not turn the music down. She was too busy staring at Priya's clothes.

"Pleased to meet you, I'm Priya." She stuck out her hand.

"Lynette." Blondie defended the entrance like a goalie.

Priya thumbed Tonya a quick text.

"We're going out tonight. Can I wait here?" Priya moved forward.

Lynette took a step back, allowing her to see the twin chairs and beds on either side of the room.

"Thanks." Priya breezed in past Lynette. "Tonight, she's joining the best club on campus. Do you like film?"

"It's a cheap date."

"Want to make a movie?"

"Oh, absolutely!" Lynette laughed. "Too bad I'm busy, going out with my boyfriend."

"Rain check?"

"You're funny."

Priya put on a smile. "How lovely to meet Tonya's friends."

"What friends?" Lynette shook her head. "She hates music, always wants quiet. It's like living with a grumpy librarian!"

"Don't worry, I'll do my best to corrupt her." Priya checked her phone, again.

Lynette crossed her arms. "So, is she coming or not?"

"She's not responding."

"Game over. Thanks for playing." Lynette hurried Priya to the door. "Better luck next time." Lynette forced Priya into the hall and slammed the door.

I think this makes us besties. Priya glanced up the hall for witnesses but she was alone.

Her phone pinged. It was Tonya, calling to say she was finished at the library.

"Let's meet at the pub," said Priya. "I just met your wonderful roommate, and while I'd *love* to stick around and lap up her charm, I wouldn't want to impose on her generosity."

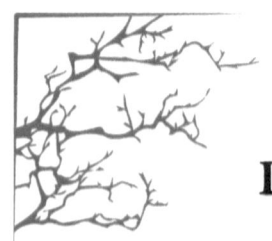

DIGITAL NINJAS

Twenty minutes later, Tonya followed Priya into the Hub Pub and immediately down a flight of stairs to the basement.

"I found these guys online before I even came to university," said Priya. "Zain does this web comic called *Monster of the Week*."

She was about to open the door when Tonya stopped her. "I'm happy to keep you company but promise you'll do the talking?"

"Relax, you're gonna *love* Duck."

Tonya had never seen Priya so animated. "Oh, I get it. You need a wing-girl. I'm only here because you want to date him!"

"Why date? I just wanna hook up with his NEX-VG30H."

"His what?"

She licked her lips and spoke breathily. "I like to take my SLR lenses and screw them onto his powerful cam."

Tonya laughed. "You're nuts."

"No, just not camera shy. But Drake and me, it's just a fling."

"You mean you and him actually . . ."

"Of course not! I want his cameras, but you," she jabbed a finger at Tonya's chest, "are just his type. Plus, tonight I want to convince him to film my installation. Ready?"

She flung open the door.

Tonya followed Priya into a cramped meeting room. It wasn't hard to figure out who Drake was from Priya's description. He had short blond hair, intense blue eyes, and wore a black, multi-pocket vest with two cameras hanging down the front. Six people in black shirts and jeans crowded around to speak with him so Tonya caught only snatches of what was said.

"You don't need film school . . .

"California . . .

"Finance . . .

"A guy I know made a horror film for $6,000.00. Got distribution, sold it on Amazon."

"Sellout!" Priya called over the chatter.

Drake smiled. "Excuse me." He escaped the huddle of would-be filmmakers and gave Priya a hug. He unclinched when he caught sight of Tonya.

"I see you've brought me the next Emma Stone. Welcome to *La La Land.*"

"Don't mind him, he's an idiot." Priya smiled fondly at Drake.

"But he's our idiot," said a guy in a Jaws t-shirt. He had slightly prominent incisors and his hair was artfully messy on top, like the hunky vampire in a teen flick. Tonya wondered if the look was achieved by product or neglect.

"Meet Tonya," said Priya.

"Hi, Tonya." Bedhead guy held his hands up, framing her face in an imaginary viewfinder.

When Drake shook her hand, Tonya couldn't help noticing his firm grip and muscled arms.

"Call him Duck," said Zain.

"Why?"

"My name's Drake."

"Why not use your real name?" asked Tonya.

"Never. A true name gives supernatural forces the power to summon you and . . ." He looked at Tonya and stopped smiling. "You don't think that's funny, do you?"

Tonya shrugged. In Loon Lake people didn't joke about such things.

"She's not into horror movies," said Priya.

"Oh, an artist like you?"

"English and History major."

His eyes sparkled when he smiled at her. "Welcome to Digital Ninjas. This is my assistant director, and roommate, Zain."

"Sorry!" said Zain.

Tonya followed Zain and Drake back into the scrum where the Ninjas were hammering out their Indie Filmmaker Manifesto.

"They have a manifesto?" she asked Priya.

"The Ninjas aren't just a social club. Stick with us and we'll make things happen."

"You sound like Lynette."

Priya made a face.

"I don't mean you're obsessed with celebrities and your boyfriend's abs. She's in a sorority to meet rich guys and make business connections."

"Smart girl," said Priya.

"You think so? I think she's fake."

"Jealous?" Priya laughed. "You know, the easiest way to finance an art career is to find a rich patron. Maybe I should join her crowd."

"Now I know you're kidding."

"Partly, but I'd do anything to mount *Man vs. Nature* properly." She jerked a thumb at the scrum of Ninjas and their cameras. "These guys are my secret weapon."

Drake was standing at the front of the room, all eyes on him. "What makes a Ninja so ninja? Is it the black clothing? The special equipment? Is it the catlike way we glide through sets and soundstages?"

"No!" The Ninjas responded.

"Why then?" Tonya asked Priya.

"They're called Ninjas for silently meeting on location, without permits, to shoot guerrilla footage," whispered Priya.

Drake continued. "The Ninja style is part art, part sport, and part black belt discipline. What is our war cry?"

"Booms down!" chorused the Ninjas.

"What's that mean?" Tonya asked Priya.

"When they film a street scene, civilians never notice cameras, but the moment somebody lifts a microphone on a pole, it draws a crowd and spoils the shoot."

"Smile everybody." Drake panned his camera across the group. "I want to document this historic moment. First we do Priya's installation."

He shot Tonya a smile. "Then we make the best campus horror movie of all time!"

The Ninjas cheered as Priya made her way through the huddle to consult a pretty black girl with a long afro. She stood next to a brown guy in a black t-shirt which listed the top ten rules of indie filmmaking. Every rule contained an F-bomb. On the far side of the room stood three dough-fleshed guys wearing Star Wars t-shirts. They chatted and smiled at Drake, who looked about six feet tall.

His enthusiasm was infectious. Tonya wondered what it would be like to go see a movie with him, but caught herself. It was easy for Priya to hang with these guys. She was a sophisticated Torontonian with artistic talent. Drake seemed friendly, but he probably already had a girlfriend.

Drake left the cluster of Ninjas to join Priya and Tonya.

"*Man vs. Nature* should open on Halloween," Priya said. "I want to put it in the cemetery."

Drake's eyes lit up.

"Perfect for a horror movie!" Zain responded from among the Star Wars shirts.

"Except it's an art installation," said Priya.

"Yeah, but a familiar place is a classic scenario," said Drake. "After your show, when people return to the cemetery, they'll expect your beasts to leap out at them,"

"Like Stephen King," said Zain, "but with maple syrup and beavers."

"People think Canada can't be scary." Drake shook his head. "But if Priya's art can make Loon Lake feel dangerous, that's scarier than Hollywood."

If only they knew, thought Tonya.

"We're going to need lots of money." Zain stepped up beside Priya. "How else can I pay for assistants to assist my assistants?"

Drake ignored him. "Horror is the perfect expression of Canadian identity. It's a cabin in the woods versus a wilderness of shapeshifters and angry spirits, spoiling to burst in."

"Like Margaret Atwood's *Survival*!" Priya said.

"Right. So, this installation," said Drake "What exactly are your artistic needs?"

"If you listen to Duck," Zain said, "we'll spend our lives making experimental films and eating Kraft Dinner. *My* big artistic need is to pay off my student loan."

"Hey," said Priya, "I'm not asking for money. There isn't going to be any money. Can we forget finance and get back to my installation?"

"Sorry." Zain pouted like a kid who'd dropped his ice cream cone. Tonya almost laughed.

Priya gathered the Ninjas around a table and started brainstorming ways to incorporate cameras and video screens into her piece. The Ninjas came with their own tech, but when Drake started tacking a storyboard onto the wall, Tonya was hooked. This guy and his friends were going to turn horror movies into Art, and Priya's Art into video.

They argued camera angles, lighting, and equipment, until Priya's stomach growled.

"Excuse me. I'm starved."

"We're all hungry," said Drake. "We've been at it for hours."

Tonya hadn't felt the time pass but the moment he mentioned it, she was hungry.

"Who wants pizza?" asked Drake.

There were cheers, and the Ninjas waved money in the air as Zain collected funds.

Tonya's stomach burbled. The thought of pepperoni and melting cheese elicited stabs of hunger, as if she hadn't eaten all day. She put a hand on the wall to steady herself. Her legs felt weak. "I have to go," she told Priya.

"Aren't you staying for dinner?"

"Sorry." Priya and the others could never understand her fear of the freshman fifteen. What, for them, would be a few extra pounds, would be doom for Tonya. She had eaten nothing but soup and salad for months in order to approach a healthy weight—for the first time since childhood. She fled upstairs, determined to leave before she lost her resolve.

"Wait!" Priya followed her halfway up the stairs.

"Sorry." Tonya didn't dare stop. Pizza was her worst trigger. Her stomach roared like a lion in the cage of her gut. She wanted to pounce on pepperoni.

Tonya emerged into the cold, pepperoni-free air outside the Hub, and not a moment too soon. In the wood fires of her imagination, she could smell caramelizing onions and crispy crust.

Of course, that was only fantasy. Why get excited about pub pizza? It was probably made in a factory, frozen, and then baked until soggy. Not worth the calories.

Before a waft of fresh-baked scent could leak under the door and change her mind, Tonya started jogging home. She had instant soup and granola bars and fruit in her room. That and a takeout salad from the cafeteria would be better than pizza. She just had to concentrate on the moment.

She jogged along the path strewn with wet autumn leaves, trying hard to think of nothing but the wind on her face, and the pounding of her feet. A couple of times she almost wiped out, the leaves were so slippery. Tonya slowed down. She had left Priya and the Digital Ninjas far behind, but her craving was harder to shake.

Tonya's breathing was getting ragged. She had shin splints and a stitch in her side. Practicing dives all summer hadn't prepared her for running, but she'd done okay. She'd gotten away, and that was what mattered.

TIED UP AND LOCKED OUT

Avoiding the cafeteria entrance, Tonya entered the lobby, her stomach growling loudly. She pressed the shiny brown elevator call button. Was it just her, or did the elevator buttons looked like Smarties? Or chocolate M&Ms . . . Her mind drifted to her roommate's stash of Halloween chocolate. How pathetic. She should have stayed with the Ninjas. She could be eating hot pizza with interesting company, but what did she do? She retreated to nibble salad in her room, and fantasize about chocolate.

She was on the verge of going back to the pub when the elevator arrived. On autopilot, she got in and got off at her floor.

The door was locked, which was unusual this time of night. Typically, her roommate left it open so her many friends could wander in and out. Tonya seldom enjoyed a quiet moment in what was supposed to be her home. When there weren't guests laughing and talking, and ignoring Tonya, Lynette would blare obnoxious Top 40 songs. Did she even like them? Tonya figured Lynette used music like hunters use duck decoys, electro pop quacking attracted drakes to her pond.

Tonya got out her keys but hesitated. The best thing about Lynette was that she went out a lot but if the room was quiet she might have company. Tonya didn't want to walk in on Lynette and her boyfriend Roberto. She put her ear to the door and listened. Nothing.

She hesitated. If her parents hadn't sold the house so fast, Tonya could have moved back home. They were the ones who had talked her into an expensive dorm room.

"You'll make friends if you live on campus," said Mom.

"Everybody lives in residence their first year," said Dad.

Tonya opened the door.

At first, she didn't know what she was seeing. It seemed too impossible. Lynette was seated at her desk, hands tied together with a handkerchief.

"Lynette, you okay?" Tonya rushed over and started untying her.

"Leave me alone. I have to stay this way, until the craving passes."

"Who did this to you?"

"Relax. I did it myself."

"What? Why?"

"I ate all my Halloween candy."

"So?"

"And all three boxes of your cereal, and I was about to eat your crappy granola bars, so I used my teeth and tied up my hands."

"So you wouldn't steal a few granola bars?"

"Plus your miso soup powder. How messed up is that?"

It was a relief that Lynette hadn't eaten all her food, but having that thought made her feel guilty. Lynette was hurting.

"Don't punish yourself for wanting to eat. Hunger is normal. Starving yourself isn't." Tonya untied the handkerchief and put her hand on her skinny roommate's shoulder. "Come with me to the medical center tomorrow? I think you need help."

"Don't look at me like that. I'm fine. I don't starve myself. If I want to eat dinner or a piece of cake or something, I eat it, okay?"

"Except today. Admit this was not healthy behavior."

"Sure. Whatever."

Tonya stood there, not knowing what to do.

"The urge has passed, finally." Lynette shook her head. "I can't believe I wanted to eat your cheap-ass granola bars."

Tonya heard the words, but she could also see a bit of drool forming at the corner of Lynette's mouth. Her roommate's eyes seemed unnaturally glossy, and she wasn't looking at Tonya. She was ogling the miso soup mix and granola bars still on the shelf.

Salad could wait. Lynette's obsession was making her crave something sweet. Tonya turned and grabbed a granola bar and gobbled it down.

"Hey, you aren't going to eat in front of me, are you?"

"Sorry." She offered Lynette a chocolate chip bar, which she gobbled in two bites. Tonya puzzled over what made Lynette do what she did, but she wasn't jealous of her anymore. This fashionable sorority girl with the athletic boyfriend only appeared to lead a perfect life. Her compulsive eating, which she had hidden from Tonya, must mean she was unhappy. Didn't it?

No. Just because a person was full-figured didn't mean she was an emotional eater, and just because she was skinny, didn't mean she had a healthy attitude to food. A chubby child who grew into a fat teen, Tonya was starting to break old habits and find healthier ways to manage her mood than by eating. When she felt down, cravings for sweets and chips still flared up, but they were more manageable.

Now, Lynette didn't seem so different. She needed to be looked after and cheered up. Tonya switched on campus radio to lighten the mood.

Lynette sat on the bed, for once enjoying tunes that weren't so plastic pop repetitive.

"You know, you're not all bad." Lynette leaned back on her elbows.

Tonya sat beside her. "Hey, sometime do you want to go to the Hub together? You can introduce me to your friends?"

"Would you like that?"

"Sure." What Tonya really wanted was for them to stop treating her like wallpaper when they came into her room.

"Why not? But not in that outfit." Lynette pointed to a box of almond crunch granola bars on Tonya's shelf. "You're not saving those, are you?"

"You should get tested for tapeworm."

"Stop overreacting."

Tonya handed one over and took a bar for herself. By the time they finished the bars, Tonya's eyelids were heavy. She drifted to her side of the room and lay down.

Lynette stretched out on her bed.

"What is happening to us today?" Tonya asked.

"I thought you were finished nagging about food."

"I am but it's good to talk, you know?"

"Like real roommates."

"Exactly. So, how is Roberto?" Tonya used a teasing tone.

"Who wants to know? Grumpy-Lights-Out-Be-Quiet Tonya, or my new roommate who actually smiles and talks?"

"Hey, I'm sorry, I just can't handle too much noise, and people. Don't you ever need to be alone?"

"I hate being alone, except being alone with Roberto . . ." She sighed.

"Oh my god. You are so obsessed." Tonya held up an invisible microphone. "Your fans need to know. Has this social butterfly fallen in love?"

Lynette laughed. "Yes, and I'll spill the details, but first I need a disco nap. Why don't you turn off that infernal indie music?"

"With pleasure." Tonya switched it off and pulled out a paperback, eager to enjoy the quiet. She switched on her reading lamp and was well into the book before soft snoring announced Lynette's arrival in dreamland.

Almost twenty minutes later, Lynette sat up with a start. Tonya watched her examine the bedspread littered with chocolate wrappers. Lynette's expression changed from soft and sleepy to surprised. "You ate all my Halloween candy!"

"You ate it before I got here, before you tied up your hands."

"Tied my hands? What are you talking about? I've been trying on clothes all afternoon, to pick a costume for Saturday."

"How do you explain the candy wrappers?"

Lynette looked around until her gaze settled on the wrappers. "What the . . . You ate all my chocolate bars!" She acted like she'd gone senile at eighteen.

"I didn't." What was wrong with this girl?

The accusing look on Lynette's face didn't soften. "You could have at least tidied the mess you made!"

"I never ate your candy!"

"Liar, but who cares. I have a life, unlike *some* people. And I have Roberto." She pulled out her phone and started texting.

"Are you pranking me?"

"Go away Tonya. I'm on the phone."

"I don't get it. The computer was supposed to match me up with someone compatible. I'm serious. You don't care about marks. You like loud music. I like ballads. I'm studying literature. You never read a book. We must be complete opposites. How did the computer give me you?"

Lynette kept texting, eyes on the screen. "Easy. On my profile, I said I needed to live with someone quiet."

"But you're not quiet."

"No, but you are, most of the time. Stop bugging me."

Tonya felt like grabbing the phone and throwing it out the window. Tonya was sure she hadn't specified selfish ass when she entered her roommate preferences. At least Lynette was quiet when she was texting. Tonya didn't think she'd ever seen her concentrate this long.

Like the movement of the sun across the sky, at first you didn't notice the change until it hit the right object and made it glow. A glow like the one lighting up Lynette's face from within. What was making her roommate so happy? She moved a little closer to sneak a peek, but Lynette started jumping up and down.

"He's coming! Okay Roomy, let's make this place shine." She cranked up her peppiest playlist and shot Tonya the open-faced smile of a child, so sweet she was almost forgiven.

It was love alright. Tonya shook her head. Roberto was so handsome, she almost didn't blame her.

As they cleaned up candy wrappers to the beat of Lynette's top ten playlist, Lynette still didn't remember her recent eating bout.

Roberto arrived. Lynette sang out "Salsa time!" and switched to something fast and Latin. Unfortunately, they skipped the salsa and started dirty dancing as if Tonya weren't there. Tonya sighed. Glasnost was over. Lynette was definitely back to ignoring her.

"Hey," Roberto said to Tonya. "Why don't you go to the movies?" He had his wallet open and was offering her a fifty-dollar bill.

"I don't want your money. It's eleven-thirty and I want to sleep in my own bed. I have early classes tomorrow. Couldn't you two get a motel room?"

"You see what I have to put up with?" Lynette fake-pouted at him.

"Shhh." Roberto kissed her quiet.

Tonya picked up the paperback and lay on her bed facing the wall. She put on her noise-canceling headphones, but they couldn't compete with Lynette's speakers. She read the same sentence over and over. Sometimes, the wild dancing caused them to crash into the wall and explode into giggles, or to land on the bed with a chorus of squeaky springs. Tonya gave up trying to read and stared at the ceiling, annoyed but too tired to fight. She rolled over, considering going to the Don to complain when, out of the corner of her eye, Tonya accidentally saw Roberto slide his hands under Lynette's shirt.

Enough! Tonya got up, took her book, and stalked off to the common room. She couldn't decide which was worse, Lynette's blind adoration, or Roberto's complete disregard for her privacy. She hoped Lynette would have the decency to come and get her when they went out.

The common room bisected two wings of the dorm. Men in one corridor and women in the other. As Tonya walked toward it, she felt an unusual tremor in the floor. Maybe somebody's bass was turned up too high. Thursday was a party night because so many students went home on weekends. Why had the computer slotted her into a course at 8:30 Friday mornings? In a just world, it would have assigned Lynette to an early slot, so Tonya could be sleeping in her bed right now.

Tonya let out a sigh. The common room was empty, and the TV was off. She set an early alarm on her phone in case she slept through the night. As she settled onto the couch, Tonya decided she preferred the popular but snotty version of her roommate to this love-struck bunny. Before she met Roberto, Lynette wouldn't have let her sleep either, because she would be flitting from room-to-room, chatting with friends until late. She was so irritatingly cheerful and liable to start dancing at the most annoying moments, but at least she didn't kiss hot boys in front of Tonya.

Public displays of affection goaded Tonya who had never had a boyfriend. Aunt Helen had made sure of it. As soon as any boy showed a flicker of interest, Aunt Helen would use her persuasive powers to repel him. Tonya had tried to confront her but, of course, she denied it.

Tonya snuggled her head into the couch pillows and hoped to be left alone. It was normal to see students visiting each other's rooms on a Thursday night. As usual, music played out of open bedrooms, and there was laughter, rowdy conversation, and the occasional thump. But underneath the ordinary, something felt off.

Have you ever stood in an empty room, aware something was irritating you, but unable to figure out what it was until you realized the radio was playing, barely audible?

Tonya glanced around the room, searching for the source of her unease. The TV was off, but she got up from the couch and checked to make sure. Something invisible was grinding on her nerves but it wasn't noise. What she was feeling came to her through senses her Pure faction parents had forbidden. She put a hand to her forehead, wondering if magic could cause a fever. Her head ached but it was probably just the stress of her roommate drama. Tonya lay on the couch and shivered, wishing for a blanket.

Just what she needed now, to get sick. She couldn't even get her thermometer because it was in the room with the lovebirds. Besides, this odd sensation didn't feel like disease. She tossed for an hour, trying to ignore her suspicions. Something here felt like magic. If only Aunt Helen were there. She would know.

Her father was a Mundane, unable to sense or use magic. Her mother was a Pure, sworn to live magic-free. Tonya was supposed to be safe from magic on campus. Like Loon Lake City, the university was considered neutral territory to the Old Families. An economic and cultural hub, they had made a pact not to spoil it with their feuds.

The university was the safest place for the daughter of a Pure family. On that Aunt Helen and her parents agreed. There was no occult energy pulsing here. Nothing was wrong. She was tired and imagining things. Tonya would feel better in the morning.

She took off her sweater, draped it over her head and shoulders and tried to think of soothing things, like lying in bed listening to rain on the roof of her old attic bedroom, or the reflection of the moon setting over Loon Lake.

FRIES WITH THAT?

The next day, Tonya sat in a packed lecture hall. Professor Rudolph was Tonya's favorite, ever since he'd invited his students to go for a drink, after their first class. His humorous rants against the "narrow, cabbage-eating island," he emigrated from also endeared him to Tonya. She had grown up in the shadow of Toronto, a "world class city," according to self-important Torontonians. Compare that to an Englishman who'd left legendary London and moved to Loon Lake by choice. Professor Rudolph not only knew history, but he shared Tonya's excellent taste in geography.

As he paced back and forth lecturing, his stomach protruded over his waistband like a wobbly shelf. While he was teaching, Tonya didn't normally notice his weight. She was too busy taking notes or looking up his erudite references on her phone. But eating and weight had become major preoccupations since she'd started dieting this past summer. Seeing the way his hips strained his pants, Tonya could see he'd gotten heavier since orientation in September.

Rudolph's lectures unraveled the complicated causes behind historical movements. Today, he was asking students what utopia meant, but Tonya was having trouble following the discussion. Priya kept pinging her phone with panicky texts. The art installation depended on cameras and lighting, but the Digital Ninjas had changed their minds about loaning her equipment overnight.

Tonya texted back: *What's wrong?*

Priya responded: *Paranoia their cameras will get stolen.*

Professor Rudolph ducked behind his lectern to grab something. Without pausing in his citation from *The Communist Manifesto*, Doctor Rudolph lifted a giant fistful of fries and shoved them into his mouth.

With a bundle of fries protruding, his face looked like he'd sprouted a deep-fried anemone. Poor man. Since September there had been whispers before class about his wife dying that spring. Some students were outraged that he posted excuses on his door and skipped office hours. Tonya agreed that it was unfortunate for the students, but the Professor had lost his wife. He needed time to grieve, although the fry thing was strange, even for an academic.

Her phone vibrated again but Tonya turned it off. Professor Rudolph's mouth was empty again and he was talking about Sir Thomas More's *Utopia*. From what Tonya understood, communal living under More's rules would afford her no privacy, no personal possessions, and very few rights, but it would be much easier than living with Lynette.

Outside the lecture hall, Priya was waiting. "Why weren't you answering my texts? This is a disaster!"

"Halloween isn't till the weekend. You have time to figure this out. C'mon, I'll skip my afternoon class and help you find materials."

Priya raised an eyebrow. "Okay. First we have to steal some lights."

When she saw Tonya's reaction she patted her shoulder. "Kidding. OK, Ms. Goody-Goody, let's check the hardware store."

A FEW HOURS LATER, Priya and Tonya were in the forested southern end of Loon Lake Cemetery, scouting sites for the installation. In town maps, Tonya thought the cemetery looked like a T-bone steak or a bull's head. The broadest section was the top, which ran in an almost straight line along the southern shore of the lake. The sides of the bull's face tapered gently to the rounded muzzle at the southern tip, where the oldest section of the cemetery stood. Just left of the center, stood an abandoned chapel at a crossroads of four paved pathways, large enough for cars. The grounds were also crisscrossed by smaller paths between the treed sections of the cemetery, each with its own era and flavor. There were a couple of pine-topped hills on the otherwise flat grounds, a round one to the south, and a lozenge-shaped one that ran down into the water to the north. Excluding the shoreline, the rest of the grounds were bordered by a tall, wrought iron fence. "To keep the living out or the dead in?" her father used to joke.

She felt less like laughing now. Her friend wanted to set up her installation in the cemetery, which was bad enough, but as they passed the chapel and continued south past the round hill, Priya noticed the most sacred site of all.

"What about that tree?" She pointed to a tall ash tree, just inside the old section of the cemetery. "Do you think we could climb it?"

"I climbed it, when I was too young to know better. We should leave it alone."

"Why? Look how big it is." Priya craned her neck up to look at the top. "The leaves have turned gold and started to fall off. It's the perfect creepy focal point for my installation."

"No, it's the Three-Century Ash."

"Wait, did you say you climbed it?"

"Yeah." Tonya shrugged.

"I don't believe you. The trunk must go up two stories before there's a branch to grab hold of. I can't even get my arms around it."

"You have to find a better place." Tonya wasn't allowed to explain to outsiders what the tree meant to the Old Families, and their ancestors buried nearby.

Priya walked around the trunk. "Hey, what's this?"

"Never mind. Let's go."

"What are these for?" She pointed to slats of wood, nailed into the bark.

"They look unstable," Tonya lied.

Priya tested them with her hand, then stepped onto the bottom rung. "Somebody built a ladder right into the tree."

"A stupid kid. Aunt Helen punished me for doing it." Mostly with long lectures on how the Ash protected them from lingering magic released by their buried ancestors.

"Why didn't you take the boards off?"

"By the time Aunt Helen discovered the rungs, the tree had stopped leaking sap and started to heal. She told me to leave them for fear of causing more damage." Her Aunt had also warned that if the tree died, the town would be in danger.

"You're making a lot of fuss over a tree."

"You hurt the tree, you hurt the town."

Priya's eyebrows shot up.

"According to my Mom. As punishment, I had to work for free in my aunt's store all summer."

"Too bad."

"It was fine. On my first day, my aunt showed me the secret merchandise, locked under the counter."

Priya quirked an eyebrow. "Your aunt's a drug dealer?"

"No. She keeps little drawstring bags, reserved for the regulars."

"What was she selling?"

"Nothing. Herbs and dried roots." In fact, they were charms, but her explanation seemed to satisfy Priya, who wandered farther into the cemetery, seemingly forgetting about the tree. Tonya couldn't get that summer out of her mind. Her aunt had made her sew sachet after sachet using an antique treadle-powered sewing machine.

"Why can't we use a modern sewing machine?" Tonya had wondered.

"Electricity interferes with the magic."

At first, sewing little bags and hanging herbs to dry was annoying because her aunt made her do and redo things until they were perfect. It wasn't until she had been working there for a couple of weeks that Tonya realized she was having fun. Something about her aunt was completely comforting in a way her parents weren't. Before long, she found herself finishing Aunt Helen's sentences, which would have irritated her mother, but just made Aunt Helen laugh.

"What are we, twins?" Tonya asked one day when it happened again.

"We're family . . ." Aunt Helen's words seemed to catch in her throat and rather than continue she pulled Tonya in for a hug. "These days, working with you, have been some of the happiest in my life."

Despite the log cabin exterior, the renovated shop was bright and airy with large modern windows. Her aunt hummed as she polished every pane of glass, as well as the long counter over the display cases lining the wall. This insistence on a clean and bright environment belied her reputation as a woman with a dark past.

Tonya could never forget the high school taunts she had endured because she defended her aunt's choices. The Herbal Healing Shop was her aunt's livelihood and her independence. So what if she was born into a Pure family who disapproved? Helen hurt no one. She kept the secret of magic from the Mundanes and mostly sold to Old Families. Tonya's mother, and a gaggle of Pure family gossips, had no right to judge her for embracing magic.

They were probably jealous of the handsome, middle-aged men who occasionally came to pick up Aunt Helen after work. It made Tonya proud when Aunt Helen trusted her to close up the shop, so she could go out.

One day that summer, Tonya got up the courage to ask, "How did you get so popular?"

Aunt Helen was threading ribbon through one of her herb bags. She put down her work and looked Tonya in the eye. "Why do you ask?"

"I'm seventeen but I still haven't had a boyfriend."

"Oh honey, don't rush it. Young love is a curse."

After each workday, Tonya found herself defending Aunt Helen to her parents. Her aunt was an infrequent visitor to their house and any impending visit caused her father to rush around putting away their valuables as if preparing for the arrival of some unpredictable animal. When Tonya was younger, this reaction simply added to her aunt's mystique, but now that they were on friendly terms, her father's behavior seemed bizarre.

"Why are you putting everything away?"

"I'm making things tidy."

As if. Her father worked long hours without tiring or complaining. He had lost jobs, buried a parent, married young. Nothing seemed to faze him, except Helen.

"She's just Mom's sister. Why do you always fuss when she comes?"

"Ask your mother."

Tonya tried to probe further but he went out to mow the lawn.

How was it Aunt Helen's presence made Tonya feel so relaxed when she made her cool-headed father jumpy as a fawn?

In the years since, his attitude had mellowed but only slightly. Why would her parents move to Toronto to care for Aunt Helen?

It gave Tonya a pang of sadness to think of Aunt Helen cooped up under fluorescent lights in a sterile hospital, all because of a so-called routine condition nobody would discuss. Did she ingest one of her own concoctions by mistake? Was she keeping a serious ailment secret? It seemed incredible that her parents refused to let Tonya visit or even know where she was being treated. Tonya took a moment to call her aunt again, but the inbox was full.

Priya came back and led Tonya to the oldest section of the graveyard. "Do you have any idea who's buried here? The names are worn off."

"The Old Families came here hundreds of years ago. I'd have to look up the records at City Hall. You can't be thinking of using burial sites in your installation?"

"Why do you think I'm here?"

"You can't put fake monsters on my ancestor's graves."

"So, it's back to the big tree then."

"Not if my aunt's opinion counts."

Priya sighed. "Let's walk over to the store. I'd love to meet her."

"She's in hospital." Probably, maybe. Tonya wished she knew.

"Oh. Sorry to hear that."

"Let me know if you're driving to Toronto some weekend? We can visit her together." Once Tonya confirmed her whereabouts.

GRUESOME PRESERVES

Friday morning, Roberto wasn't feeling well so he skipped class and drove to town on the opposite side of the lake. In the pharmacy, the clerk showed him diet pills with caffeine, and imported slimming pills but Roberto didn't want to lose weight. He was in great shape from daily runs through the wooded cemetery near campus. Even doubling up on food since September, he had gained only ten pounds. No big deal. What bothered him was the constant hunger.

This persistent desire had started a couple of weeks ago but lately it was getting so bad, it distracted him when he wanted to study, and he was losing sleep to a new compulsion for midnight snacks. Last night, rather than going out and buying himself a bag of chips or a sandwich and returning to bed, he had gorged himself on ice cream. He didn't even like sweets, but he had driven to the convenience store, grabbed a bag of corn chips on the way in, and finished them while foraging in the freezer.

The next thing he knew, he was back in his car hunting for a spoon. He had a big tub of Kawartha Dairy maple walnut. He'd never seen such a flavor before, and didn't expect to enjoy anything so sweet, yet he couldn't wait to eat. There were no utensils in the glove box, so he spooned huge globs of ice cream into his mouth with his fingers. Once he got to the bottom, the last bits melted, and he tipped up the container to drink syrupy dregs.

Roberto stood staring at a shelf of useless medications in the diet aisle of the biggest drugstore in Loon Lake, but nothing there could help. He didn't need his poncho-wrapped *abuela* to tell him this eating compulsion wasn't natural. He came from a family that recognized magic.

He had caught the right kind of vibe from Helen's Herbal Healing Shop when he passed it on his training runs through the cemetery, in what locals called the Village. He decided to get back in the car and go for a drive.

After the high-rise lifestyle of Lima, buildings here seemed ridiculously small. As he drove south out of downtown, the roads were lined with single family houses with backyards. He passed parks without fences, then turned west along Lakeshore, marveling how much public greenspace encircled the water.

At Kenny Road, he turned south and crossed the bridge, passing close to the cemetery on his left. The open fields to his right soon revealed a two-story log cabin. He had reached the Herbal Healing Shop, according to the sign painted across the front but he wasn't quite ready to go in.

On a whim, he parked on the shoulder and crossed Kenny Road to have a look at the tree-filled cemetery. September's changing colors intrigued him after the sparse vegetation on Peru's coast, but by October the leaves were gone, leaving bare branches to scratch the sky. Shivering, he braced his foot on the fence's lowest crossbar and leaned his forehead between the posts.

The people beneath these old stones would never move again, and the land looked like it was dying too. Roberto had seen too many withered faces in town, old people like leaves, waiting for their turn to fall to earth. Only Lynette made him feel alive. Without her he'd have flown back to Peru, even against his parents' wishes. Let them disinherit him. He wasn't helpless, at least, if you didn't count this helpless craving for food.

Used to Lima's ten million people and diverse districts, Loon Lake was simple and boring. When his parents had first tried to convince him, they claimed a town with 135,000 people would be comfortable and safe. He didn't want comfortable and safe. He wanted thrills, and neighborhoods where life was passion. Campus was tame and generic, so he went hunting for real life, night life, the dangerous and exotic. In Loon Lake, sadly, the enticing English idiom "wrong side of the tracks," meant nothing more exciting than a cheap subdivision north of town. Loon Lake's main products seemed to be diplomas, cemetery plots, and trees. Why was magic attracted to such an ordinary place?

A few steps inside the fence, his eye was drawn up the side of an enormous tree, the tallest he had seen outside the rainforest. The earth around it was mounded and uneven and, when he strained to look, Roberto noticed ancient gravestones flush with the ground. The lettering was so weathered it was difficult to read. He would have liked to check them out, but not until he got treatment for this hunger.

The shop stood opposite the cemetery, banished from sanctified ground. He took a package of biscuits from his pocket and munched on them as he walked to the building.

Two stories tall and constructed of weathered logs, with modern windows, and a painted sign over the door; the shop stood behind a gravel parking lot. This wasn't some multinational drugstore. It was special, but not centuries-old special, like Pucllana Temple in Lima. It was old by Canadian standards and as he approached, he sensed an aura of power.

With renewed optimism, and cookie crumbs on his hands, he tried the door. Locked. The lights were off. Odd. It was already 10:30, but the posted hours were 10:00 a.m. to 7:00 p.m. He knocked hard, and when that didn't work, he shouted:

"Anybody there?"

There was a crash inside the shop. His first instinct was to back away. The locked door and crash meant a robbery was in progress—except the guys on the cross-country team had told him Loon Lake had no crime. Could somebody be hurt?

He thought he heard a woman's voice, muffled by the door. He didn't want to run afoul of police or criminals, but it would be wrong to walk away. Roberto couldn't force the door, so he pulled his fist into his sleeve and punched through the little window beside it. His heart accelerated, like the final push at the end of a race. He reached in through the broken window and unlocked the door, throwing it open.

"Hello? Everybody okay?" He took a step into the dark foyer and let his eyes adjust. Entering the shop, the wall to his left was dominated by a long glass case. It was the kind used for pastries, but this was no bakery. Exotic objects and herbal ingredients crowded the glass. Mounted on the wall opposite the counter, shelves displayed jars of odd preserves. He stepped closer, still unsure where the crash had come from. There was nobody here. He went around the counter to investigate a doorway which opened into the back room. Inside, there was a work table, floor-to-ceiling canning jars and, at the far end, a window. Curtains waved inwards with a cold draft. Broken glass glittered on the floor. He *had* interrupted a break-in.

Roberto wondered if he should leave when a feeble moaning came from close by. He stepped around the work table and found a woman, kneeling on the hardwood. The *Señora's* thinning white hair was pulled back in a ponytail and her hands trembled.

She was stuffing handfuls of something into her mouth that dribbled down her chin. It was pinkish, pickled. It looked like a jar of fetal pigs! Her face twisted into an expression of disgust, and yet she kept shoveling it in without even pausing to look up. This was worse than his junk food compulsion, but would it be his fate? He looked at her chicken-bone frame. She might be eating uncontrollably now, but she was too thin to have been doing so for long.

Between mouthfuls she spluttered, "Don't just watch me. Help."

He reached out to her but although she looked at him with tears in her eyes, her body kept on eating.

Roberto came from behind and slipped his arms through hers. "*Vámonos.*" He dragged her gently away from the fleshy preserves. She clutched the last bloody morsels to her chest, but when they were almost at the door, he pried them from her fingers and tossed them into the garbage can.

"Don't worry, *Señora*. I will take you to the medical center and they can tell us both what is making us sick."

She nodded her head and let him lead her away. She was still chewing furiously and choking as she tried to swallow everything packed into her mouth.

"Take your time." He led her toward his car.

"He's getting away." She pointed to a stand of trees behind the shop. "Stop him!"

Roberto could see a man in a leather jacket trotting away unevenly, as if one of his legs was longer than the other. His hair was a flash of white against brown as he receded into the trees.

"Run! Len's had a hip replacement. You can still catch up. Bring him to me and I'll know what to do with him." She shot Roberto a lopsided smile.

"Are you sure?"

She wobbled and grabbed the side of the car to steady herself.

Why did she want to confront the intruder? It was dangerous, and he wanted to refuse, until she turned her deep blue eyes on him. He felt himself falling into their liquid depths, until they were linked and helping her felt as natural as breathing.

"Go," she said. A whispering voice in his mind told him her name was Helen and he knew he couldn't let her down.

Roberto jogged toward the trees at a rate that would easily catch the limping man. Question was, what would he do when he caught him? The old guy wasn't feeble, despite his bad leg, but it wasn't a fair fight. How could a big strong guy like Roberto tackle him? He was an old man, and he wasn't carrying off any loot. It was confusing, but he felt strangely compelled to bring him back for Helen.

The man stopped running and turned to face Roberto. A smile crossed his face. Deliberately, he lifted his hands above his head.

"It's okay," said Roberto. "I don't want to hurt you . . ."

A fireball came at Roberto. He dove to the ground but knew by the painful heat that his hair, and the clothes on his back were burning. Roberto rolled in the damp October leaves until he felt wet. He remained lying on his back, panting and thanking the Saints he wasn't dead. What kind of burglar was this?

"You're next, Helen!" The old guy strutted back toward Helen's property. Roberto could see him, but no weapon. Had he used magic? No time to wonder. The flames had set several fires in the grass. He had to get back to Helen and protect her.

Flames streaked past Roberto as a bigger fireball struck the back of the shop. The back window was obliterated, replaced by a jagged hole in the charred cabin wall.

Roberto ran but couldn't reach the *Señora* in time. Her legs collapsed under her and she fainted onto the parking lot.

Seconds later, he knelt and put a hand to her chest. Her heart was beating fast but feebly. She breathed in ragged little gasps. He dialed for an ambulance, but by the time he described his location to the dispatcher, the mysterious stranger was gone.

LUNCH WITH A ZOMBIE

Tonya, Priya, Zain, and Drake were eating lunch in the cafeteria of Mackenzie College.

They had a table next to the floor-to-ceiling window which overlooked the tree-rimmed lake.

"When do they turn off the fountain?" Priya asked, referring to a jet of water offshore in front of campus.

"When it freezes I guess." For Tonya, the picturesque view was commonplace. During lectures, she preferred sitting close to the building's southern walls which overlooked the broad lawn where athletic guys habitually threw Frisbees over the bronze head of sour-faced railroad baron, Sir William McKenzie.

"Tonya? Earth to Tonya?" Priya swept her hand in front of Tonya's face.

"Sorry, what were we saying?"

"We think you should be in the movie," said Drake. Tonya admired the way his shoulders filled out his checked shirt.

"We need a couple of girls for speaking parts," said Zain. He was wearing a black t-shirt with a great white shark printed on it and a ball cap that said, "Fear Me."

"Are you directing?" Tonya figured he belonged in front of the camera.

"That's Drake's job. I'm grip, best boy, bottle washer, prima donna, muse and auteur all rolled into one manly package."

"You forgot egomaniac," said Priya.

"Out of modesty." Zain bowed.

Priya pointed out the window at Lakeshore Drive. "Don't you love watching them scurry this way and that while we sit here enjoying our mango shakes?"

"That will be us in another half hour," said Tonya.

"Not all of us," Priya smiled. "Drake and I are skipping this afternoon, so we can figure out how to record my installation."

"It's a mistake," said Zain. "What if people break our cameras as a Halloween prank?"

"When's the last time you heard of someone pranking an art gallery? This is an installation, only for the interested," said Priya.

"They could be interested in stealing cameras," said Zain.

"They won't even see them," said Drake. "I'm going to mount them way up in the trees."

"They could watch us put them up and steal them when we leave." Zain pointed an accusing French fry at his friend. "What would you do then?"

Drake pointed a long fry at Zain's heart and put on a cheesy French accent. "I would defeat them with ze Blade of Orléans. *En garde*, coward!"

Zain brandished his own deep-fried weapon and started to thrust and parry across the table. Drake stood up to gain some reach, so Zain leaped to his feet, and the two of them took the fight to the floor. All across the cafeteria, Tonya noticed people staring.

Let them. If Drake could let loose, she could too.

"Would you idiots sit back down," said Priya. "You'll embarrass Tonya."

"Speak for yourself." Tonya grabbed a fry and held it *en garde*. "I was known as ze Ketchup Killer of Loon Lake High."

Priya raised an eyebrow at Tonya. She smiled until Zain put a hand on Tonya's shoulder, his face suddenly serious. He pointed out the window.

"Isn't that your Professor?" said Priya.

Through windows on the opposite side of the cafeteria, Tonya saw Professor Rudolph on the lawn. He was walking blindly up the path as students dodged out of his way. On the lawn, the statue of Sir William Mackenzie stood in his path. The Professor walked right into it, stumbled back and continued past, lumbering into a student and causing her to drop an armful of books.

"He looks sick or something. C'mon." Tonya leapt to her feet and went outside to see what was ailing her beloved History professor. His eyes, when she caught up with him, were unfocused and dull, coated in a bluish film. He staggered blindly toward the west end of the grounds, headed toward the wooded path between campus and the cemetery.

It wasn't difficult to keep up with him. He walked with the grace of Frankenstein's monster. "Professor Rudolph," she touched his shoulder. "Are you okay?"

No reaction.

"Can you hear me? It's Tonya, from Philosophy of History."

He kept lumbering forward, unhearing as well as blind.

Priya and Drake caught up.

"What's wrong with him?" Priya stared.

"He won't answer. Watch this." Tonya waved her hands in front of his face. He didn't react, so she stepped into his path and stood there. Professor Rudolph was huge and closing on her fast. She waited, blocking the way in the hope he would come to his senses. When he was about to plow into her, she leaped clear.

"We should follow him," said Drake. "My brother used to sleepwalk so badly, my parents had to tie his leg to the bed, so he wouldn't wander down the stairs."

"If we wake him suddenly, could he have a heart attack?" asked Zain, who was drawing even with Rudolph.

Priya took the Professor's shoulder and gave it a gentle shake. "Wake up Professor. Wake up!"

That didn't work so they tried grabbing him. Gently at first. Then they tried poking. Tonya watched Drake pinch him, hard, but the Professor didn't notice or slow down. He left the college behind taking the path into the trees.

Zain stopped, arms crossed. "I refuse to be a part of this. You're going to hurt him, and then we're going to get sued."

"Don't you need to have money to get sued?" Drake asked.

"Hey, I resent that. Someday I'll be worth millions of bucks. Don't say I didn't warn you."

Priya rolled her eyes.

Tonya understood her frustration. While they were arguing, the Professor was getting away.

"Wait!" Drake yelled, but the Professor lumbered farther from campus.

"*Adios* suckers! I'll be in Economics." Zain waved over his shoulder and headed to class.

"Let Zain go," said Tonya. "We have to stop the Professor, or he might walk into the road and get killed." She hurried after him.

"How are you going to do that?" Priya jogged to catch up. "You're a head shorter, and you're a cream puff."

"No problem." Tonya caught up and rushed ahead of the Professor. Smiling confidently, she placed herself in his path, straight-armed her hands at chest height and planted her feet. She gave him a stern look and shouted "Stop!" but the blue film on his eyes told her magic was involved. Rudolph kept coming so Tonya resisted with all her force, for at least half a second, until he tipped her back and she crashed onto her ass. Before she could stand, the Professor stepped forward raising a foot so large that from this angle, it blocked out the sun. He was about to bring it down on her head!

Drake grabbed her hands and pulled her aside, just averting the Professor's trampling feet.

"Thanks." She brushed wet leaves from her jeans.

After that, the three of them tried everything to wake Rudolph: grabbing, shouting, and even kicking at the backs of the Professor's knees. That made him stumble, momentarily, but nothing could stop or wake him. Giving up on individual efforts, they grabbed onto his belt together and dug in their heels, but soon found themselves water-skiing along the path, sitting on their own heels as their feet slipped across muddy leaves. Three determined Ninjas were no match for the sheer forward momentum of Professor Rudolph.

"It's like trying to stop a rhino," said Drake "What do we do now?"

"I don't know," said Tonya.

"He ruined my good shoes." Priya frowned at her Victorian booties.

"We have to do *something*," said Drake.

"Call the cops," said Priya. "He's a clear and present danger to leather goods."

"Not funny," said Tonya.

Nothing helped. Like god in his Greek philosophy lectures, the Professor moved as inexorably as the Unmoved Mover. What was next, perpetual motion?

Priya was panting. "Let's get ahead of him and clear a safe path. It's all we can do."

"We need professional help," said Tonya.

"Who? Campus police? The Provincial Police?" said Drake.

"The OPP would laugh at us," said Priya.

"You have a point." Tonya couldn't imagine the OPP investigating a runaway sleepwalker. "So, we steer him clear of obstacles until he wakes up naturally." Although she feared he could only be awakened supernaturally.

The professor had almost crossed the well-trodden path through the woods. Tonya said, "He's headed for the cemetery."

"That makes sense," said Drake, "since he lost his wife. Maybe he fell asleep in class and he's dreaming of visiting her grave."

"Very poetic," said Priya, "but shouldn't we call an ambulance?"

"Yes. Do it." Tonya wasn't allowed to mention magic to Mundanes, but the man needed to be stopped before he hurt himself. Professor Rudolph wasn't from one of the Old Families which meant using magic on him was prohibited. It looked like a rogue magic user was breaking the highest law of Loon Lake.

"Tell them we're headed for the cemetery, and Priya, don't forget to describe his eyes."

Priya dropped back to make the call while Tonya stayed ahead with Drake.

"This is hopeless," Drake said. "What if he walks into a car crossing the road?"

Approaching the cemetery, the gravel path changed to asphalt. This was the route runners took on their long circuit from the Athletic Center to the east, west along the south shore of the lake out of campus and then through the Eastern Gate into the Loon Lake Cemetery. All summer, Tonya had watched from the Herbal Healing Shop as they emerged from the Western Gate of the cemetery and turned south to run through Loon Lake Village in their team jerseys. Their typical route ran from Mackenzie College, in through the East Gate, along the path that ran past the chapel, out the West Gate and then around the outside of the cemetery and back up to campus again. How odd to be following the same paths chasing a runaway professor.

Somebody wanted to hurt Rudolph, but even the Mods wouldn't curse a university professor, would they? It was such a blatant, public flouting of the rule of secrecy that kept Trads and Mods from settling their disputes in the street. *Could it be related to her aunt's mysterious illness?*

He stepped blindly into the road.

They tackled him, trying to alter his course.

The force of their combined weight should have turned him, but they slid off as if he was coated in Teflon. He staggered across the road, oblivious to horns blaring.

A car was headed on a collision course with Rudolph.

Tonya was too far away to intervene.

The car squealed the brakes and Tonya watched helplessly as Professor Rudolph continued blundering forward, into the path of the approaching car.

Priya sprinted up from behind and shoved him across, clearing the road just in time.

Drake cheered and followed after them, but this tiny victory worried Tonya. It demonstrated that Rudolph could be hurried along, but he couldn't be slowed or deflected from his objective.

And then, up ahead, Tonya saw salvation. The tall, wrought iron fence around the cemetery was right in the Professor's path. A conscious man could turn and walk to the front gate, but Rudolph was in a mindless state. He would wash up against the gate like a fish in a net.

"I see the end of the road," said Drake, echoing her thoughts.

The Professor shambled up against the gate where she expected him to stop. Instead, he placed one foot onto a crosspiece and boosted himself up.

Drake whistled. "Who knew he was so spry?"

"How's he doing that in his sleep?" asked Priya.

"His eyes are open," said Drake. "My brother used to open the refrigerator door when he was sleepwalking."

The next bit was harder. The Professor had to get a leg over the top of the fence. Drake rushed over and tried to pull him back.

"Stop! What if you knock him down and he hurts himself?" said Priya.

"What if he falls on top of you?" Tonya stood helpless, her own body swaying in sympathy as the Professor teetered with one foot set halfway up the fence, the other in the air, straining his weak muscles to lift it over.

When he finally succeeded Drake said, "I thought he was going to rip something."

Tonya clambered over the fence. "Stay here," she told the others.

She followed his halting steps as he took the circular drive that led around the wooded hill and then continued, walking across country, between the weathered monuments in the oldest section of the cemetery. From here, she could already see her aunt's shop through the trees, on the other side of Kenny Road. There was no doubt about it, as much as Tonya wished she was wrong. The Professor was headed straight for the Three-Century Ash. This confirmed her fears that the Professor's problem was magic-related, but would the Ash protect a Mundane as it protected Tonya and other members of the Old Families?

The Professor stopped dead in front of the tree.

She heard feet crunching through the leaves behind her. *No, no, no.* Tonya was going to have to explain the tree's powers to her friends.

How else could she make them steer clear of the danger? Her dream of popularity and a normal life was over. So much for keeping magic hidden from the Mundanes, the one issue Mods and the ruling Trads all agreed on.

Loon Lake Village, and the ancient section of the cemetery where the Old Families were buried, exuded supernatural energy. These powers were not supposed to leak onto campus, territory of the Mundanes. Tonya wrestled with what to do. If she told her friends about magic, the Pures like her mother (who never practiced magic) and the Trads (who hid magic from the Mundanes) would punish them severely.

"He stopped walking," Tonya said. "We should go back to campus."

"Not till the ambulance arrives," said Priya.

Before Tonya could answer, the professor sat down on the dirty roots, and then lay out flat with his head pointing toward the Ash. He moaned and started to agitate his arms.

"What's he doing?" asked Priya.

"Making snow angels with the leaves?" said Drake.

"Freaking me out." Tonya's phone shook in her hands. "I'm calling the hospital."

"I already called 911," said Priya.

"Calling the hospital direct is better. This isn't Toronto," said Tonya. She turned her back to finish the call. Afterward, she explained. "The firefighters are volunteers and the OPP are outsiders. I want to make sure they send first responders from Loon Lake Hospital," *who had seen weirdness like this before.*

She had made sure to mention the Ash Tree and the frosted look in the Professor's eyes to tip them off that magic was involved. Something was going on, something a lot bigger than one sleepwalking professor.

When Priya and Drake went to bend over the body, Tonya said, "Stay back. He might be dangerous."

"A dangerous sleepwalker?" Priya raised groomed eyebrows.

"We were all over him a minute ago," said Drake.

"Just back off!"

Priya looked hurt but Tonya couldn't stop to explain her darkest fears. She was desperately calling her parents, the Herbal Healing Shop, and her Aunt Helen's number, leaving messages everywhere when nobody picked up. Even her Dad's cell, which should have been switched on for emergencies, went straight to voicemail. In desperation, she sent him a text, even though he hated texting.

The ambulance arrived, rolling along the paved road which crisscrossed the cemetery. When the paramedics came out—a man and a woman—they looked so young, they could have been students too. He stood a head taller than his partner, but both had light brown hair, similar features, and dark green eyes. Were they twins?

Tonya and her friends answered their questions, then stood and watched as they slid Professor Rudolph's portly body onto a stretcher. With a grunt and muttered curses, they lifted the heavy man and the gurney and rolled it to the back of the ambulance.

"Can I come along?" Tonya asked. She felt responsible, especially since she hadn't been able to stop his blind walk to the Three-Century Ash.

"We'll take it from here," said the young woman. "Unless you're a relative?"

"I'm not, but I'm from Loon Lake, and I think this is a *local* problem," Tonya said. "He walked from the middle of campus to the Three-Century Ash with his eyes open but not seeing." It was the most she could say in front of Priya and Drake.

Tonya watched their faces for reaction. A local from an old Loon Lake family would hear those clues and suspect magic right away. Unfortunately, these two didn't react.

"Make sure they know about the Ash Tree when he gets checked in," Tonya added.

"Don't worry," said the male paramedic. "He'll get the best possible care."

"He's my Professor. Let me come with you."

He shook his head. "You can visit him in hospital once the doctors okay it."

As the ambulance rolled away, Tonya wondered what to do next. Could the professor's illness be related to Aunt Helen's and to her parents' sudden move? Something was wrong. Her parents would never leave without giving her a forwarding address or telling her which hospital Helen was in. They were hiding something from her. Too many strange events at once had to be related, but how?

She looked at Priya and Drake, innocently watching the ambulance drive away. How long could she protect them from magic if a Mundane like Professor Rudolph wasn't safe? Had he learned something he shouldn't? The Old Families could be cruel to those who discovered Loon Lake's secrets. When she was only sixteen, her mother made her attend a meeting where City Council wiped some poor Mundane's memory. He had stumbled across some Mods using magic, and so, to protect their secrets, the Council made him forget several months of his life.

"Now do you see why using magic is wrong?" Her mother had smiled at her, eyes glinting.

After the ambulance left, Drake and Priya turned to go. Tonya followed without saying a word.

The three of them were nearing the Eastern Gate when Tonya stopped. "I'm going back to the shop."

"What about class?" Priya asked.

"And Rudolph?" said Drake.

"I'm worried about my aunt. She isn't answering her phone. I want to make sure she's alright."

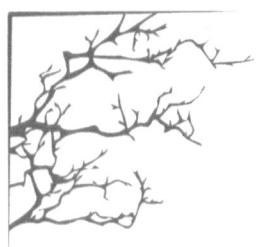

DRAKE

Drake watched Tonya head across the cemetery toward the Village. "Aren't you coming?" asked Priya.

He shook his head. "I'm going with Tonya."

He let Priya go in the opposite direction and strode after Tonya. As he caught up, Drake couldn't help admiring Tonya's long, shiny hair, and hourglass figure.

"Are you following me?"

He drew even with her in two long strides. "I hope you don't mind me coming along?"

"No, it's fine," she said, but her crumpled brow said otherwise.

"Do you smell that?" Acrid odors wafted toward him on the breeze.

Tonya stopped in his path. "Maybe I should go alone. My aunt is kind of a *special* person. I shouldn't just walk into her place with a stranger."

"Isn't it a store?"

"She has an apartment upstairs, but she's disappeared. I might have to go through her stuff looking for clues to where she went."

"I get it. It's personal."

"Don't be offended."

"It's fine. What do you want me to do, wait in the shop downstairs?"

"You should go back. Look at you, without a jacket. Your lips are turning blue."

"Really?" Drake put a hand to his lips. He watched her eyes linger on them a little too long and smiled. "I feel fine." He stifled a shiver. There was no way he was going back now. Something weird was going on and he wasn't going to let her walk into danger alone.

Drake picked up the pace. "What's that burning smell?" What if the store were on fire?

"Coming with me is a bad idea," said Tonya.

The night they met, Tonya had seemed excited about Priya's installation and the Ninja's film plans, at least she did until she bolted.

"What's really wrong, Tonya? What aren't you telling me?"

"Nothing."

"Why did you leave the Ninja meeting so fast? Did we offend you?"

"No. Everything's fine. You should go back to class."

He looked at her, standing arms akimbo, her frown set. Clearly something was bothering her.

"You're private. I respect that, but I'd like to keep you company."

He waited for her to put him off again but finally she said, "Okay."

Near the center of the cemetery stood an old church with broken windows. To the north he spotted glimpses of the Lake through pines and leafless trees. Tonya was headed west, past crumbling marble angels and monuments, at a pace that meant no fooling.

She didn't slow until they reached a small break in the fence. Across a meadow he glimpsed a two-story log building. The Herbal Healing Shop looked like an old-time settler's cabin, although there was nothing historical about the cluster of emergency vehicles flashing their lights in the parking lot. One firefighter stood talking to a police constable while other firefighters rolled up firehose.

"What happened?" Instinctively, Drake rushed forward, but Tonya pulled him back.

She took his hands and looked him in the eye. "Promise you won't touch anything, and let me go in first."

Without waiting for an answer, she raced across the field.

Suddenly, Tonya stopped and covered her ears, crouching in pain. Drake didn't hear anything unusual.

He caught up and offered her a hand. "What's wrong?"

Tonya stayed limp, her eyes glassy. Drake pulled her to her feet and propped her against his shoulder, draping her arm around his back for support. They were so close he could see right into her unseeing eyes. "What's wrong?"

She pointed away from the store. Tears rolled down her face and she started to thrash. Was she having a seizure?

As he walked her away from the store, her movements calmed, and she pulled away. Putting one arm on his shoulder, she walked steadily until they were back in the cemetery. She sat down with her back to a small tree.

"Are you okay?" Drake crouched in front of her.

"Yes," she answered through gritted teeth, her eyes focused again.

"I'm taking you back. One of the ambulance people should check you out."

"No!" Leaping to her feet, she hurried toward the chapel, hands clamped over her ears.

Drake hurried after her. "What's wrong?"

"Leave me alone!"

Drake let her put some distance between them. What was wrong with her? Her breakdown near the shop, her glassy eyes, and the look of pain on her face . . . If Tonya was ill, why wouldn't she accept help? Drake followed her at a respectful distance, determined to make sure she was okay.

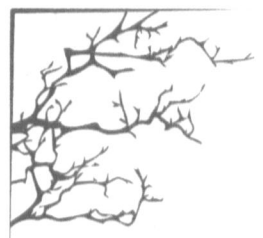

SUSPICION

Roberto didn't have a lot of experience with ambulances and police. In Lima, his family used private security companies and hospitals. The Canadians had free health care, like ordinary Peruvians, although from what he could ascertain from casual conversations, public treatment here took place in less crowded, well-equipped hospitals. Still, he wondered if he was doing the right thing, letting them take the lady to a public hospital.

She was frail, hardly solid enough to fill the thin blanket on the gurney in front of him. Most of her face was covered in messy white hair that had escaped its ribbon. He reached out to take her hand.

"Step back, sir." The attendant's voice was loud, his lips set in a frown. The police had asked him to leave her, several times. Roberto stood with his hands at his sides, unsure what to do. The compulsion to look after her was so intense, it was painful.

"Come with us," said the police officer.

"Can't I go to the hospital first, just to make sure she's okay?" He should never argue with police but couldn't fight the compulsion.

"We need you to make a statement." The officer came right up beside him now. His partner in the cruiser watched Roberto closely.

"You say Helen was attacked by a man with white hair, carrying some kind of flamethrower?"

Roberto nodded. Magic was involved but he wasn't fool enough to mention it.

"Catching him is our first priority, before he hurts someone else."

"So, I can leave?"

"We want you to give a full description, look at some pictures. We'll give you a ride to the hospital after."

"I have a car."

"I'm sorry. It's part of the crime scene. You have to leave it for now."

62

Roberto didn't like the sound of that. They didn't say he was under arrest, but he was forced to go to the police station. He would be a fool not to cooperate, but couldn't master his urge to stay with the old lady.

"All right buddy, let's go."

"Please." Roberto stood with his arms crossed, unable to overcome his compulsion or to explain it to these Mundanes.

The second officer got out of his patrol car. Now there were two of them standing either side of Roberto.

"Everything will be fine. Get in the car." The second cop's tone made that an order, no mistake. They were about to quick march him to the police car, only that couldn't happen. He was linked to Helen and where she went, he must follow.

"Just let me . . ." He took a step toward her, but the police took him by the arms and held him back.

"Calm down, nobody's going to hurt you," said the first cop.

Roberto was about to fight his way free when attendants slammed the ambulance doors and hopped in. They couldn't leave without him! Who would watch over Helen?

As it drove away, lights flashing, Roberto felt increasing pain in his chest as if a cord was stretching between him and her. What powerful magic, unlike anything he had suffered before. The pain increased with the distance between him and the ambulance until, like a cable, the link between them snapped. He was released. The compulsion to protect her faded sharply.

"I can go now."

He let them put him in the back of the car, mentally preparing himself for interrogation. Police were police, even if they were Canadian. What if he had incriminating ashes on his body from the explosion? As they drove away, his situation seemed increasingly dire. They had caught him at the scene of the crime and the real criminal sounded like a made-up story. Who seemed the more likely suspect, a young foreigner in custody, or a limping white-haired pappy who had conveniently disappeared?

"Are you okay back there?" the first officer asked.

"I'm fine. Sorry, I didn't want to leave the old lady."

The driver gave Roberto an odd look in the rear-view mirror.

Roberto took a deep breath and tried to let it out slowly. In North America, you were innocent until proven guilty, and nobody said the OPP were corrupt; but of all the things that had happened since he flew into Toronto, this ride was by far the scariest.

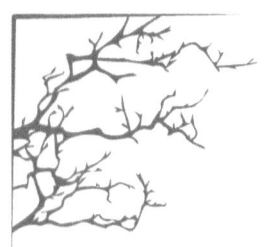

AUTHORITIES

The officers escorted Roberto into the foyer of the police station, took his international driver's license and student card, and told him to wait in line. When it was his turn, the officer behind the front desk typed Roberto's particulars into a computer then handed his cards to another officer who took them out of the room. Roberto felt naked without his ID.

A pretty, fresh-scrubbed officer beckoned him to follow her into a sparsely furnished room. "You can give your statement here." She set a wrapped sandwich and a paper cup of coffee on the table in front of him.

The moment he saw them, Roberto was ravenous. In six bites, the sandwich was gone. "Can I have more?" He opened his wallet and started to count out bills.

She scowled. "Do I look like a waitress?" She turned away and adjusted a camera mounted on the ceiling. "The red light means it's on. Tell me exactly what happened, starting at the beginning."

"How is Helen?" Roberto tried to keep his voice even.

"In the hospital getting excellent treatment, but the perpetrator is getting farther away every minute. We have cars out looking for him." She rubbed her forehead. To Roberto her concern seemed genuine. They believed him.

"Tell me everything you can remember about the attacker."

It was weird. She had Roberto tell his story over and over, then asked a bunch of questions she should know the answers to, if she had listened. So, he was being interrogated after all. These Canadians. They appeared soft and friendly and brought sandwiches, all the better to trip you up.

Many hours later, Roberto re-emerged from the station. The officer who released him told him to wait by the curb for a ride. It was already dark. October days were so short here. One of many things he could never get used to: long nights, the wind and the cold. It was threatening snow. Specks of white flew into his face with a burning chill.

Roberto hated his parents for sending him to Loon Lake. Why not somewhere warm, like California? What was special about this small university surrounded by forests, lakes, and fields?

"It has a strong aura of magic," Madre had said. Informants had brought the news all the way to Lima and she had to know more.

"We have magic at home," he had protested.

"We buy you everything you want, let you see who you like, go where you like, but when we ask for one little favor . . ." His dainty mother looked up at him and sighed.

"I won't be your lab rat. Why don't you go yourself?"

His mother fussed with the buttons of her lace blouse. "It's just a year. We're doing you a favor."

"Hilarious. As if you don't have enough problems with magic here."

"Respect your mother." Papí imposed his barrel chest between them.

"I won't go."

He had tried to refuse but they threatened to disinherit him and cut off his hefty allowance.

If they knew what he was going through, they would apologize. Tomorrow, he would call his parents and tell them everything he had survived, but right now Roberto yearned to go back to the dorm, order pizza, and collapse into bed.

A cruiser pulled up to the curb, his ride home. He got in and asked the officer to take him directly to the school cafeteria. He had a sudden craving for gravy, mashed potatoes, and meatloaf.

"Are you sure you don't want to go home and change your clothes first?" The officer raised an eyebrow. It was the same one who had brought Roberto in.

Roberto remembered that his jacket was singed. He ran a hand through his fire-crisped hair, stirring up a terrible odor. "I really need to eat."

Roberto's ribs ached where he had thrown himself on the ground to escape the fire ball, but the ravenous emptiness of his belly was much worse. If he didn't eat soon, he would bite into his own arm just to chew on something.

FORTY MINUTES LATER, Roberto drove a friend's car to the hospital, feeling stuffed from gorging on cafeteria food. His hair was damp from the shower and it sent shivers down his spine. More than ever, all he wanted was to sleep, but as strong as his need to eat had been, the minute he had looked at his empty plate, all he could think of was Helen. He thought the compulsion to look after her had ended when the ambulance drove away. No such luck. Once he lost his fear of the police, and fed his raging hunger, it came back again. She had bewitched him and without his *abuela* or his mother to help, he couldn't lift the spell.

The sensible thing would be to call the hospital and see if she was alright. Then he could go to bed in peace. Instead here he was, nearly falling asleep at the wheel one moment, and shivering the next, anxious to see she was okay with his own eyes. Roberto couldn't feel more concerned if this stranger was his mother. It was wrong, and he knew it by moments, but then his attention would drift, and he'd forget again. Roberto's brain was a muddle of sleepiness punctuated by moments of urgency, like two people trapped in one overfed body.

He opened his eyes to the sound of gravel under his tires and realized he was drifting into the unpaved shoulder. This was insane. He was going to get himself killed. The logical thing to do was to pull over and take a quick nap, before he crashed the car.

It was the sane thing to do, and yet Roberto couldn't stop driving. He was too worried, his head looping and looping with questions. Was she alright? Her quick pulse and funny breathing were worrisome. Did that mean heart attack? And why had she been eating a jar of pickled monstrosities? It was repulsive and unnatural. Helen needed help and Roberto was letting her down.

The thought filled him with a deep sadness that served to keep him awake and on the verge of tears until he turned into the hospital parking lot. What was happening to him? Roberto never cried, and yet as he got out of the car, the cold wind on his cheek iced a rolling tear.

At hospital reception, a back-combed brunette with scarlet nails sat inside a Plexiglas box. Roberto had to stoop to talk to her through the bottom of the wicket because she slid the divider only halfway up. Her cell phone sat on the desk beside her and she kept glancing at it, and chuckling.

"Hi, hon, what can I do for you?" She gave him a toothy smile through the Plexiglas barricade.

"I'm looking for a lady named Helen. She came in by ambulance this afternoon."

"Helen, eh? Is she a relative of yours?"

"No. She's a thin, white-haired lady. I was there when she took ill. I called the ambulance for her and now I just want to make sure she's okay."

"How sweet. You're a real life Good Samaritan, am I right? Well, I'd love to help you out, hon, but we get lots of old ladies. Loon Lake attracts more retirees than the early bird special."

"I'm afraid she was having a heart attack. Could you check the Emergency Department?" *Why was this cow making jokes? This was serious.*

"No need. Give me her last name and I'll look her up." She tapped a computer monitor with her pen.

"She's the owner of Helen's Herbal Healing Shop. Maybe you know her?"

"Don't you know her last name?"

"I found her when she needed help."

"How do I know you're not some kind of stalker?" She stood up, hands on hips, the teased top of her hairdo standing just above the Plexiglas barrier.

"Why would I do that?"

"I wonder too. I also wonder why your family sent you here." She put a hand up to cover her mouth, but not before he caught her smirk. "I'm sorry, but if you're not family and can't even give me her name, you're obviously not a friend. I'm going to have to ask you to leave."

"Can't you just tell me if she's okay?"

"Who?"

"Helen."

"I don't know who you're talking about." This time she didn't even try to hide her smile. "Is there something else I can do for you? Maybe have somebody take a look at your back to check for burns?"

Roberto had showered and changed his clothes. He was wearing a hat that didn't smell of smoke.

"How do you know—

"News travels fast in Loon Lake. I think you'd better be on your way, Roberto."

"I never told you my name."

"Which was very rude of you. I thought Peruvians were friendly." She shook her head and sat back down.

"What?" How did she know where he was from? "Why won't you let me talk to Helen?" He moved closer to the desk, fingertips on the glass.

Clearly the Canadians were spying on him, and maybe planning to pin something on him too. First the three-hour grilling in the police station with the too-nice policewoman, and now this? The receptionist avoided his gaze, tapping on her phone as if he weren't standing right in front of her.

Behind him, Roberto heard grumbling from the line of people building up. Didn't she care? Shouldn't she be doing her job?

Ostentatiously, she started playing a game. He banged on the glass, but she ignored him. He felt like reaching through the glass and crushing her phone but what would be the point?

He decided to go out the front door and come in another way. The hospital was pretty big. He just needed to find a sympathetic nurse on another floor. Women liked Roberto and he liked them. He would give the new nurse a friendly smile and ask politely for the room number. Problem solved.

With new optimism, he tried to leave but someone took his shoulders and pressed him against the Plexiglas. Roberto struggled and craned his neck to see the same two attendants who had taken Helen in the ambulance. The man shot him a nasty grin just as Roberto felt a needle stab his leg.

He staggered free. Roberto's head spun, and his knees went weak. He closed his eyes and felt himself hang-gliding off the cliffs in Lima again. His head climbed in a lazy circuit around a thermal until the fishing boats in the harbor shrank to bath toys. Picking up speed, he spiraled faster and tighter, the sky getting brighter with every spin until he merged into the sun.

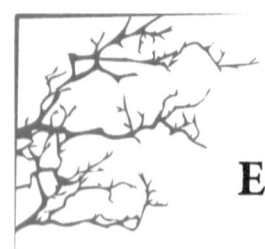

EATING CONTEST

After the head pain from her aunt's protective ward faded, Tonya attended the rest of her classes. At the Athletic Center after school, she stood waiting for Priya in the stands overlooking the pool. At one time, Tonya dreaded the prospect of exercise, but now it was a relief to smell chlorine and anticipate a nice, normal lane swim with her friend. Magical madness could wait. Below her, the diving team were cooling down with a few laps. She watched them glide through the water with barely a ripple. If only her life were so smooth.

Her aunt's wards hadn't repelled her like a stranger. They had felt personal somehow, as if her aunt's own hands were driving a stake through her head. How could someone she loved hurt her so much?

This brutal tactic doubled her determination to find out what her aunt was hiding. Someone else would have to do her snooping, but who? Priya would think she was crazy if she asked her to search her aunt's apartment. If she mentioned her aunt's magic to Priya, her friend would be in danger. Once Mundanes knew about magic, they were no longer off-limits. If they discovered Priya knew about magic, anyone in the magic community would be allowed to curse her until City Council ordered an amnesia spell. Tonya shivered. That wasn't something she'd wish on anyone, not even the mean girls back in high school.

Drake was sweet and knew nothing. He also had the equipment to make a video inside the shop. All she had to do was convince Drake to go through her aunt's place with a camera, as if he was making a documentary, and without mentioning magic. Piece of cake.

She sighed. Her parents forbade her to use or learn about magic, but she was tired of living by her mother's Pure rules. Tonya knew she had a talent for magic. None of the Mods in her high school could sense life energy like her.

Aunt Helen could, but she studied all types of magic. Flouting her Trad heritage, she made her living selling cure charms, occasionally to Mundanes. "What does it hurt?" she told Tonya when she first caught her at it. "I tell them it's traditional medicine."

She was always experimenting with new materials and spells. Could that be the real reason she was sick?

The coach blew a whistle and the team lined up for the last dives of the practice. Idly, Tonya scanned the pool for Marta's orange and blue swim cap, but she was absent. As the last swimmer got out of the pool, Tonya was sure of it. Could Marta be sick again?

Ten minutes later, Priya still hadn't come up to meet her so Tonya left the stands and went downstairs to get changed. She was crossing the foyer when Shin came out of the men's change room, walked past her, and doubled back.

"Hi," he said.

"Hi?"

"I want to apologize for Marta the other day. She's under a lot of pressure."

"Don't worry. I should never have tried out."

"Yeah. Anyway, a bunch of us are hanging out at her room tonight if you want to come. No hard feelings?" He smiled broadly at her.

Tonya couldn't believe it. Shin Chang was asking her to a party!

"Okay."

"Great. Ask your friend to come too." He gestured at Priya, who was just coming in.

Tonya managed to keep her voice calm until he left. Then she bounced up and down on the balls of her feet, tripping over her words as she told Priya about the party.

"I love divers with their big shoulders and tiny waists." Priya outlined an invisible hottie with upheld hands.

"So, you'll come with me?"

"Yes, and stop bouncing. If I'm gonna be seen with you, you have to pretend this isn't the first time your parents let you out of the house."

"What?"

Priya rolled her eyes. "I'm kidding. Sounds like fun."

THAT EVENING, TONYA wished she had shampooed her hair three times. Did she still smell of chlorine? Probably. Maybe at a divers' party others would too.

Choosing clothes for the evening was excruciating. Tonya was nervous about meeting the same diving team girls who had witnessed her crash and burn at the tryout, but this wasn't high school. University kids should have better things to do than bully her for making a pathetic dive. At least, that's what she told herself but just in case, she wanted to look great. Because of her summer weight loss, she had to try on three pairs of jeans before she found some that didn't look sloppy.

She hadn't bought tops in her new size yet, so she took the stairs up to Priya's floor. Her friend was shorter and slim, but her clothes were so original. Maybe she could loan Tonya something stretchy but devastating.

"What would you like?" asked Priya.

"Oh, not much. I want girls to envy me and guys to notice me—but I don't want to look like I'm trying too hard."

"Call me your fairy godmother." Priya scooped up some accessories. "I don't have your size. Let's try your closet."

Hours later, they got in the elevator. Priya had loaned Tonya a wide belt which cinched her roomy top and emphasized her cleavage. Would people stare?

"Maybe going to Marta's party is a mistake."

"Too late to back out now," said Priya. "I straightened my hair for this."

"It was Shin's idea, not Marta's. What if she tells me to get lost?"

"You worry too much. She was embarrassed you caught her being sick. That doesn't mean she'll hate you forever."

"She did in high school. What if Marta set this up so she can laugh at me in front of her friends?"

"Don't be paranoid. She's probably forgotten her embarrassment by now."

When they arrived on Marta's floor, Tonya could hear indie music playing. She smiled at Priya. "Thanks for calming me down."

"Deep breath," said Priya as she opened the door.

Tonya wasn't sure what to expect. She never got invited to the cool kid parties in high school. She had all kinds of fantasies about how exciting and exotic their lives must be, like the rich kids in American movies. So, when she saw a bunch of students in jeans, sitting on the chairs, tables, and the bed of a dorm room just like hers, Tonya felt a bit let down.

She looked for Shin or Marta, but the room was all sparkles and shadows. They had doused the fluorescents and hung strings of pumpkin lights. There were glowing Halloween decorations stuck to the walls and at the study desk, a scarecrow sat guarding the punch bowl. The kids who weren't on the floor or sitting on the window ledge, were crammed together on the bed. As her eyes adjusted to the low light, Tonya made out Marta, holding court to a circle of students. Pulling Priya by the hand, she went to say hi. No reason not to have manners.

"Hey Marta. How are you?" Tonya tried to act casual.

"Mmm," said Marta. Her acolytes were playing a strange game. There was a huge aluminum bowl between them, filled with porridgy goop. Tonya couldn't look away as, one after the other, they scooped out handfuls of oatmeal and ladled it into their mouths. When they had gone around the ring once, Marta started them off again.

Tonya nudged Priya. "What the?"

Priya shrugged. "They're your friends."

Tonya recognized some of them from the diving team.

"What is this?" Priya stepped closer to the circle, "a dare?"

"Join us," said one of the guys, spraying oatmeal as he spoke.

"No thanks," said Priya. "I'd rather eat chips."

"Those are long gone," said one of the girls. "We had to make porridge because we ran out of everything else."

"What about ordering in?" Tonya suddenly wished she had brought snacks.

Shin threw open the door. "Pizza's here!"

He held stacks of pizza boxes in front of him, his broad shoulders filling the doorframe as he came through. Looking at him and his buddies with their perfect faces and beautifully molded arms, Tonya didn't care about Marta anymore. These guys were so symmetrical, they were godlike.

So she wouldn't stare, Tonya got herself some punch labeled "witch's brew." It was dark with disgusting brown foam on top but tasted like a Coke float. There were bottles of rum and other liquor bottles on the side. Priya offered to add a shot of vodka to their glasses but Tonya declined.

"To partying with the cool kids," Priya toasted, softly enough to keep it between them.

"Cheers." Tonya was finally here, at one of those university parties she had always heard about. It was weirder than she expected but in Loon Lake weird *was* normal, especially around All Hallow's Eve. That was the time of year the Mods really let loose, practicing magic openly under the guise of Halloween illusion.

Priya, meanwhile, was going around the room, talking about her art installation and handing out flyers. When she got to Shin, she stopped and waited for him to finish handing out pizza.

"This is for you. I'd really like you to come to the cemetery Halloween night and see my art display."

"Okay..."

Tonya noticed him glance at Priya's cleavage then back at her face. He grinned like a kid.

"I'm premiering an art installation called *Man vs. Nature*. There's also going to be a bonfire."

"Does the university know?"

"No, it's close by but off campus. Bring your friends but don't tell everybody. We don't want to attract attention from campus police."

"Okay." He took the flyer, which looked small in his long fingers, and shoved it into his pocket. "Pizza?"

"Thanks, I'm starving." Priya took an enormous slice and somehow, using folding techniques Tonya had never mastered, ate it in a graceful and ladylike manner.

Tonya stepped up to take a slice just as Shin walked off with Priya on his arm. He seemed awfully excited to be speaking to her, right in front of his girlfriend.

A buff guy stood on top of Marta's swivel chair. "Alright everybody!" A couple of his buddies grabbed the chair and started rolling it back and forth, so it pulsed in time with the music.

"It's showdown time! Clear the floor."

A group of spectators formed around a clear spot in the center of the room. Priya joined Tonya, but Shin wasn't with her.

"The athletes have been preparing themselves all night," said one of the chair rollers. He pointed to the bowl of porridge and everybody erupted into shouts of "Ew!"

"Bring it on." Marta stepped up and motioned for someone to challenge. At last another girl was pushed into the ring, facing Marta.

The guy on the chair said, "Each athlete will be given a pizza. The first to finish wins."

Eager hands pushed four pizza boxes onto the floor as a couple of guys stepped up as well.

"Let the eating begin!"

The contestants dropped to their knees and started wolfing down food like dogs.

"And you wanted to come to this party?" Priya rolled her eyes but she was smiling.

They were shoveling pizza into their mouths so fast, Tonya knew they couldn't be chewing. It was disgusting!

"Marta's in the lead!" said the chair guy. "No wait, it's Paul. Paul's ahead by a pepperoni . . . Wait, now Tyrell is coming up from behind. It's Paul and Tyrell, nose to nose with four slices left."

"I don't think I can stand the suspense," said Priya.

Suddenly Marta stopped eating. Her distress was subtle, until her face contorted and she struggled to her feet, stumbling out of the circle. Her milk-white face turned bluish. Tonya wanted to help but she hung back, not wanting to provoke another conflict. Marta put her hands to her neck in the universal choking sign. Tonya rushed to her side.

Marta started to wobble but Tonya supported her. Tonya leaned her over and delivered five back blows then joined her arms around Marta's chest, placed a fist below her xiphoid process, and gave five quick upward thrusts.

"Call 911," she ordered Priya.

She repeated the five and five procedure, but no matter how hard Tonya tried, she couldn't get Marta to breathe.

Marta collapsed almost taking Tonya with her. It was the first time Tonya had done the Heimlich maneuver on a real choking person instead of a rescue dummy. *Why wasn't it working? Please, please, please let the ambulance come fast.*

Marta lay on the floor, her lips blue. When her eyes rolled back in her head, Tonya knew. No ambulance could get there fast enough.

COIMETROPHOBIA
(FEAR OF CEMETERIES)

Tonya stood looking at Marta collapsed on the floor. The rest of the partygoers were crowding in to see what was wrong.

"Back up!" It was the loudest she'd ever shouted.

They obeyed, and Tonya dropped to her knees, positioning Marta on her back, lifting her neck to open her airway. She swept a finger through Marta's mouth to check for obstructions. At the back of her throat she felt the hard edge of pizza crust and tweezered her fingers together and pulled, but it slipped through her fingers. Tonya tilted Marta's neck higher, gave her a rescue breath and then joined her hands over her chest to give thirty chest compressions. By the time she completed the last one, a faint gurgling came from the girl's mouth. This time when Tonya breathed into her, Marta's chest rose a little. Encouraged, Tonya slipped her fingers back into Marta's mouth. The pizza had shifted forward. Tonya reached in as far as her fingers would stretch. She pulled, extracting a wide piece of crust.

Marta coughed and started thrashing on the floor.

"Are you okay?" Tonya examined her face.

Marta's complexion went from bluish to white to pink. When she stopped gasping, her first words were, "Out of my room!"

At first, Tonya thought Marta was joking, but the girl's face was red, and her eyes stood out of her head, cartoon furious.

"But . . ."

"Don't come near me!" She shot Priya a look. "Or near my boyfriend again!"

"You're welcome!" Tonya stood up and marched to the door.

Priya tried to leave with her but Tonya put a hand up to stop her. "Stay and make sure that harpy doesn't die. I'm going to wait for the ambulance before I strangle her."

Outside was a lot colder than Tonya expected. The wind blew through her thin red top and made her wish she was wearing one of her roomy old sweaters. At least *her* discomfort was temporary. Marta was in real trouble.

Priya joined her. "They're panicking, hiding the alcohol in case the cops come upstairs with the ambulance people. Marta wants you to turn them away."

"The paramedics should see Marta. I think she needs help."

"She'll be delighted when she finds out you insisted," said Priya.

"Too bad." After seeing Marta vomiting in the change room and now gulping pizza like a starved wolf, Tonya was afraid for her.

The ambulance pulled up and she recognized the same paramedics who came for Professor Rudolph.

"Where is she?" asked the woman.

"Priya can lead you up," said Tonya. "I gave her CPR and got the food out of her airway. She might try to tell you she's okay, but will you take a look at her anyway? She's been purging, and binging . . . I'm worried about her."

As they waited for the elevator, the attendants stood on either side of a stretcher. Things were getting out of hand. Marta was from a Mod family but there were Mundanes on the diving team. One individual could suffer from bulimia but the way those divers were eating seemed unnatural. Could they be cursed?

Tonya turned to Priya. "Something's wrong about the way Marta and the divers were eating."

"Like what?"

"Pigging out on porridge doesn't seem natural." Would keeping Priya ignorant of magic put her in more danger than knowing?

"It was an eating contest."

Tonya tried again. "What did Professor Rudolph and Marta have in common?"

"Passing out?"

"Eating like crazy. He stuffed his face full of fries in the middle of a lecture and then wandered off, blank-eyed." *All the way to the Three-Century Ash*, but Tonya wasn't going to explain to Priya that the ancient ash, the same species as the Old Norse World Tree, concentrated power. Until she had evidence to prove supernatural forces were involved, mentioning them would make Priya think she was crazy. Given recent events, Tonya feared she'd get proof soon enough.

The elevator arrived and Priya followed the attendants in. "Aren't you coming?"

"You go with them. I want to check something."

She could feel it coming. Tonya reached out with her mind and detected an extra current of energy in the earth beneath her feet. Pure power was moving and shifting but this was nothing like the little currents of life force that sometimes ran through the Herbal Healing Shop. In the summers when she worked there, life magic gave her a warm feeling or made colors look brighter for a while.

This underground energy felt cold and dark, like something bad was coming. It must all connect somehow: Marta, the professor, the porridge-eating divers . . .

Then it hit her. The cemetery. The diving team kids cross-trained by running through it. Professor Rudolph visited his wife's grave there, and the ash was just inside the cemetery, near her aunt's property. Lynette took her boyfriend on romantic walks through the cemetery's winding paths. Marta didn't have an eating disorder. She had caught some kind of supernatural disease in the cemetery. Was that even possible?

Aunt Helen would know. Tonya sighed.

With a clattering sound, attendants emerged from the elevator pushing an empty gurney. Priya was with them, as was Marta, shoulders squared, face neutral. Her mask only slipped when she caught sight of Tonya and wrinkled her nose.

"I hope you feel better . . ."

"Shut up!" Marta strode past to join the ambulance attendants at the side of the road. She told them something Tonya couldn't hear, but which cracked them up. Still laughing, they loaded the gurney into the ambulance.

Marta waved them off as they drove away.

"C'mon," Priya said, "let's take the stairs."

On the way up to Priya's room, Tonya tried to compose a rational argument to convince her friend to stay out of the cemetery. Priya was so excited about her art installation, but if she went ahead with the plan to set it up in the graveyard, the whole campus could wind up like Marta. Supernatural curse or airborne disease, everybody who spent time in the cemetery had been struck with compulsive eating. Her need to eat had gotten so extreme, Marta would have choked to death if Tonya hadn't intervened.

They went into the room and Priya gave her a hug. "What you did was brave. That ungrateful witch should be thanking you." Priya's hug made warning her friend away from the cemetery that much harder but it had to be done.

Tonya sat on the edge of Priya's bed and gestured for her friend to take the desk chair. "I have to tell you something important. I think I know what's happening, to Marta, to Lynette, and Professor Rudolph."

"Lynette your roommate?"

"They're all eating uncontrollably. Something takes over their minds and, well, you saw the diving team."

"Peer pressure at its worst, right?" Priya shook her head. "If Marta told those kids to jump off a bridge . . ."

"It's not peer pressure. It's a curse that spreads like a disease."

"A what?"

"This town hides a lot of secrets. The ground beneath us is full of magical energy. You don't notice them, but the Old Families in this town are constantly negotiating and fighting with each other to control that power."

Priya crossed her arms. "You must be joking."

"Magic is real."

"Very funny. Nice Halloween prank."

"I'm not kidding. This eating problem is coming from the cemetery."

"Don't be stupid. Aren't you learning anything in first year Psych? People in groups do nutty things. That doesn't mean they have a magic virus."

"So how do you explain Professor Rudolph stuffing his face with fries and bumping into things all the way to the graveyard?"

"Narcolepsy?"

"I'm telling you, a magical force drew him to that cemetery."

"You don't really believe that." Priya stared at Tonya, her eyes a little too wide. She hadn't told her she was crazy yet, but Tonya figured it was coming.

"You saw my roommate Lynette. She doesn't seem the imaginative type to you, does she? Well, she ate four boxes of Halloween candy, for no apparent reason. People are binging compulsively because they caught something in the graveyard."

"That's insane," said Priya.

"What if I told you it wasn't magic? What if I said the cemetery was spreading a contagious disease and the only way to save them was to shut down the cemetery."

"I'd say shut down the bakery too. Every time I walk by that place I smell cookies and I want to buy some." Priya pretended to sniff heavenly baked goods.

"I'm not kidding."

"You're overreacting."

"Can nothing convince you to stay out of the cemetery?"

"I've been building my animatronics for months and you're telling me to scrap everything? Halloween night is my debut, my one shot. Local TV is going to cover it. I won't get a chance like this again."

"Marta almost died tonight."

"She has a problem. The rest is your imagination."

"You saw the professor's face yourself. And I told you about Lynette. She's binging too."

"How do you know the Professor is still sick?" asked Priya. "Maybe he signed himself out of hospital."

"Look, I know, okay? People in my family have kind of a connection to .
. .

Priya frowned. She held up her hand, ready to cover Tonya's mouth.

How to make her listen? "Something weird is going on in that graveyard. I can sense it."

"Good. That makes it even spookier."

"I'm serious."

"An eating contest is not a virus, and bulimia isn't a contagious disease. Do you know how crazy you sound?"

"People here know I'm sane. Loon Lake isn't like other places."

"Right. Your auntie sells herbs and calls it medicine. People in your family believe a bunch of superstitious garbage."

"Her cures work!"

"Sorry. No offense to your sick aunt, but before I believe in magic, you have to show me some."

"Magic isn't like card tricks. There will be consequences."

"And lame excuses."

There it was. Initiating Priya into the magic world was dangerous, but there was no choice. "C'mon, we have to take this outside."

Tonya led a reluctant Priya outside and along the path toward the edge of campus. She stopped under a pine tree. "I hoped I wouldn't have to do this."

"Let's go back, I'm cold." It was the first thing Priya had said since Tonya hustled her into the elevator.

"Stand back. I'm untrained so things might get out of control."

Priya didn't move. Tonya walked to the far side of the tree and pulled down a bough by the tip. She closed her eyes and concentrated on the life inside, her mind lighting up with green traceries of sap running through fractal channels like veins. She took a deep breath and willed that life force out through the pine bough, along her arm, and down through her body into the ground.

"Nothing's happening."

Tonya lost her concentration and had to start again. This time she ignored Priya's questions and tried to become one with the ground and feel its thirst for life.

"All things die and return their energy to the earth. I'm just speeding up the process . . ."

There, the pine needles went crispy dry in her hands. Tonya opened her eyes.

Priya took the branch from her, turning it over to examine the dead needles. "How did you do that?"

"I drew out some life force and returned it to the ground."

"You killed a branch with your touch."

"Now, do you believe me?"

"Maybe. What did you say? Magic can speed up the natural process of death and decay. But if magic is real and dangerous, that gives me a whole new reason to spread my message. My art scares people. People think art is pretty but pointless. When they walk through that cemetery, I want them to feel primal vulnerability, like their ancestors, surrounded by wild beasts and scared of the dark."

"The forest south of campus is creepy too. Why not move it there, just to be safe?"

"Are you joking? It took me a whole day to install the mounts. Besides, we've already handed out the flyers and announced a bonfire in the field just outside Loon Lake Cemetery."

"On my aunt's property!"

"She won't mind if we use her empty field. Didn't you say she was in the hospital? Besides, the swimmers are already bringing wood for the bonfire. If I don't light it, they will."

"Tell Shin to make them move it."

"Too late. People are going to show up whether we like it or not."

"Make an announcement. Rope off the area and put up signs or something. We can't lead a hundred people through the cemetery tomorrow night. They'll get infected."

"You can't prove that."

"Isn't the risk enough to convince you?"

"Building my creatures has taken years, and preparing them for installation took weeks. I've already installed most of the pieces. You can't tell me to dismantle my masterpiece. I could never move it in time."

"There are powerful forces you are messing with, extra-powerful on All Hallows' Eve."

"These forces are all over Loon Lake. You said so yourself."

"Something's changed." Tonya put her hand on the grass. An extra energy thrummed beneath the earth. "Feel it?" She took Priya's hand by the wrist and placed it where it vibrated most. "There's something wrong with this magic."

"I don't feel anything." Priya snatched her hand away. "You're tired. It's late. You're getting emotional. Go to bed."

"Tell me you'll call it off."

"Sure, don't worry. Now go to bed before you fall over."

"So, you'll do it?"

"First promise you'll get your ass into bed."

Priya's half-smile gave Tonya a nagging doubt, but how could she argue with yes? Besides, draining the branch had worn her out, as though some of her energy had flowed into the ground with the tree's.

Tonya couldn't help it. She leaned on Priya's shoulder as they walked back into the dorm.

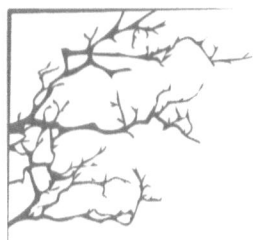

LEGENDARY

Drake's phone woke him before sunrise.

"Priya gave me your number."

Like a sleepy Klondike prospector, Drake let the girl's words pass through his groggy brain pan, but he couldn't sift out a nugget of meaning. "Who is this?"

"Tonya. I hope you don't mind."

"It's 5:30 in the morning."

"Talk to the Ninjas for me? I don't have their numbers, and this is urgent. The art show is canceled and so is the bonfire."

"No, it isn't. We're set to start in twelve hours."

"Priya promised."

"When?"

"Last night."

"Funny, we were on the phone past midnight, running down her checklist. The installation opens tonight."

On the other side of the room, Zain groaned. "What in the name of Bruce Campbell!?"

"It's Tonya."

"How dare she wake me! I was dreaming of zombies."

"Go back to sleep. It's a mistake. She thinks we have to cancel the installation."

On the other end of the phone, Tonya's voice shot up. "You have to stop people from going. There's something evil in the cemetery air. It made Professor Rudolph sick and Marta and the diving team. If you go into those woods, you'll get sick too."

"I walk by the cemetery all the time without even sneezing."

"I'm not talking allergies. Stay out or you'll end up like Professor Rudolph."

If he hadn't seen Rudolph with his own eyes, Drake would think Tonya was crazy. Cute but crazy, and prone to strange headaches, but he *had* seen Rudolph, which made Tonya's early morning call seem less insane.

"I get that you're worried, but Priya isn't. The Ninjas aren't."

Zain staggered over and grabbed the phone out of Drake's hand. "What's this about?"

Zain listened, eyes widening with every word until Drake got so curious he wanted to snatch the phone back.

"You can't cancel the movie." Zain started doing his Godfather voice. "It would kill Priya and then I'd have to kill you, and all your little friends, except you won't have any friends because you want to kill our movie!" Zain handed back the phone and flung himself on his bed.

"Zain! Zain?" Tonya shouted into his ear.

"It's me again. I agree with Zain, except for the killing part. Are we done here? I want to go back to sleep."

"Sorry. Go back to sleep. I'll come see you later."

Drake was concerned about recording Priya's event, but not for Tonya's reasons. The university installed surveillance cameras without student protest, so Zain argued that nobody would mind a harmless recording of Halloween hijinks. He swore he would only use footage of people disguised by their costumes. It was already an ethical gray area, but what if Zain got too enthusiastic and crossed the line? He could jeopardize everything.

"Hey Zain, you awake?"

"No."

"I was thinking. Maybe we shouldn't film people in the cemetery tonight. Tonya says Professor Rudolph visits his wife's grave there all the time."

"So? We won't run into him Halloween night."

"It isn't respectful."

"You can't change your mind now. Screaming students and Priya's monsters will make priceless footage. This is our chance to make the Great Canadian zero-budget horror movie we've always wanted."

"But—"

Zain got up and started pacing the room. "This is our big break." He conducted invisible orchestras with his hands. "Priya's concept is brilliant. Using a centuries-old graveyard will give our movie a look you can't find anywhere else."

"Or residents could complain, and the cops could take our cameras."

"Don't be stupid. Tonight will launch our careers like a rocket, leaving YouTube stars moping in the cinders as we rise into the galaxy of pro film. Want me to leave you behind, or will you be flying Ninja Spaceways?"

"Beam me up, I guess."

"Good." Drake clapped him on the shoulder. "When I'm big in Hollywood I might need a pre-fame friend."

Hours later, Drake finished loading his car with cameras, tripods, and brackets. He also had spare pieces of wood, clamps, an electric drill (sorry trees) and rolls of duct tape. It might take hours to rig, but people's reactions would make it worthwhile. Zain was right. By daylight, Priya's animatronic monsters were fascinatingly creepy. Tonight, when they leaped out of hiding in a centuries-old graveyard, the students would feel legendary terror.

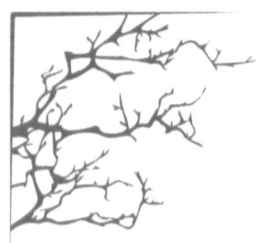

GONE

Tonya found herself in a dark forest. A hidden assailant had cut off her friends' legs at the knees. Tonya rushed from victim to victim, twisting tourniquets onto their thighs to stop the bleeding. The leafy earth beneath her shoes puddled with blood. She ran but slipped on gore. She felt herself falling backward when someone grabbed her shoulder. She lashed out to save herself from amputation.

"Hey, it's me! Calm down."

That didn't sound like a serial killer. Tonya opened her eyes.

Lynette stood over Tonya's bed, her hair a golden halo in the morning light.

"Shouldn't you still be sleeping off Friday night?"

"Roberto's missing," said Lynette. "We were supposed to meet yesterday but he isn't answering texts or calls. The guys on his floor haven't seen him. Nobody has."

"Maybe his phone died." Tonya rubbed her eyes. Things were coming at her too fast. There was something she had to do. Something urgent . . . Oh yeah, she had to stop *Man vs. Nature* from happening in the cemetery, or a lot of people could end up like Professor Rudolph.

"He should have borrowed a phone and called. I'm worried."

"He probably had a few drinks and crashed at a friend's place." For all she knew, Roberto got tired of Lynette. Tonya had.

"He texted me that he wasn't feeling well. He was supposed to call when he got home."

"Lynette, when you were pigging out on candy, did you ever feel the urge to walk to the cemetery?"

"What?"

"Or to go to the Ash Tree?"

"You're even weirder than I thought." Lynette spoke slowly, enunciating every syllable. "Roberto is missing."

"Tell campus police."

"They said he hasn't been missing long enough to report. Help me?"

What a choice. She had to help Lynette look for Roberto, but that would leave her less time to stop the art installation. If she refused, Lynette would probably kill her in her sleep.

"You don't need my help."

"Please." Lynette crossed her arms, her pretty face crumpled in a scowl.

"Why don't you wait and see if he shows up in an hour or two?"

"I want to look now."

Tonya sighed. "Let me throw on some clothes."

They went to the cafeteria to grab coffee. Students in line gossiped about a fire at the Herbal Healing Shop. Tonya shivered. The shop was full of dangerous items that posed a threat to the ignorant if her aunt wasn't there to supervise . . . but what if she had been there?

"I still haven't heard from my aunt and that's her store."

"Roberto texted me he was going there last night." Lynette's bottom lip trembled.

"I'll call the hospital to check for Roberto while you drive us to the shop."

Tonya had Loon Lake Hospital on speed dial. She called on their way out to the parking lot. During the short drive, Tonya waited on hold until a chipper voice answered and told her Roberto wasn't there.

"You sound familiar. Do I know you?"

"Doubt it, hon. Goodbye!" The connection clicked off.

Minutes later, Lynette drew near the Herbal Healing Shop. Tonya expected a painful repeat of yesterday's ward incident so she dry-swallowed a couple of aspirins. Her aunt might use magic to repel her, but a headache was physical, right? And painkillers prevented physical pain. That was her theory, anyway. She braced herself as they got close. Even ice pick stabs of pain couldn't keep her from investigating.

"Did Roberto do any binge eating?"

Lynette hesitated. "I don't know. He's an athlete. He eats a lot, all the time."

Not good. He sounded sick too.

When they pulled into the parking lot, Tonya anticipated knitting-needle-through-the-head agony. They parked near the store, but the pain never came. That worried her even more. Did her aunt have to be nearby to keep up her wards? Tonya didn't think so. Did she need to be alive?

Lynette opened the car door and ran across the parking lot which was littered with broken glass. She picked up something gray, a fine wool scarf patterned with geometric condors. "This is his!" Lynette held the scarf to her face.

"I'm sure he's okay." Tonya came up behind her.

"I'm not." Lynette slipped the scarf into her pocket.

Tonya put a hand on Lynette's shoulder. "We'll find him."

Aunt Helen lived above the shop, part of the massive two-story log cabin she had inherited from Tonya's great-grandparents. It was drafty in the winter, and attracted mice in fall, until Aunt Helen resealed the outside walls and modernized. As a child, Tonya remembered walking through the gutted building, asking her aunt why she didn't just tear it down and build a new one.

"History," was all her aunt would say.

Aunt Helen tolerated a filthy building site for months during renovations, despite her obsession for order. Mom always said she should have been a scientist. Before, after, and somehow even during the reno, she kept her counters sterilized like a laboratory.

As they approached, Tonya noticed the window beside the door was shattered. She stepped over a black puddle onto the stoop and pulled away yellow police tape sealing the door.

"Hello? Aunt Helen?" It was as cold inside as out and reeked of smoke. The small foyer where they stood opened into the shop, giving them a clear view of the premises. To Tonya's immediate left, a door marked "private" stood between her and the staircase up to her aunt's apartment.

Wind gusted in through the end of the shop, which was punched through, leaving a large, charred hole. The walls were streaked with soot near the floor, but the A-frame roof remained pristine. The countertop, ahead of her and to the left, remained untouched, but the glass case beneath it, and every jar and container inside, seemed to have exploded. *This was no natural fire.*

Tonya opened the door to the staircase, but a female constable rushed out from the workroom behind the sales counter. "You can't come in here." She had mousy hair and pale eyelashes like a child.

"I'm looking for my aunt."

The woman tilted her head slightly and squinted at Tonya, despite the light streaming in from outside. "You're Helen's niece? I didn't recognize you."

Without the extra pounds and bulky sweaters. "I remember you. Didn't you volunteer at the hospital?"

"Not anymore. Constable Purrell." Her hands stayed on her hips, but she nodded at Lynette and Tonya. "I'm sorry about your aunt. She's in hospital."

"What? When?"

"They sent her, after the fire."

"She was here?" *Her parents had lied. Aunt Helen wasn't away, being treated in Toronto.*

"What happened?" Lynette asked.

The constable's face gained twenty years as she snapped into authority mode. "This is an active investigation. You have to leave." She moved forward, crowding them.

"What about my boyfriend, Roberto Alvarez? This was where he was going last night, and now he's disappeared."

"Your boyfriend must be the guy who called us. Probably saved Helen's life." The officer backed them to the door. They lingered in the parking lot.

"Was my Aunt Helen living here or did she just come back last night?"

Purrell shrugged.

Lynette waved her hands in distress. "Is Roberto okay? Where is he?"

Purrell pulled out her phone. "Let me check." The woman gestured for them to stay outside as she walked back in. Through the broken window, Tonya watched her disappear into Aunt Helen's workroom.

"Shhh. Stay here." Tonya slipped back in and crept upstairs. She hoped to find clues in her aunt's apartment, something to explain why everyone lied about her whereabouts.

At the top of the stairs was the start of the living room, narrow like the workroom below it. Tonya ran her finger across the china hutch. Dustless. A few steps in, the living room opened into the kitchen where the counters gleamed. Either her aunt had been living here recently, or she had found a cleaner as fussy as her.

Tonya decided to check the 1940s Frigidaire which her aunt refused to replace. If it was stocked with fresh produce, it would confirm her aunt never left. She pulled the chrome handle. Inside, the light had burned out, so she swung the door wide, illuminating darkly filled preserve jars, and bowls with lids. No boxes, no store-bought condiments, not even a carton of eggs. *Didn't Aunt Helen eat anything from the grocery store?*

She moved aside to let more light in. No aluminum takeout containers. Not even a plate of leftovers.

Tonya fished out a bottle of milk and sniffed it. She poured a bit down the sink to see if it looked sour, but it was fresh. She was replacing the milk, angry with her aunt and her whole family for lying to her, when she saw it. A glass jar filled with smoky fluid and pale, thin, pointing . . . fingers. Ugh! A hand.

Of course her rebel aunt had a hand in a jar.

Heavy boots stormed up the stairs. Tonya grabbed the jar and shoved it deep into the pocket of her coat, hoping nobody would notice the bulge.

"Hey! What are you doing up here?"

Tonya slammed the fridge door shut and scooted out of the kitchen. She recognized Constable Cram, a fleshy local man with a buzz cut. He swaggered across the living room, forcing Tonya to take a step back into the kitchen.

Tonya didn't know what to do. She needed to dispose of the hand without getting caught, but Cram wasn't letting her pass. He towered over her, so close she recoiled from his coffee breath.

"Well? What are you doing here?"

"This is my aunt's place. I'm worried about her."

"She's in Loon Lake Hospital, as you probably know. This is a crime scene. I should arrest you for interfering with a police investigation." He crossed his arms and puffed out his chest.

At times like this, Tonya wished she had her aunt's gift of persuasion. She'd love to magically send this lunk butterfly hunting.

"Oh my God. You're *that* kid."

He didn't say "that fat kid," but Tonya could tell he was thinking it.

Cram stepped back to look her up and down. His eyes rested on her new-found waist and then uncomfortably long on her chest. This was a new sensation for Tonya. She used to feel self-conscious about her chubby belly, but men staring at her chest was worse. She zipped up her coat.

"Can I go?" She stared him down.

He stepped aside to let her take the stairs. Tonya imagined his eyes following her.

Downstairs, she told Constable Purrell. "Your partner's a creep. He was staring at my chest."

"How did you get upstairs?" Purrell backed Tonya into the wall.

"This is my aunt's home."

"You're interfering with a crime scene!"

"I'm sorry. It won't happen again."

"You ignored the sign and the police tape."

"My aunt and I are really close. She'd want me to check on her apartment."

Purrell took a step back and pulled out her notepad. "Do you know anything about what happened here?"

"No."

Purrell handed Tonya her card. "Call and set up an interview. You need to answer some questions."

"Am I in trouble?"

"Not unless you're hiding something."

Tonya heard Constable Cram's heavy steps overhead. He was poking around but at least she'd gotten the hand out of the fridge. *They'd better not find anything else.*

"Aunt Helen is sick. She's supposed to be in the hospital in Toronto but yesterday you're telling me she was here. Looks like you know more about it than me." She wrote her phone number on a scrap of paper and handed it to Purrell. "I can't contact my parents. They sold our house and moved and now they won't answer their cell phone. Can you help me? They're missing."

Tears sprang up in Tonya's eyes. This fire and their disappearance couldn't be a coincidence. She massaged her throbbing temples.

As Tonya described the last time she'd seen them, Purrell jotted details in her notebook.

"They told you they were moving?"

"My aunt did."

"So, it isn't a surprise they left?"

"I moved into residence in September and then, without saying goodbye, just before Halloween, they were gone."

"What's your relationship like with your parents?"

"I love my parents. They would never leave without a goodbye."

Purrell rubbed a creased brow. "So, why didn't you report them missing sooner?"

"Their emails said they moved to Toronto, to look after Aunt Helen. I'm worried because I can't contact them anymore."

"Hmm." Purrell snapped the notebook shut. "We'll be in touch."

A horn honked outside.

"Your friend is waiting for you."

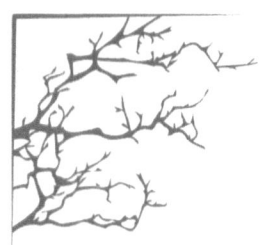

CACTUS LADY

As Tonya got into the car, her roommate was running the engine. "What took you so long?" Lynette pulled onto the road and headed for town.

"The cops wanted to speak to me."

"About Roberto?"

"My parents. I'm worried they might be mixed up in something bad. I need you to drive me by their house, so I can check something." She didn't say, *to make sure they aren't still in the house, dead.*

"And Roberto?"

"For all we know they're together. They were the first ones to start acting strange, but I think this is some kind of epidemic." Tonya didn't say *a curse that spreads like a disease.* Showing magic to Priya had been hard enough. She couldn't imagine showing it to Lynette, who didn't respect her.

"I can't believe you want me to look for them now. Why did you wait until my boyfriend disappeared?"

"Trust me, this will only take a minute. Either the new owners of the house will come to the door or I'll figure something out."

"I'm not helping you break in."

"Fine, I'll ring the doorbell." She would only break in if she really had to.

Lynette sighed and goosed the accelerator.

Tonya wanted to reveal more, but she had no idea what anything meant. The jar Tonya had taken from the fridge didn't square with the helpful aunt she worked for as a teenager. Her aunt was caring and kind, and swore she made her cures from plants and minerals without drawing on dark sources of power. Only a necromancer would use human body parts. Could it really have been her aunt who put it there, or was it planted by someone to get her in trouble with City Council? Mundane law could put you in jail, but the Old Families could erase your memories and strip your powers.

The fiery explosion suggested Aunt Helen was in magical trouble. Was she hiding more skeletons in the closet to go with the pickled hand? Did her parents know?

In minutes, Lynette raced over the bridge and entered the subdivisions north of town, arriving almost too fast for Tonya. She had to know what happened, but she was afraid of knowing. As long as she didn't find them, she could pretend her parents were alive and well, living in Toronto to visit her sick aunt. Except since that was a lie, Tonya wondered what else they were hiding.

Strange cars sat in the driveway. Lynette pulled up to the curb.

"I'll wait here while you ring the bell. If you go around the back to break in, I'm going."

"You can't leave me here!"

"You've been twitchy since you talked to the cops. What are you planning?"

"Nothing, I have a key." Tonya conveniently failed to mention the locks had been changed.

"Alright, hurry up!"

Tonya got out of the car, curiosity pushing her forward, even as dread slowed her steps.

She tried the door. Locked. She rang the bell and waited.

After four evenly spaced rings, Tonya was ready to give up when a rumple-faced man answered the door. He had a comb-over and a stained undershirt.

"Sorry to bother you. I was wondering if you've seen my parents?"

He stared at her, blinked a couple of times before clearing his throat. "We just moved in. We don't know anybody here."

"We used to live here. Jim and Barbara?"

He smiled and put his palms together, releasing a cloud of stale cologne. "Such a cute couple. They sold us the house, really wanted us to have it. I haven't seen them since." He shrugged his hairy shoulders.

"Did they leave a number? Some way to contact them?"

"No. They were in a hurry to get out of the country, but when you see them, tell them Phil says hi."

Out of the country. Her parents had left the country? Mom was strict, but she would step in front of a charging rhino for Tonya. Her parents avoided magic—and with it, Old Family politics—but abandoning Tonya to face danger alone wasn't like them. Something made them leave, against their will.

While Lynette drove to the hospital, Tonya called the local police and reported her parents missing, again. Purrell wasn't from an Old Family so she wouldn't know how to help. Only an officer briefed by City Hall would.

"Before we check the hospital, I have to visit City Hall," she told Lynette.

"You must be joking. This is no time to pay your parking tickets!"

"In Loon Lake we do everything through City Hall. It acts as our law court and local police." She didn't say magic police.

"What about Roberto?"

"I'll be fast. You can stay in the car and call the hospital while you're waiting for me. I'm sure they just kept Roberto for observation. Purrell would have told you if he got hurt."

"I can't wait for you."

"Come on, Lynette. I came with you, so now do something for me. It'll only take a few minutes."

"Be fast."

As they drove through city streets, Tonya wondered who might help a Pure from a disgraced family. Trads and Mods alike called Pures ignorant for denying their magical heritage. It had scandalized both groups when Mom refused to shun Aunt Helen for selling charms to Mundanes. Between her Mom's Pure, anti-magic upbringing, and Helen's maverick attitude, all three factions had reasons to reject Tonya.

In high school, Tonya had tried to make Mod friends, but they scorned her lack of magical training. Tonya hated that her father was a Mundane and her mother was a Pure. She wound up with Mundane acquaintances and Mod enemies, but yearned for a best friend she could share her secrets with. The closest she came to real friendship were the summers she worked for Aunt Helen.

They parked in front of City Hall, a pink granite building surrounded by fallow gardens. She hoped to find an ally who could see her issues in shades of gray but in this emergency, she'd take anyone from an Old Family. Tonya pushed through the glass door, her eyes adjusting to filtered light from a skylight in the cupola. The round atrium of City Hall echoed as she crossed the marble floor. By habit, she looked up. A mosaic depicted the top of the Three-

Century Ash Tree, encircling the skylight centered in its leaves. A beam of sunlight cast a pretty glow on the stone below her feet.

Behind the reception counter, a lady with long, ash-blonde hair appeared to be scolding a cactus. She was willowy and smiling, wearing a crocheted vest over a long floral dress. It wasn't until Tonya got close that Tonya noticed her hair was streaked with gray. The lady's crow's feet crinkled but her gaze remained on the cactus, even when she began to speak.

"Some of us were wondering how long it would take you to come." Her voice was clear and passionless, a cold breath blowing from a snow-capped mountain.

"Who?"

"You're going to have to be brave."

"Are my parents okay?"

"Helen predicted you would come."

"How did you . . ."

The lady picked up the plant pot and held it between them, her eyes never leaving the spiny green succulent. "She says your parents are alive and well, but they can't come back to Loon Lake right now. They can't even come back to the country."

"But I need them. Aunt Helen does too."

The lady smiled and shook her head. "An Entity is rising, and the Trads are losing control. Anyone who can't use magic will be caught in between."

"Tell me where they are." Tonya's voice cracked, and she struggled to compose herself. She shouldn't show weakness when she didn't know if this lady was friend or foe. Delivering a message for someone, she appeared to be in a trance.

"Aunt Helen, is that you?"

"Your parents are well."

"Give me a phone number, an address . . . I need to talk to them."

"She warned me you would insist but they must be protected, even from you. If you find them, you will put them in danger."

Tonya considered the lady behind the counter. Could she be speaking for the enemy? Was this a tactic to put Tonya off the scent?

"Why would Aunt Helen leave me here if it isn't safe enough for my parents?"

"She predicted that question."

"And?"

"Helen is working to make sure you never have to know."

"What do you mean?"

With a cough, the lady's eyes came back into focus. Her voice turned raspy. "Why am I talking to a plant?" She frowned down her nose at Tonya. "What can I do for you?"

"I need help from the Old Families. There's some kind of eating disease on campus."

"Campus? Well, if it's just at the university . . ." The aging woman smiled, looking less like a fading flower child now than a shark with her bleached teeth.

"My aunt seems to be affected, and my parents have left town." When she caught the pleased look on the woman's face, Tonya decided not to mention her own cravings.

"If the disease only affects outsiders, I don't think the Families need to intervene, do you?" The lady's eyes sparkled.

Tonya shivered. "Mundanes are getting sick."

"Good riddance."

"What?"

"Look at the time!" The lady grabbed her purse. "Be careful." She swung open a door in the counter, forcing Tonya to hop out of the way. "We don't want Family secrets blabbed to outsiders, do we?"

Before Tonya could reply, the lady strode off with a strength that belied her previously gentle demeanor.

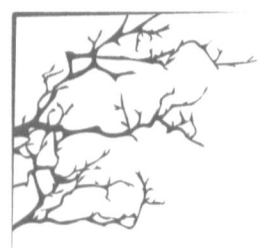

HAIRS AND HOMEWORK

Tonya got back to the car and Lynette sped to the hospital. They didn't speak again until they reached Reception in the front foyer. It was a relief when Tonya recognized Donna Ashton, seated behind the glassed-in desk. The middle-aged brunette from a prominent Mod family was a member of her Mom's choir. She was also Marta's mother, but Old Family was Old Family. In an emergency, Tonya couldn't be choosy.

Tonya stooped to speak through the window in Donna's Plexiglas box. "We're here to visit my Aunt Helen."

Donna typed a few words into her computer and pronounced Aunt Helen discharged.

Lynette nudged Tonya aside. "What about Roberto Alvarez?"

"Not here either." She didn't check.

"Are you sure?"

Lynette spelled his name and provided information as Donna checked her computer.

"He was never admitted."

Tonya stooped to speak through the window. "What about Professor Rudolph? I know *he* was here."

"Full name?" Donna's voice was chipper.

"Professor Frank Rudolph and I know he was here. My friends and I called him an ambulance because he sleepwalked off campus, all the way through the cemetery, and then lay down at the base of the Three-Century Ash." Tonya gave her a significant look.

Donna's kohled eyes widened. "Did your aunt know about that?" Donna tented red, manicured fingers.

"I haven't been able to reach my aunt or parents for days."

"That is a problem." Donna stroked her chin. "What are you going to do?"

"I have to see the professor. Are you sure you can't find him?"

"I probably shouldn't tell you, since you're not family, but he checked out this morning." She beckoned Tonya to lean in closer and whispered, "Against doctor's orders." She shook her head. "His color was terrible, and he walked like a robot. He had the nerve to steal the cookie tin off my desk!"

Tonya inhaled sharply.

Lynnette asked, "Know where he was headed?"

"No idea. He just walked out."

"I'm finding him," said Tonya.

"We still have to find Roberto," said Lynette.

"Try his phone again. He might be home by now."

Tonya checked her phone while Lynette checked hers. She had sent a text to Priya, reminding her she had promised to cancel or move the show. Still no reply.

Tonya followed Lynette back to the car. "We should go back to campus. Somebody must have seen him."

"I hope so."

During the drive back, Lynette was quiet. Tonya tried to distract her with chit chat, but the conversation died every time.

"At least you know Roberto is okay."

"He's been acting funny."

"Maybe he lost his phone in the fire. I'm sure he'll call as soon as he can." Tonya tried to sound hopeful but suspected a darker reason for his silence. *What if he spent too much time in the cemetery and wound up like Professor Rudolph?*

They drove west, then south over the bridge, and back east. As they entered campus, Tonya noticed a telephone pole papered with flyers for Priya's installation. Thinking she might have missed stripping one pole, Tonya didn't worry until a few poles farther on she saw more. Priya's flyers fluttered on lampposts lining the drive and the walkways between buildings.

"Let me out in front of the dorm. You're going to have to keep looking for Roberto on your own."

"Why? What's going on?"

"No matter what happens, don't go into the cemetery tonight."

"I'll be too busy looking for Roberto." Lynette pulled up outside the dorm.

"I know you'll find him." Tonya leaped out.

In the front foyer, on the bulletin board, Tonya saw shiny posters advertising *Man vs. Nature*. Flyers covered the first-floor doors. Tonight, the cemetery would be full of innocent students expecting a party. Whether the eating disease spread person-to-person like an infection, or whether it was a curse cast on the cemetery, Priya's installation would put people at risk. She'd seen what this affliction did to Marta. Nobody could save a crowd, compelled to eat until they choked.

She had to stop Priya. Tonya took the elevator to her friend's room, but Priya wasn't there. She didn't have mobile numbers for the rest of the Ninjas, but she guessed where to look. She rushed down the stairs and ran for the cemetery.

She had slowed to an out-of-breath jog as she reached the path leading off campus, but didn't dare go slower. Only she could stop this catastrophe. The bonfire would draw a big crowd, so she had to convince her new friends to move it far away from the cemetery.

Her feet pounded the path and her labored breaths turned to cloud in the chilly air. Hitting a patch of ice, her legs flew up from under her and she slid along on her backside. When she came to a stop, Tonya sat for a moment, waiting for the pain to ease. What made her think she could convince them of anything, especially without demonstrating magic? If only her aunt were here. She could charm the hair off an orangutan.

Tonya got up and jogged on, despite a stitch in her side. It was a small campus with few Halloween parties advertised. Most of the student body would have heard of the bonfire. How could she, one lowly freshman, stop the majority?

She crossed the street dividing campus from the cemetery. As she passed through the wrought iron gates, Tonya saw hairy things, up in the trees. Priya had shown Tonya sketches, but in person her monsters were hyper realistic.

Priya was a macabre genius, with a theme-park mentality. From now on, every time she walked this path, Tonya would expect to get ambushed by Toyota-sized tarantulas.

Tonya was so impressed with the giant rabbit with sad eyes and blood on its chin, that she wanted to forget why she was there. She had to keep everyone from seeing this masterpiece. Somehow. Her confidence collapsed. To stop mass infection, she was going to need more than circumstantial evidence. She needed proof the cemetery could kill.

Marta's near-miss could be explained away as an eating contest gone wrong. Tonya believed the feeding frenzy was caused by magic, and suspected the curse was related to the unnatural explosion at her aunt's shop. A nasty magic user was at work here, one who had probably hurt her parents or forced them into hiding. She suspected their spells caused irrational binge eating, and the mindless stagger of Professor Rudolph, but how to prove it?

And what was so bad about a little binge eating? If a victim didn't choke on their food, would the need to pig out wear off? How did she know Professor Rudolph wasn't home right now, doing a crossword and drinking tea? Just in case, Tonya pulled her turtleneck up over her mouth and nose to keep out airborne contaminants. She feared it wasn't only Egyptian Pharaohs' tombs that could inflict airborne curses.

Tonya followed a meandering path through the cemetery. At the southwest end, in the oldest section, where time and rain had eroded the names off the marble headstones, she approached the Three-Century Ash. She slowed, walking with dignity in this holy place.

The Ash was revered by the Old Families who had buried ancestors there for hundreds of years, the source of their power. The longer the family had been settled here, the more powerful the magic of the descendants.

They would all be angry if they could see this. Priya had turned the tree into a monster, with slits for eyes and a mouth that looked like a slash in the bark, with fangs. At its base, the clean-picked skeletons of manufactured prey were piled in a jumble, as if the tree had devoured them and spit out the pellets like a giant owl. She did a double take. Priya hadn't actually cut into the Ash, had she?

She rushed up to take a closer look but there were no cuts in the bark. Priya had applied a mask to the tree trunk that blended so perfectly, it looked like it was part of it. In any other place, her handiwork would be beautiful but here it was an abomination. She was surprised someone from the Old Families hadn't discovered it and punished her already. If they discovered Priya's blasphemy and found out Priya knew about magic, there would be a heavy price to pay.

It was a price she had paid herself. Tonya had defaced the Ash in childhood when she nailed slats of wood like rungs to help her climb up the back. Her parents had been livid when they caught her, and her aunt could hardly look at her. That was so many years ago that the Ash had long since started to grow around the rungs, but her guilt still stung.

Tonya went around the back of the tree to look for traces of her forbidden ladder. Lying on a bed of yellow leaves at its base, lay Professor Rudolph. Up through the ground, hair-like roots were growing into the unconscious man's ears, nose, and mouth. A few more were growing upward and around the side of his face, preparing to enter through his eyeballs.

"Professor!" Tonya tugged at his arms, poked him with her toe. She slapped his cheek, but nothing would rouse him. Slowly, being careful not to disturb or touch any of the white tendrils, she put a hand on his chest. He was cold. His chest was still, without a heartbeat. His wrist lacked a pulse. He was dead.

Tonya, have you done your homework? His voice demanded inside her head. His unseeing eyes opened. She ran.

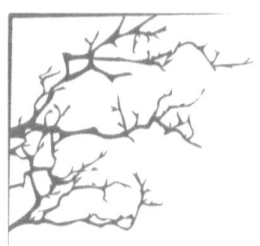

WHISPERS

Tonya ran up the path that skirted the west side of the cemetery then, eventually, slowed to a walk. Her chest heaved, and her mouth escaped her turtleneck. Listening to her breathing she wondered if she had already inhaled the contagion that killed Professor Rudolph. Would she die too? How much time before the infection took effect? His voice in her head reminded her of a gravedigger fungus she'd once stumbled upon as a child, in a dark corner of the cemetery.

She still remembered how it sent wordless whispers through her mind. In a panic, she had rushed to the shop to ask Aunt Helen about it.

"Gravediggers grow into the brains of the dead. Their telepathic whispers frighten outsiders away."

"And if they don't?"

"Don't look at me like that. It's harmless."

"You planted it, didn't you?"

Her aunt looked away, but not fast enough to hide her smile. "Of course not. Everybody knows I avoid death magic."

The Professor's voice in her head had sounded ten times more powerful than the telepathic fungus of her childhood memory. She stretched the neck of her sweater over her nose and went back to look for telltale signs of fungus. Normally, a gravedigger just gave you that cemetery feeling, like raised hairs on the back of your neck, or rustling sounds in the bushes. It was a harmless guardian but the way it propagated itself creeped Tonya out. It sent up one kind of shoot to sense movement, and another to spread spores. Tonya didn't like to think of it spying on her, then releasing a cloud of spores as she passed by.

Tonya wished her aunt had explained how to destroy the fungus. She suspected Aunt Helen knew more about it than she would admit. Her aunt claimed to create folk cures from natural elements like herbs and minerals, but there was another kind of spell, cast purely through the will of the caster. Such spells required dark energies, the kind it would take to boost the powers of a mindless, mildly telepathic fungus into something more sinister . . .

Tonya tried to swallow the lump that rose in her throat. Her parents were mixed up in this with Aunt Helen. They never spoke of the danger, but the warning, delivered by the entranced woman at City Hall, confirmed it. Whoever was behind this must have defeated Aunt Helen and done something to her parents. Helen wanted to fight this battle alone, but there had been some kind of magical showdown at the store which sent Helen to the hospital. She had checked herself out but still hadn't contacted Tonya, leaving her niece alone and surrounded by unknown enemies.

Even in daylight, this forested patch on the edge of the cemetery was half-dark. She shivered and zipped her coat up to her chin, scrunching her face into her collar in case of spores. *What if they didn't only grow in the brains of the dead? What if they could grow inside her living brain?* The wind blew through her hair, whipping it around and making the trees hiss and sway, lending life to the artificial creatures Priya had hidden there. Tonya closed her eyes and stood still, wondering how far the Dead Professor's mind reached. Did the link work in two directions, allowing him to overhear her thoughts, and broadcast his? Could he feel her shivering right now?

Tonya sped up. As she passed through the Eastern Gate and crossed the road back to campus, she had a new theory which would explain Professor Rudolph and Marta. It had to be the gravedigger plant, enhanced by dark magic. This gravedigger couldn't just broadcast whispers into people's minds, but implant ideas as well. Ideas like the compulsion to eat.

She had to stop tonight's gathering at all costs. Tonya started jogging toward campus.

She yearned to leave this to the authorities, but the Provincial Police would laugh at her. And campus administration? She'd never find somebody to talk to her on a Saturday. Besides, they'd think she was crazy.

With no other choice, Tonya pulled out her phone and called.

"Loon Lake police." The chipper voice didn't sound familiar to Tonya. Was the receptionist mundane or Old Family?

"Miss, are you still there?"

"Uh, I want to report a death." Tonya didn't risk saying more.

"Where are you?"

"Loon Lake Cemetery."

"Young Lady, we don't tolerate pranks! I should warn you this call is being recorded."

"Something terrible is happening to my Professor Rudolph. I just found his body, laid out at the base of the Ash Tree."

"Now aren't you smart, to know the kind of tree. What's your name, Miss?"

"Tonya."

"I guess that makes you Helen's . . ."

"Her niece."

"Hm. Well, don't trouble yourself about Rudolph."

"You'll take care of it, then?"

"In a way. Some things have a way of taking care of themselves."

"Should I stay with the body?"

"Leave him to us. I'm sure you've done enough."

Tonya hesitated. "Warn your personnel to wear masks. I think he's *contagious*." She emphasized the word, hoping the woman would understand this was a special, magical kind of contagion.

"You sure know a lot for someone who just found the body."

"Yeah, well, send the right people and they'll understand." She hung up but, in her mind, Tonya saw him again, white shoots snaking up from underground to invade his lifeless body.

She didn't trust the police. The lady on the phone had recognized her and acted like she'd been expecting her call. The receptionist sounded like she was working for the Old Families but if so, why hadn't she seemed more concerned? Professor Rudolph had died under suspicious circumstances. Were the Old Families and the police working together to cover it up?

At City Hall, the lady with the flowery dress had brushed her off. It made Tonya want to march into City Hall and complain to the Mayor—if that would do any good. Tonya wondered if the councilors actively opposed Helen. They were mostly Trads, and some were Pures, which didn't help her aunt's case. Tonya wasn't supposed to know, but when Helen's hair turned white overnight in her late teens, she had been accused of using death magic.

The mayor had exiled Aunt Helen for ten years right around the time Tonya was born.

Since she couldn't count on the police or the Old Families, Tonya had few places to turn for help. She had shown Priya magic. Maybe together they could convince the Ninjas to move the festivities out of the cemetery.

She phoned and sent Priya urgent texts, but she didn't answer. Time to make house calls.

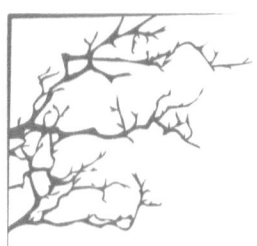

DRAKE

When she reached the Hub Pub, Tonya double-timed down the stairs almost colliding with Drake who was walking up, carrying a box full of cables and equipment.

"Am I glad to see you!" Tonya let him pass.

"Me too. You want to tag along? One more run and I'm finished." He hefted the box.

Tonya joined him at the top of the stairs. "That's what I want to talk to you about. The cemetery is too dangerous."

"We already talked about that. Priya's concept is to scare people." Drake walked to his car at the curb. He arranged the box in the trunk and shut it.

"Wait! Let me explain."

"Okay." Drake smiled at her like she was a piece of chocolate cake.

"Professor Rudolph is dead,"

"What?" His smile vanished. "Wasn't he your favorite prof? Are you okay?" Drake took Tonya's hand and led her to sit on the bumper of his car.

"What happened?"

"Bad magic made him sick, in the woods by the cemetery."

"What do you mean magic? They took him away to the hospital." Drake sat on the bumper beside her.

"He checked himself out and went back to the cemetery and lay down at the foot of the Three-Century Ash to die."

"Did they figure out what was wrong with him?"

"He was eating all the way. Donna, at reception, said he swiped the cookies off her desk."

"That's terrible." Drake knit his brows. "So, heart attack?"

"That tree is supposed to protect the town. It has for hundreds of years, but now I don't know. Somebody is using its power to do terrible things."

"Tree power?" Drake quirked an eyebrow at her.

Tonya shifted her feet. "I know it's hard to believe, but my family knows things." Uncomfortable under his stare, she shoved her hands into her coat pockets until her right hand encountered the jar and she snatched it back as if burned.

Drake pulled out his phone. "Did you call someone to deal with the Professor's body?"

"Yeah. I wish I could show it to you before they collect it."

"No thanks."

"I know it sounds crazy but Priya's installation is wrong. The cemetery is a sacred place and the Ash Tree—"

"Has spiritual value, and your professor's dead, and Priya built a nasty monster on it."

Tears welled up in her eyes. "He won't be the only one to die if I can't stop her show."

"You still believe that?" He stood, and the bumper lifted beneath her as she stood too.

"Sounds crazy, until you believe in magic."

"Priya told me about the thing you did with the tree branch. She called it sleight of hand and swore you wouldn't be able to do it in daylight."

"Why won't she just believe me!"

"Show me?" He held his hands out, not quite touching her.

"No. Until you've witnessed magic, the Old Families aren't allowed to use their powers against you."

"That's lame. You might as well say if I tell you, I'll have to kill you."

"I won't have to. Somebody wants to do it for me." Tonya sighed. At least Drake wasn't laughing. She watched his expression change as he tried to process the idea of real magic.

Finally, he held out his arms and Tonya crumpled into them. Everything was wrong, except for his warmth. She leaned her head on his firm chest and some of her tension drained away.

"I'll talk to Priya," he said gravely. "She'll be disappointed, but we'll clean up your aunt's tree."

Tonya backed away. "That's not it."

"The spot where Professor Rudolph died deserves a memorial. We'll put a picture and flowers there so his students can pay their respects."

"People should stay out of the cemetery."

"You're against a memorial?"

"His corpse could be contagious," she remembered the shoots growing into his eyes. "Something evil is growing in the cemetery and it's making people sick."

"Who?"

"The diving team were competing to eat the most bowls of porridge and stacks of pizzas. Marta couldn't stop eating. She choked on a piece of pizza until her face turned blue. If I hadn't been there to give her CPR, she would have died."

"That's disgusting but an accident isn't a disease."

"My roommate Lynette has been eating so compulsively, she tied her own hands together." Lynette's concern for Roberto was all-consuming and that might have distracted her for a while, but the compulsion to eat must mean she was infected. How long until she went frosty-eyed and brainless?

"The thing they all have in common is the cemetery. The diving team runs through there to train. Lynette and Roberto go to the graveyard for picnics. I'm afraid if you set up your cameras in the cemetery, you'll end up like Professor Rudolph."

"That's all coincidental."

"Don't ignore me and get sick, I'll never forgive myself."

"Stop worrying, nothing's gonna happen." Drake stepped close and brushed the hair out of her face. He was so close she could see right into his bright blue eyes.

She sighed. "If you go into those woods you'll die like Professor Rudolph."

"He was old. He was grieving for his wife. Maybe he was sleepwalking or had a mental breakdown." The angular planes of Drake's face were like porcelain, subtly strong but not unbreakable.

"This thing could become an epidemic."

"Sit here." Drake offered her the driver's seat, but she remained standing.

"You saved Marta from choking to death. You said she looked like she was dead when you started CPR. You're still in shock, that's all . . ."

"Promise me you'll help me cancel the installation, and the bonfire too."

"Sorry." He looked at his phone. "I'm late. I promised Priya I'd get the last cameras to her half an hour ago."

"A few more minutes won't kill you. C'mon." Tonya led him back into the pub and downstairs to the Ninjas' meeting room. She had been going about this all wrong. Drake was rational, and he wasn't going to see a supernatural cause for anything, no matter how much evidence she could tell him about. He wasn't going to believe until he saw for himself.

He sat down at the table. Tonya pushed her chair far away from him and, breathing softly into her turtleneck, began to explain. "Lynette and I went looking for Roberto this morning." Tonya described the Herbal Healing Shop after it got hit with the unexplained fire, the shattered jars, and the unnatural burn marks. "My aunt and Roberto went missing from the hospital. The strange eating compulsion must be related. I think they wandered out of there, unconscious, just like Professor Rudolph."

"I'm sorry about your aunt." Drake reached for her hand and, although she probably shouldn't have, she let him take it. His hand was warm and calloused, and holding it made her feel calmer.

"You have to believe me. Something bad is happening. Help me convince Priya to move the installation. I can't fight magic and Priya all by myself."

"Forget Priya. Tonight, we should remember Professor Rudolph. The bonfire will be his wake."

"Not in the cemetery."

"Why?"

"It's contagious, like a mummy's curse."

"There's no such thing."

"Isn't there? Rudolph was eating himself to death, just like Marta, and then a magical force drew him to the Ash Tree. Remember, we couldn't stop him, no matter how hard we tried? Look, I know it sounds nuts, but this was no natural disease." Could the gravedigger fungus have infected her? Could she be shedding infection onto Drake right now?

"You really *do* believe in magic."

"For hundreds of years, the Old Families have used magic in Loon Lake."

"I live here. Why haven't I seen magic?"

"We don't practice in front of Mundanes. The mayor and his councilors are Trads who enforce steep consequences on anyone who breaks the rules."

"By telling me, aren't you breaking their rules?"

"If they find out you believe, you could get your memory wiped."

"Gee thanks."

"It's better than dying like the professor."

"I want to believe you, mostly because I don't want you to be crazy, but I don't believe in horoscopes, or bad luck on Friday the thirteenth, or unicorns."

Tonya wiped her hands on her jeans and took a deep breath.

"Of course you don't." She phoned the hospital and asked for Reception. When Donna answered, she set it to speakerphone, so Drake could hear everything.

"Hello, this is Tonya. Remember Professor Rudolph? We found his body lying under the Three-Century Ash in the Loon Lake Cemetery."

Donna sounded excited to hear this. She listened as Tonya described the hair-like roots growing out of the ground and into all orifices of his head. "How terrible," she said. "Evil forces are at work in Loon Lake for sure."

"What's with the sarcasm?"

"No sarcasm. Tell me how I can help, hon."

Finally, somebody who believed her! She arched an eyebrow at Drake and smiled. To Donna she said, "Do you think you could get word out to the other Old Families? I need help right now."

"I'll see what I can do. Tonya, take care of yourself."

"About that. I must go into the cemetery tonight, but first I need to take some precautions. Could you loan me some equipment, off the record?"

"Sure."

Tonya was surprised she agreed so quickly but she thanked Donna and hung up.

"Well, that makes one person who believes you," said Drake.

"You still don't? Donna is from an Old Family that has been practicing magic for hundreds of years. Anyone from an Old Family knows about magic, they just hide it from outsiders like you. I wish my Mom were here, or Aunt Helen. They could tell you."

"I admit, Professor Rudolph's sleepwalking, and his eyes, didn't seem natural."

"Finally." Tonya took a deep breath and sighed. Drake knew, which meant with him, she didn't have to hide who she was anymore. It would have been a perfect moment, if they weren't all doomed.

"So, magic is real, and it can kill you." Drake stared at his hands, as if the town's secrets lay there.

"Can I borrow your car? I need to pick up a box of equipment from the hospital."

"I'm coming with you."

"Sorry. Somebody might figure out that you know."

"So, they'll make me forget it. Big deal."

"A mind wipe is serious. It erases months of your life, not just the thing they want you to forget."

"But you need help."

"Just stop the party tonight—without telling anybody else what's really going on. Can you do it?"

"I'll try, but it's Halloween. The students are expecting a keg party, *Man vs. Nature*, and a bonfire." You'd need armed guards to keep them out of the cemetery tonight

Tonya held out her hand. "Give me the keys."

If Drake couldn't stop the students she needed a plan B, and for that she had to visit Donna at the hospital.

He surrendered the keys. "Stay safe."

"See you soon." Maybe, unless Rudolph's condition spread unchecked and this was their last moment together. On impulse, Tonya kissed him on the cheek.

He smiled, eyebrows raised. "Hurry back."

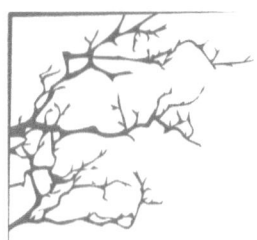

PLAN B

D onna would know what to do. Donna was a familiar face in Loon Lake, particularly after last year's fall fair when she won first prize for heaviest gourd. Her giant pumpkin made the record books and sparked controversy. Mom had suspected she'd cheated with magic, but the judges couldn't detect spell traces on the winning gourd.

Tonya was relieved to find Donna at Reception. She stooped to speak through the slot in the Plexiglas.

"We spoke on the phone, about Professor Rudolph?"

"I haven't got around to sending an ambulance but don't worry." She shot Tonya a smile.

Mom knew Donna, but they weren't quite friends. "I was hoping you could loan me some equipment."

The smile faded. "Not my department."

"I need to avoid breathing some very bad stuff."

"Safety equipment has to be inspected and accounted for."

"I promise to bring it back in perfect condition. It's only one night."

"Oh, I see what this is about." Donna leaned back in her swivel chair. "We don't loan medical equipment for Halloween costumes."

"Of course not. I suspect somebody cast a curse on the cemetery."

"Recently?"

"I think it's contagious."

"Really, how would that work?"

Tonya didn't want to tell Donna her gravedigger fungus theory. While it was possible to enhance living things with magic, like Donna's pumpkin, a gravedigger fungus wasn't exactly alive. It increased in size by feeding on dead things, and could be only manipulated by death magic.

"I'm not sure, and I don't want to find out the hard way."

"Don't you think you should be telling City Hall about this?" Donna tented her fingers.

If somebody was using death magic they were powerful and unethical. Before making accusations, Tonya had to know who she was up against. "I'll tell the mayor once I have proof. Help me?"

Donna shook her head. "Leave it to the authorities."

"I will. The equipment is just in case they don't listen. I'll probably return the stuff tomorrow without taking it out of the box.

Donna shot Tonya a tight smile. "All right, hon, but only because your Mom makes the best coffee cake in town."

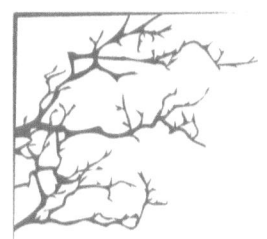

HALLOWEEN

The sun was low in the autumn sky when Tonya pulled up in front of her dorm. She had texted Drake and there he was, arms crossed.

"I'm going with you."

"Sorry, I only have safety stuff for one." She dashed around to the trunk and hauled out the box of hospital equipment. "Promise me you won't go in and make yourself sick?"

Tonya looked at Drake over the cardboard lid, but he wouldn't make eye contact. "I have bad news."

"What?" Tonya set down the box and slammed the trunk.

"I believe you but Priya doesn't. They're going ahead with it."

"I'll try her again." Tonya hoisted the box in front of her.

"Let me carry that."

"I'm fine."

"No, really. I got this." Drake carried the box into the building and held it as they stood in front of the elevator. Tonya called Priya who answered on the first ring.

"I already talked to Drake."

"People's lives are at risk." Tonya described finding Professor Rudolph's body. The elevator arrived, and Drake came up with her.

"I know you're trying to do the right thing," Priya said, "but walking through a cemetery on Halloween will not make people sick."

"I can't protect you Priya. I showed you my magic so now you have to be careful."

"I'm not falling for your optical illusion. You can't suck the life out of a branch."

"I did. You just refuse to admit it."

"People walk through the cemetery every day. The diving team and cross-country teams run there to train."

"Which is why Lynette and Marta are sick. Lynette says Roberto is having uncontrollable food cravings too."

"It's fall. People eat more when the weather gets cold."

"The Old Families of Loon Lake have been burying our dead by the Three-Century Ash for hundreds of years, accumulating power. Now somebody is using that power to kill people."

"We're done here."

"I get it. You refuse to believe in magic. I don't blame you, but you have to admit we have a contagious disease problem. People are getting sick."

"I worked hard. I burned through all my savings to create this installation. My art, the Ninjas' film . . . There's too much at stake to indulge your paranoia," said Priya.

"Last night you promised to stay out of the cemetery."

"You were supposed to come to your senses after a good night's sleep and apologize in the morning."

"Trust me or people will die."

The elevator stopped, and they got off at her floor. She walked down the hall, unlocked the door, and Drake followed her in. Priya's voice was getting louder.

"First, it's evil magic, now it's a scary epidemic. You know what I think? You're jealous. Your family doesn't even return your calls but mine crowded around to listen when I got interviewed on campus radio."

"I was happy for you."

"After Halloween, the whole town will know my name." Priya's voice went up an octave. "You were my friend when I was nobody, but now I'm a tall poppy you want to chop down."

"This isn't about you. It's about Rudolph."

"One sleepwalker doesn't mean panic."

"Not yet."

"We found him wandering around the courtyard so maybe the courtyard is contagious. If people go see my show, at least they'll be safe from the dangerous courtyard."

"Not funny. You *have* to move your art thing."

"Art thing! I've been working on my *installation* for months, and nobody, especially not a jealous frenemy can ruin it." Priya disconnected.

Tonya stared at the phone.

Drake raised an eyebrow. "Want me to talk to her?"

"Too late." Tonya sat on her chair with the hospital box at her feet. It gave her a shiver. Drake and she were alone. A boy was sitting on her bed.

"Give."

She handed over the phone and let Drake redial. He put it on speaker phone.

"Tonya is right," he said.

"I thought about this all night." Priya's voice was strong again. "Seeing Marta almost die affected Tonya. I don't blame her for getting upset but now it's time to look at the facts."

"Why are you so stubborn?"

"I can't believe you're taking her side."

Tonya took the phone from Drake. "All right, I give up. There's nothing we can say to stop you." She directed her words at Drake too. "At least aim some of the cameras at the Ash Tree. There has to be a way to monitor things, so we'll know when to call the police."

"No police. Are you crazy? I'll never live this down if my friends get carted away."

"Now who's being over-imaginative? I just want a camera and a monitor. The Ash Tree is where Professor Rudolph died."

"Drake told me you thought the man-eating tree concept was in poor taste so I'm turning it into a memorial. You should be happy."

"Good. Let's set up a web link from the tree to people's phones, and a laptop in the common room back at the dorm."

"So absent students can pay their respects. Good idea. I'll get Drake to help me. And Tonya, I'm sorry I called you a frenemy. Of course, we're still friends. It's just that this installation took me years to make. So, are you mad or can we still have fun together?"

"I'm not mad."

They might never have fun again, but at least Tonya would have video proof if people passed out under the Ash, and rootlets started growing into their brains. She had been so panicked at the time, she didn't think to get a picture of Rudolph with her mobile and by now his body would be gone.

"Drake's on his way now."

"Tell him to hurry. You just wasted fifteen minutes I didn't have." Priya ended the call.

Tonya looked at Drake. "Promise you'll stay out of the forest."

"Where will you be?"

"Don't worry, I'll be safe." She patted the side of the box at her feet, pretending confidence she didn't have.

She walked Drake to the door, but they lingered, neither wanting to part. Tonya made comic shooing gestures. It wouldn't do for him to see how worried she was. "Go on. Priya's waiting."

When the door closed behind him, Tonya shuddered. Ever since she heard the voice of Professor Rudolph in her head she'd been worried about her friends. Tonight, the nocturnal gravedigger fungus would rise to feed and send out spores. She had to keep people out of the cemetery! She paced the small room. The equipment Donna gave her would help, but she still had to think of a way to turn back the crowds.

Her stomach growled. Normally not a big deal but right now any urge to eat made her suspicious. She hoped it was just her mind playing tricks with her stomach. Trying not to think about eating always made Tonya hungry.

Tonya went into the bathroom and ran cold water over her hands and face. She stood up and admired her healthy new form. She was getting strong and her curves were firmer now. She was healthier than she'd been since she was a kid. Turning sideways, she sucked in her gut, which was still round. It reminded her of all those times she had looked in the mirror and hated herself as a young teen.

"Hey, you're kinda cute," she told the mirror, and blew herself a kiss. "But tonight, you have to be kickass."

Her stomach growled like an angry raccoon. Why were her cravings back? Was it because people around her were pigging out? Or was this hunger and Rudolph's voice in her head symptoms of infection?

She steadied herself on the bathroom counter and stared down at the tiles, remembering Marta. She was doomed. Rudolph's voice in her head was just the final stage. She'd been craving food non-stop since September. What if *she* had given it to Lynette, and Lynette had given it to Roberto, plus all the love-struck boys who hovered around her?

That couldn't be. It was the cemetery, the trees, the terrible roots growing into Rudolph's head through his ears. As the sun set, Tonya unpacked the hospital box to get dressed. By the time she was through, she would be completely unrecognizable. Good thing too. Getting caught doing what she had planned would make her a social outcast, forever.

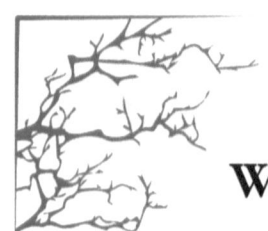

WORLD PREMIERE

Priya felt like a director on opening night. The lights dimmed with the setting sun and the audience filed in by twos and fours. After weeks of planning, costume, and rehearsal, it was show time for her creations. She sat on a folding chair in the control tent, observing events from her laptop via six cameras Drake had rigged amongst the cemetery's mature trees.

There was plenty of action: the animatronic arm that came out of a gap in a tree trunk as you entered the east gates near campus; the giant constrictors that lurked amongst tangled tree roots along Loon Lake's southern shoreline and, continuing west all the way to the fence; the Volkswagen-sized tarantula poised to pounce from above. She loved to hear the whoops and screams of teens as they stumbled upon her "actors." How could Tonya have tried to deny her this? With its meandering paths and ancient, indecipherably weathered tombstones, this place was perfect. She avoided the chapel of course, although Zain was dying to record in it. Her installation steered clear of modern gravestones and concentrated on the parklike areas of the cemetery where she could use trees to trigger people's eternal fear of the Wild.

She left the tent to find Shin. She had to see his reaction when he saw her werewolf sculpture, an Adonis caught halfway through the change, his powerful shoulders modeled on Shin's own. She thought she was finished sculpting her last creature before she met him, and she had tried to resist using Marta's boyfriend as a muse, but his athlete's anatomy was too perfect to overlook.

She took the path leading out of the western gates and turned south toward the bonfire, through the wooded strip between the cemetery gates and Kenny Road to the west. This patch of ground was even more wooded than the cemetery.

As she walked, Priya was disappointed by this year's female costumes. She passed one scary Bride of Frankenstein, but the rest of the co-eds defaulted to the standard hot chick combo: heels, cleavage, and short skirts. By the time she reached fireside, Priya had passed sexy witches, sexy devils, sexy cats, and sexy pirates who all looked the same. Not that she had a problem with sexy, but couldn't they show more imagination?

The bonfire was built in a clearing just outside the cemetery, almost opposite the Herbal Healing Shop. Around the fire, Priya recognized a cluster of guys from Shin's party wearing capes, swords, and cowboy hats. It made her wish she had a costume. Too busy primping her monsters these past few weeks, she hadn't thought about her own appearance.

"Hey." Shin was coming toward her, silhouetted against the flames.

Priya dusted bark and twigs off her jeans and heavy lumberjack shirt. Her hair was clean at least. For convenience, she had braided it and pinned it to her head in a pair of tight coils.

The light caught the side of Shin's face and she could see him staring, first at her plaid jacket, then up at her face and hair.

"Who are you supposed to be?"

"Uh . . . Princess Leia, disguised as a Canadian."

He smiled and pointed up into the trees where she had installed a hundred glowing eyes.

"So, all these crazy monsters are yours?"

"I confess. I am the mad artist."

"Well, don't cut your ear off, Van Gogh. Can I get you a drink?" He thumbed over his shoulder at a keg on the far side of the fire.

With a flourish, Marta strutted out of the shadows wearing a floor-length gown with an embroidered bodice worthy of Queen Elizabeth I.

"Your costume is fabulous!" Priya tried not to stare.

Marta's cleavage welled up from the beaded neckline of her dress and even the corset underneath couldn't hide the fact she looked fifteen pounds heavier than in her diving team picture on the university website.

"Shin likes it." Marta spun, sending multiple layers of skirts floating.

Priya saw Shin frown, as Marta wobbled to a stop. Was there something not right between them?

"So, about that drink." He shot Priya a gaze so steely she felt like it could nail her to a tree. *What was wrong with this guy?*

"No thanks. I'll get my own." She strode around the fire to where a couple of guys were selling cups of beer for a buck. Priya wasn't thirsty but she found a place to stand in the shadows. She was intrigued by the firelight effect, flickering over the circle of faces. *Paintable. Definitely paintable.*

She was so lost in this living chiaroscuro that it took her by surprise when somebody sidled up to her.

"Here's to the Mistress of Darkness and Special Effects." Shin toasted her with his plastic cup.

"It's supposed to be Art."

"It's incredible." He closed the gap between them and spoke softly. "Me and Marta are just about finished."

"So?"

"I thought you might care," he looked back at the fire.

"Has she stopped training? She's gained some weight."

"D'ya think? Lately she eats like nothing else matters. We go on a date and she ignores me. Won't look at anything but her plate. It's like she's trying to push me away."

"You're not supposed to love someone when they're rail thin, then dump them the minute they don't fit your idea of perfect."

"Is that what I'm doing?"

"Yeah it is, but how you feel about your girlfriend is not my business."

"That could change." He took her hands in his and Priya didn't know what to do. He was so forward, and she was more comfortable pursuing rather than being pursued.

"You sure are friendly." She gave his hands a little squeeze and broke away. "Want to see something cool?"

"And leave the bonfire? This is where the party is."

"C'mon, you have to see this!"

She led Shin through her carefully constructed monster experience. As the path wound deeper into the wooded section, glowing eyes gave way to hints of things that swished and howled in the bushes. Shin tried to take her hand again, but she evaded his grasp. His nearby presence felt magnetic, but she couldn't decide whether to encourage or reject him. He belonged to Marta.

Priya led Shin off the path.

"Where are we going?"

They were approaching the tent. He looked at her, then back at the tent. He grinned. "Looks like your lucky night!"

"Calm down, Diver Boy." She unzipped the tent flap revealing the laptop and chair.

He raised his eyebrows. "You brought me all the way here, to show me a computer?"

"Patience." She pointed to the laptop screen which was divided quilt-wise, showing images from six different cameras.

"Watch camera four." She indicated a couple strolling through the cemetery.

"What are they doing?"

"Getting close to Tonya's famous Ash Tree. Watch what happens."

The camera was mounted high in the branches, yielding a foreshortened, bird's-eye view. At their leisurely pace, it was taking them a while to get to the tree and, while Shin watched the screen, he snaked his arm around Priya's waist.

It sent a shiver up her spine.

She stepped out of his reach. "Look."

Camera three showed the same scene from the opposite direction. In it, they could see what the couple was seeing: the tallest tree in the cemetery.

There was a flash, then a trembling in the branches and out leapt Priya's *pièce de résistance*, Artemis, goddess of the Hunt. After a whole forest of creepy, fierce-looking creatures, Priya wanted to end the show with something magical.

"Is that Marta?" Shin stooped closer to the screen.

"Not exactly. Months ago, I used a volunteer in a wig for the hologram, then spent a day last week manipulating the face. It's her portrait."

Projected in holographic light, Artemis glowed like a goddess. The couple in the forest stood still, watching from behind as the huntress drew her bow and shot at something unseen beyond the cemetery fence.

"What's she aiming at?" asked Shin.

"Exactly! That's the effect I wanted to create."

"She's so perfect."

"Do you want to see her live?"

The way Shin's eyes looked her up and down told her he'd rather get lively in the tent, but an object on the screen caught her attention. A bulky dude passed right through the hologram, dispersing Artemis into haze.

Priya was annoyed. Some lunkhead student had ruined the recording, except his suit and hair weren't student-like. Was he wearing a costume?

He turned to face the camera.

"It's Professor Rudolph!"

"Didn't you say he was dead?" asked Shin.

She watched the professor lumber after the couple, hands outstretched like a sleepwalker. There were no microphones, but Priya saw the girl's mouth open wide and her hands go up to protect her face. As the couple sprinted away, Rudolph blundered after them, passing out of camera range.

"We should check that out," said Shin.

They jogged along the path by the bobbing light of Priya's phone, but when they reached the Ash Tree Professor Rudolph was gone.

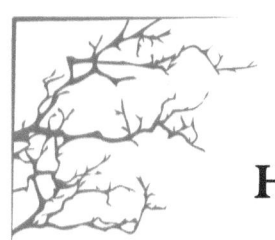

HERO COSTUME

Tonya rode her bike along the path between campus and the cemetery. It was getting dark and she didn't have time to walk or even run. She must have looked unhinged, wobbling along the path with the yellow Hazmat suit tangling and impeding her legs as she pedaled. With the hood limiting her vision to one small plastic window in the front, it was hard not to drift off the path.

She crossed the road, walked her bike through the Eastern Gate and rode west. This was it, the moment which would define her career at the university and her life in Loon Lake.

There are those who give their lives in battle. Others sacrifice themselves at sea like the captain who goes down with the ship. Tonight was Tonya's weigh-in on the scales of Fate, and henceforth she would know her worth. Heck, the whole town would know. And so, for the good of the many, she had come equipped for self-sacrifice on the altar of social suicide.

The yellow Hazmat hood made her stumble by limiting her vision, but it protected her from inhaling infected air. She walked her bike into some bushes and left it hidden, beside the abandoned chapel. With gloved hands, she pulled a penlight out of her plastic pocket.

Inside, the chapel ceiling was too high to illuminate with her little flashlight, but she could see a set of dusty wooden steps which took her up to the choir loft. At the top of the stairs, gauze blurred the mask of her hood. Ugh! She had walked through a cobweb. She wiped her mask and walked toward a patch of moonlight.

Peering through a gap in the broken stained-glass window, she spotted a bonfire just outside the cemetery. To get there, the students would have passed the great Ash Tree. She shivered. They could already be infected.

Tonya left the chapel and took the southward path. She was familiar with every cemetery trail. The Old Families treasured their graveyard and revered the ancestors buried there. They were the first Europeans to settle the area who, legend had it, survived their first winter by using old country magic.

Tonya could hear the shouts of students coming through the Eastern Gate. Through the trees, she heard laughing and screaming as they encountered Priya's monsters. Tonya hesitated. Every moment they spent in the cemetery put them at risk. Should she break up the bonfire first or turn back the arriving crowds? She decided to detour east.

Students strolled in through the gates and cut south on the path which led around the hill into the old section and the Three-Century Ash. Tonya rushed to intercept them. When she got close enough, she yelled through the plastic window of her Hazmat suit:

"Leave the cemetery immediately!"

A couple stopped and stared.

"This area is quarantined!" Tonya shouted.

"Funny!" said the guy.

"Who are you supposed to be?" asked the girl.

"I mean it. It's not safe."

"Don't worry," said the guy. "We'll use precautions."

The girl giggled and punched him in the arm. They brushed past her as if compelled to visit the Ash Tree.

Tonya watched couples, singles, and groups take the path leading to the ash, drawn by some unseen force. To anybody else, they might appear to be wandering randomly but Tonya was convinced the gravedigger plant was manipulating them, drawing in victims for a sinister purpose. Professor Rudolph's behavior had proven it. Yet how could the beloved tree of her childhood have been corrupted to cause harm? There was dark magic at work here, but who was behind it?

Another handful of students approached Tonya who was blocking the path.

"Go back or die!"

"Very scary," some said. Others mocked her plastic suit but not one listened. For a moment she stood, too frustrated to move. Their refusal to listen brought back high school memories of rejection, like being chosen last in Phys. Ed., except there were no captains to pick or leave her anymore. She had volunteered for this job herself.

Tonya walked to the pinch point in the pathway between the small hill and the cemetery gate. They would have to get past her to reach the Ash Tree and the bonfire beyond. Squaring her shoulders, she pressed the button on the loud hailer with her bulky gloves and shouted:

"Attention! Attention!"

No sound came out. All she could hear was her voice, muffled by the thick Hazmat hood. She held the handle up to her face and angled it this way and that in the moonlight, trying to see what was wrong, but it was too dark. She pulled a flashlight out of the suit pocket and looked again. The buttons were clearly labeled. She tried again. Nothing. Even the power light didn't come on.

Fumbling with her gloves, she pressed a release and snapped open the back. No batteries. Donna said the equipment was tested. What now? With the suit and hood on she could never shout loud enough to warn people. If she took it off, she would be infected. There had to be another way.

Tonya replaced the flashlight and took out her phone. She removed the plastic glove, so she could work the touch screen. Video cameras fed online images. She would be able to see whatever was happening by the tree as soon as the page loaded.

The first thing she noticed were the flowers, garlands, and photos attached to one side of the massive trunk in memoriam for Professor Rudolph. Priya had removed the evil-looking mouth and teeth as promised.

A woman carrying a bow came around the side of the tree. She was dressed in white. Tonya had another look. The woman wasn't visible because of light reflecting off her white toga as Tonya first thought. She glowed from within. It must be Artemis, Priya's showpiece.

Tonya watched as Artemis knocked an arrow to her bow, stepped around the tree, and fired a shot into the darkness beyond. She blinked out of sight much too soon.

Why did Priya's creations have to be so breathtaking? It made what Tonya had to do that much harder.

With a few taps on her phone, it was done. Priya would never forgive her.

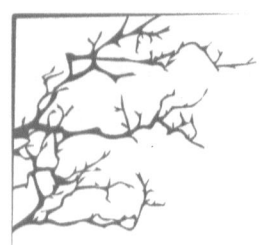

HOLOGRAM

By the time Priya and Shin arrived at the Ash Tree, not only had the Professor left but a new group of students were marveling at Priya's hologram. Too bad there was no time for Priya to bask in their appreciation. "Professor Rudolph could be anywhere by now."

"Not our problem." said Shin.

"How can you say that? You saw him chasing people on the monitor."

"I saw him stumbling around and one couple running away, but this is Halloween. How do you know he wasn't just fooling around?"

"We made a memorial for him. Tonya says he passed away, right here in the cemetery."

"Weird."

"Tonya wanted to cancel tonight. She said something here was making people sick, but I wouldn't listen."

"And you believe her now?"

"We saw the Professor stumbling around blindly on the campus lawn. Three of us couldn't wake him or stop him. We were afraid he would walk into the road and get hit by a car."

"Tonya's mistaken. If he's here tonight, he must feel better."

Priya's stomach did a fish flip. "Or he's dangerous." She took out her phone and tried first Tonya and then Drake, but there was no answer. "What if Tonya's right and he's contagious?" Priya searched Shin's face for a sign he believed her.

He frowned. "We should get Marta."

"If Tonya's right, Marta's binge eating was caused by the same disease. Stay away from her or she could give it to you."

"Let's find her." Shin grabbed Priya's hand and started running toward the bonfire. His long legs made him impossible to keep up with. She stumbled until he slowed down a little.

She was panting as they jogged into sight of the bonfire. She scanned the crowd ringing the flames, but couldn't see Marta's face.

"Do you think she wandered off?" she asked.

Shin didn't answer. He searched the bushes and clearings nearby until they found her, sitting at the base of a tree, with her head tilted against the trunk.

"Marta, are you okay?" Shin went down on one knee and put his hand on her forehead.

Marta didn't move. Priya touched her shoulder. No reaction.

"Wake up." said Shin.

They each took one hand but when they tried to lift Marta up, she shook them off. Marta started to rise, hands out for balance. She wobbled up to her full height and opened her eyes.

"How long have you two been together?" Marta's voice sounded groggy.

"Priya's worried about you."

"That's your excuse for going off into the woods together?" Marta steadied herself against the tree.

"Want to come back to rez?" Shin held out his hands.

"Not with you two." Marta closed her eyes and slid down the trunk. "Nap time."

Her gentle speech and the way her legs practically collapsed beneath her surprised Priya. Where was Marta's attitude?

Shin stepped forward and took Marta by the shoulders, "You can't sleep here. It'll freeze overnight." He laid his hands gently along the sides of her face tilting her head up, but Marta wouldn't open her eyes.

"C'mon, I'll take you back to your room." The tender way he kissed Marta's forehead took Priya's breath away.

"So much for breaking up," said Priya.

Shin still had feelings for Marta and they were putting him in danger. What if Marta was infecting him right now? Priya wanted to protect Shin, but he was right. It was chilly and would get much colder. If Marta fell asleep out here, she'd get hypothermia.

Marta made a vague mumbling sound and swatted in Shin's direction before her arms fell limp at her sides.

"You see the strange way she's moving," Priya said, "like Professor Rudolph, sleepwalking." *They had to act, before she got out of control like him.* "Maybe she is sick."

"I got this." He lifted Marta into his arms and strode back toward campus.

WHAT'S WORSE THAN SNAKES?

I t was dark when Roberto awoke. He was outside, his back uncomfortably pressed against something hard. He tried to move his arms or stand but strong ropes held him in place. He was tied to a tree.

"Hey! Help! Help!"

Nobody seemed to hear him, despite a cemetery filled with people. He could see flashlights moving between the tombstones and among the trees. Halloween. Roberto heard the faint shouts of university kids, partying somewhere nearby. Closer, he heard individual shouts and cheers coming from every direction, but nobody responded to his cries.

The moon peeked out from behind the clouds allowing Roberto to make out his surroundings. He was tied to a tree of average size, behind the big Ash Tree he used to run by in the cemetery. Why had somebody left him just inside the cemetery, near the break in the fence? He remembered the white-haired man, the surprise injection, and passing out in the foyer of Loon Lake Hospital. This must be the work of Helen's enemies. Did they put him here for Helen to find him?

Poor boy. Don't bother your head trying to figure it out. Just relax.

Roberto tried to locate the source of the voice, but nobody was there.

Roberto, you are outranked, outflanked, and you surrendered before you knew we were at war. When it comes to strategy, you flunked the final exam.

"Professor Rudolph?"

I am Rudolph, yet so much more. Let go. Join the amalgam of consciousness. I can already taste your memories and thoughts. Peruvian archeology. Your abuela's magic. Delicious visions of Machu Picchu in sunshine, and the smell of rain on the Inca Trail. It's a shame I'll never walk it with my wife . . .

Roberto felt hundreds of disjointed images and sounds stream into his mind, making his head spin. He strained against his ropes not wanting to hear Rudolph's silky words in his head or relive the Professor's memories, but he couldn't resist forever. The pull of something under the ground crooned at him to surrender.

He felt himself slipping into a murmur of voices gathered somewhere in the earth below. With every minute, they sounded louder, the words and images more fascinating. He felt his body relax as his mind opened to it and all pain faded away. Even if someone were to cut his bonds right now he might be tempted to stay a little longer. Long enough to understand what he was feeling—

—unless the person cutting the ropes was Lynette. The memory of her face and her slender arms returned to him and he wanted to escape again.

Don't struggle. You'll only make it worse.

Roberto tried to wriggle free of the fibers. They moved like pythons, cinching him tighter each time he exhaled, winding relentlessly up and around his chest, compressing more and more of his ribcage.

"Help! Help!"

His cries started out strong but petered out as constriction made it hard to breathe, and fibers began growing into his mouth. He gnawed them off and spat them out, but a new crop forced their way in. The second he stopped fighting he would stop breathing, asphyxiated by the living gag, and coils crushing his ribs.

And then, salvation. A couple came along the path, laughing and talking, unaware of his plight. Roberto was so tightly bound he couldn't move an arm to wave, or use his fiber-filled mouth to shout.

If he could just make a sound they might look his way. Inhaling through his nose, Roberto tried to yell.

Whistling through roots that clogged his throat, a scream came out, too muffled to hear. Roberto took a second breath and waited for them to get closer. The coils kept tightening around his ribs but if he kept his lungs full, he should have enough breath for one last sound as they passed.

The coils seemed to anticipate his strategy, cinching his chest until he felt a rib waver, then snap under pressure. Through agony, Roberto felt the coils tighten around the break to take up the slack. Everything went cold except the pain. His body shook, and he had to fight to stay conscious. The vines were crushing his chest, rib by rib, and there was no way to stop them. If he died he'd never see Lynette again.

Give up, Roberto, you can't resist. The pain will end when you let go.

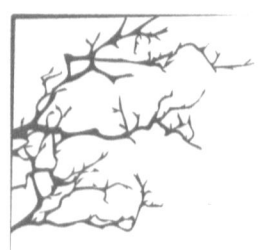

BANG!

Tonya came up behind a dark figure, leaning against the Ash, half hidden by the enormous trunk. Her flashlight revealed the arm and side of his rumpled suit. As she closed in, stench washed over her. Stepping around in front of him, Tonya noticed white roots trailing out of his eye sockets.

Tonya, don't go. Stay with me.

Professor Rudolph used his calm, history lecture voice, which made everything worse. Tonya backpedaled until she was up against the fence. Outside, she could see happy students standing around the bonfire. She wanted to scream at them to evacuate the area, but it was hopeless with a malfunctioning loud hailer. She would be ignored or laughed at again.

Tonya knew she'd probably regret it but there was no choice. She pulled off her Hazmat hood in order to shout louder. As she did, a cluster of dark slashes in the fabric stood out in the moonlight. With her flashlight, she examined a series of razor cuts, deliberately punched into the back of the hood. So much for an infection barrier. She hadn't noticed the sabotage when she got dressed, but it explained how she could smell Professor Rudolph's corpse.

At the hospital, Tonya had told Donna her plan. She had needed help and didn't know who to trust. It looked like she had made the wrong choice, but how was she to know? Marta's mother had never treated her badly. In middle school, she reprimanded her daughter when Marta snubbed Tonya for being a Pure. Tonya shook her head. Donna's treachery proved Donna knew there was something contagious in the cemetery, and she wanted Tonya to catch it.

Mom never would have suspected Donna's politics. For hundreds of years, Trads and Mods had fought for control of Loon Lake, but Mom willfully ignored such struggles. Trads controlled City Council and they, like Mom, wanted to regulate magic use and hide it from the Mundanes.

As a child, Tonya thought Mom's anti-magic stance unfair. Arguments usually ran like this:

"The other kids at school use magic, why can't I?"

"Because you're a Pure."

"You're a Pure. I can be whatever I like."

"As long as you live under this roof, you won't touch magic."

Tonya obeyed until, as a teen, she learned by watching the other kids. They laughed at her but didn't chase her away. Maybe they felt sorry for her. And why shouldn't Tonya learn a little? It wasn't illegal to use magic discreetly, among Trads.

One day, Mom caught Tonya with her hand on a tree, sensing life energy. She kept Tonya home from school and banished her to her room. At the end of the day, Mom brought dinner.

"Why can't I use magic like Aunt Helen?" asked Tonya.

"It's dangerous."

"You want me to be just like you."

"I want you to be happy."

"So, let me learn magic."

"Magic broke Helen's heart."

"That's stupid."

"It's true."

"Is that why she never married?"

"Ask her yourself." Mom left abruptly, and refused to talk about it, ever.

SIRENS WERE APPROACHING the cemetery. *Time to get out of here.*

The police would probably enter through the eastern gate and drive through and out the Western Gate to reach the bonfire. To see the Ash Tree, they would have to walk along footpaths.

Tonya hurried west. She didn't want to run into police. If she did, she'd be tempted to rush over and warn them of the epidemic. Drawing attention to herself would be a mistake. The cops would be looking for a perpetrator after she'd called in the anonymous bomb threat.

Tonya's stomach growled. She wanted chocolate, and steak. Maybe together. Although she was prone to nibbling when anxious, Tonya wondered if her cravings proved she was infected.

A widespread shuffling blocked the road ahead of her. Out of the trees and descending the hill, frowning, foot-dragging beings shambled toward her en masse. Tonya paused, unsure whether it was safe to walk through this tide of . . . sleepwalkers? Zombies?

No. Judging by their swearing and muttering, and by a few wearing beer guzzler hats, these students were dragging their feet to delay leaving the woods, and to express their annoyance at the cops for breaking up the party. As the slow mob of pissed-off party-goers continued east toward campus, one pointed to Tonya.

"That's her! The one in yellow. She wanted us out. She must have called the cops!"

"She was weird in high school," said a girl.

"Get her!" called a guy wearing a funnel hat.

Tonya thought about standing her ground. She was acting to save them. She shouldn't be afraid. This wasn't high school anymore. She stepped forward to explain the danger . . .

A wave of shouting people charged.

Tonya ran off the path and up the hill. Branches caught at her Hazmat suit. She didn't dare sneak a glance, but she could almost feel their beery breath on the back of her neck. Tonya tossed away her hood and raced up the hill, hoping they wouldn't follow, but they did. Like a pack of wolves, the leader barked orders at them, describing how to outflank and capture Tonya.

Descending the other side, she continued north and ran through the bushes. The woods weren't as thick here, but she tripped over headstones and roots in the dark. The sound of her pursuers was softer now, but she didn't dare turn on her flashlight. She could hear them fanning out, looking to see where she went. As quietly as she could, Tonya slipped behind a large monument to think.

Tonya had to get to the chapel and find her bike.

Dashing from bush to tree to headstone for cover, she peered into the black. Was she still going the right way? She searched the sky ahead for the familiar chapel spire but couldn't see it, like a black cat in a coal mine.

She angled her head this way and that, peering intently. Something glinted up ahead. Bingo! Moonlight on the chapel windows. She closed the distance quickly and groped the bushes until she found her bike. She swung a leg over and had just pushed off when the students swarmed her.

She rang the bell and ploughed into the crowd, which instinctively stepped back just long enough for her to get free. She circled around the chapel but there were teens clogging the main road between the Eastern and Western Gates. With no other choice, she headed north toward the big hill overlooking the lake.

The group stayed with her, no matter how hard she pedaled, so she cut sharply onto what looked like a deer path. It was a hard slog uphill, but she kept pumping her pedals. Thank goodness for all those summer workouts.

At the summit, she intended to hide out in the base of a hollow tree she remembered from childhood. Nobody would think to find her there. She smiled to herself despite the sweaty Hazmat suit. She had escaped the pack of beery nutcases, or at least she thought so, until she heard footfalls on the path behind her.

They had caught up and she couldn't go any faster uphill. One guy was so close she heard his heavy breathing and thumping tread. He must be massive to make that much noise on soft ground, but Tonya didn't risk turning her head to look. On a path this narrow, a moment of inattention could slam her into a tree. The only way was to outdistance him. Tonya pedaled until her thighs burned. She should be out of reach soon. The terrain leveled out and she was going faster.

What was with this guy? He didn't seem to tire. He was gaining on her. There was a whoosh of air at her back, as if he had tried to grab her and missed. Pain forgotten, she pedaled faster than ever in her life.

"I got her!" he announced in a powerful bass voice.

Tonya snuck a glance back in time to see him lunge. She feinted to the left, but it would only be seconds before he caught up and pulled her off the bike.

With the puffy Hazmat suit encumbering her legs, she could feel herself losing speed when she needed it most. She would never get away without an incline. The only hope left was to somehow descend toward the water, but the top of the hill was studded with trees. She didn't dare go off the path, so she circled around in a clearing, looking for a way down.

She spotted a faint track leading southwest. She could roll down it faster than anyone could run. She swerved and headed for the dip which twisted right, then left, before suddenly turning into a drop.

She hurtled down the hill on a tiny track, visible like a pencil line on charcoal. Keeping clear of the trees was hard as speed turned them to a midnight blur. The only sounds were the wind rushing past, riffling the plastic legs of her suit, and her gasping breaths. At this speed, it was hard to keep control. She could brake, a little, and steer even less, but she needed both hands on the handlebars. She would just have to—

Bang!

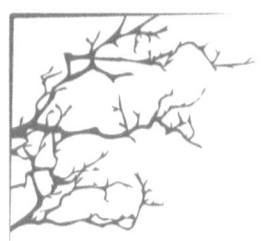

CAUGHT

Tonya shivered, laid out on leaves edged with frost. Her head spun when she tried to raise it and her stomach roiled. It was difficult to order the thoughts ricocheting inside her tender skull. *What time was it? How long had she lain there?*

Her ears were ringing, distorting sounds of police shouting and dogs barking. Through the trees, an officer wielded a powerful flashlight. Every few paces his German Sheppard sniffed at the fallen leaves then led his master in a circle, looking for a bomb that wasn't there.

Last night in a panic, making a bomb threat to evacuate the woods had seemed like genius. Tonya hadn't anticipated endangering the lives of these officers who might be breathing infected air as they searched under every leaf. Unless she confessed, they would keep looking.

Admitting she made a false bomb threat would get her charged, but it couldn't be helped. That is, unless she could think of a good excuse for her actions? Tonya shook her head at her own folly, making herself dizzier. There was only one way out of this mess. She had to invent a rational, believable explanation for crying bomb, one that didn't involve magical fires or mysterious eating epidemics. Trying to think made her head throb more.

She tried to sit up, but the world wobbled. She touched her forehead and felt a teacup-sized bump.

That's it! I'm faking amnesia.

The sky disappeared, blocked out by a monstrous head. Black eyes stared into hers and a deep growl sent her neck hairs standing. She wanted to flee until a gleam of light highlighted the beast's enormous teeth. She froze. Its rotten breath invaded her nose.

"I found somebody!" said an officer. He recalled his dog, but not before it dribbled slobber onto her face. Tonya groaned. She hated dog slobber.

A second officer approached. "Are you okay?"

She nodded, then winced as that movement sent pain through her head.

As the first officer rejoined the search with his dog, Tonya wasn't sure what to do. Should she protect this cop by telling the truth or deceive him in case Donna's family had infiltrated the police?

"What happened?" he asked.

"I hit my head on a tree." She cupped the goose egg on her forehead.

"You were riding your bike off the path, in the dark?" He stood with his hands on his hips.

"I was being chased by angry students."

He raised an eyebrow.

"They were upset because I called about a bomb and they had to leave." Tonya sat up gingerly.

He stroked his chin and got down on his haunches. He pointed a flashlight into her face. "What bomb?"

"I saw suspicious wires in the trees and I thought, terrorists for sure, right?" *Better sound as ditzy as possible if she was going to sell this tale.* "Then everybody got mad and came after me."

"We haven't found any bomb."

"Thank goodness! That must be why I'm still alive. I was sure everything was about to blow."

"Where did you see these wires?"

"It was dark." She looked around pretending to search for landmarks. "I don't know but somewhere on the path, near the small hill."

He extended a hand and helped her to her feet. Tonya groaned. Her leg muscles were in agony from running and pedaling, and stiff from lying on the frosty ground. She took a step forward, but her leg refused to extend fully, and she stumbled.

"Easy there, lean on me." The police constable took her right arm and pulled it around his broad shoulder, at the same time wrapping his other arm around her waist. "Do you think you can walk? My car's back at the road."

"I'll be okay," She wobbled as the world spun, forcing her to lean into him more than she intended. Beside her he felt warm and solid. At another time, she might daydream about a uniformed hero come to rescue her, but she was too suspicious to enjoy it. For all she knew, he would take her straight to Donna.

They walked until the trees thinned and she could see a car passing on the road beyond the cemetery gates. She wriggled away from him. "I'm okay now," she lied, "just a bit stiff from sleeping on the ground. Can I go back and get my bike?"

"Your bike?" His expression was perplexed.

"Campus isn't far."

"Let me give you a ride. You're covered in scratches and that bump on your head needs treatment."

"But my bike . . ."

"I'm sorry but the bike is a write-off. Come with me." He took her arm and steered her westward through the trees.

"Oh. Good thing I don't love cycling." It was the first true thing she'd said to the constable. She was glad he wasn't looking at her face, in case he could tell. Under interrogation, she'd probably crack and tell this handsome policeman everything. If he was a Mundane, the truth would earn her psychiatric attention. If he was Old Family, who knew where his loyalties lay?

They went through the Western Gate and walked to his patrol car. In a moment, he would lock her in the back, behind a heavy grill. It might as well be a jail cell. She had to get away before she was trapped.

"Wait." She retreated a few steps and unzipped the Hazmat suit. As she stepped out of it, the wind cut through the jacket she was wearing underneath. She turned the Hazmat suit inside out so any fungus spores on it wouldn't get airborne and infect him.

"Let me take that."

"It's dirty," she ran a hand through her hair, knocking out some dry leaves. "I have to return it. Thanks for offering but I'd rather walk back."

He shook his head. "You can sit in front." He took her hand and helped her in like a gentleman. Was that to put her off guard? She had lost. She sat back, and her eyelids drooped.

Tonya sat bolt upright and forced her eyelids open. It seemed right to trust this handsome policeman and let him look after her. Besides, her eyes felt so heavy . . .

Her mind drifted away from Donna and gravedigger fungus, and Rudolph's creepy voice in her head. It would be so sweet to relax and let herself sleep.

As the car pulled out she was hardly conscious of it moving until he said: "So, describe this equipment again?"

Her eyelids snapped open. His stern tone meant she was in trouble. With effort, she ordered her thoughts. "Up in the trees. There were wires and boxes and blinking red lights."

"Uh huh. And why were you riding your bike in the cemetery?"

"It was Halloween. I'm too old for trick-or-treating."

"I also want to know how you got a hospital Hazmat suit." He shot her a crooked smile then looked back at the road. "I'm going to take you in and get a formal statement, but not until a doctor declares you fit. You really cracked your head."

"The bike took most of it. No doctor necessary."

"I'll take you to the hospital, to get checked for concussion, before we go to the detachment." His tone made clear that this was not negotiable.

What should she do? Tonya didn't want to make a false statement, and she was afraid to face Donna at the hospital. Once she discovered what Tonya knew, the evil choir lady might schedule a lobotomy!

"I hate hospitals. Besides, I'm fine." She moved her head around in a circle, pretending it didn't make her woozy. "Can't I give you my statement now?"

"Sure." He pointed up the road to where an ambulance was parked on the shoulder. "First let's get you a second opinion." He pulled alongside and rolled down his window to talk to the driver.

"This girl hit a tree on her bike. Real feisty. Says her head doesn't hurt but . . ." He shrugged and got out of the car to talk to the driver.

Tonya wanted to flee, but she couldn't outrun this young cop. Just turning her head made her stomach heave.

When he had finished talking the officer returned, offering her a hand out of the car. "They're just going to make sure you're okay."

"And if I don't want to go?"

"Then come with me." His smile was tight. "You need to report to the station for questioning, as soon as you feel better."

"I do have a headache. Maybe they should check me, to be sure."

He nodded and tried to take her hand again. Tonya insisted on climbing into the back of the ambulance without help and stood, pretending she wasn't desperate to lie down on the gurney.

"Lie down, I have to strap you in," said the attendant.

Lying down sounded too tempting. "I'm not sick,"

"Sorry, but you have to. The less your head moves the better." The ambulance still wasn't moving. "Now."

"Please? I hate being strapped down and I hate hospitals."

"Sorry. I need you strapped in. You look kind of green."

Tonya didn't see a way to refuse that wouldn't put this nice young ambulance attendant into save the uncooperative victim mode. She was familiar with it from lifeguarding, and feared the restraining moves he might execute to force her compliance.

"All right, but don't strap me in tight. It makes me claustrophobic." That at least was true.

The minute she lay down, Tonya's eyes closed. She was on the verge of passing out. As the ambulance pulled onto the road, she allowed herself sixty seconds with her eyes closed as the vehicle did a U-turn. Forcing them open, she craned her neck to look the attendant in the eye.

"So, do you live around here?" The attendant was muscular but not nearly as handsome as the police constable.

"I'm from a village North of Loon Lake. Do you know Rural Route . . ."

She let him describe the tiny intersection closest to his father's farm, but she was more worried about the dwindling distance between the ambulance and the hospital. Surreptitiously, she loosened the straps each time he looked away, all the while encouraging the attendant to tell her about the horse he was going to buy someday.

"What are you going to call him?"

"I don't know. That depends on what he's like."

The attendant seemed like a decent guy. She hoped he would get his horse one day, but when the ambulance stopped at a red light, she slipped off the far side of the gurney and shoved it at him.

She leaped from the ambulance and ran. Although she had pushed the gurney hard, Tonya figured the attendant would be fine. She, on the other hand, was so dizzy she could barely see where she was running. The horizon kept circling around her.

Straining to put maximum distance between herself and the ambulance, she tripped over her feet. *Slow down.* If she fell again she would pass out and they'd carry her away. Her only hope was to duck into a backyard before the driver got turned around.

At least she hadn't leaped into farmland. Here, the houses were grouped along a handful of loosely interwoven streets. She sprinted across a lawn and found a chain link fence. She got her shoe tips stuck in and climbed over easily. Dashing across the lawn, she emerged between two houses and crossed a small street. She crossed another set of lawns and another street before she saw a shed where she could hide and catch her breath.

The darkness inside the shed tickled her nostrils and watered her eyes. The arterial *stab, stab, stab,* of pain in her temples dulled to a steady throb as she caught her breath. The shed was safe but also a dead end. This was a residential area to the northeast of the lake, nowhere near campus or friends who might give her a lift. The ambulance driver would spot her the minute she went near the highway, or tried to walk home.

Home. The cut grass scent of the shed triggered memories of Dad pushing the mower on Sunday afternoons. It worried her how he and Mom had suddenly moved, like refugees leaving everything behind. Tonya blamed Old Family magic but to what purpose? What did Donna gain by perforating her Hazmat suit? She hadn't sent an ambulance to pick up Professor Rudolph's body from the cemetery, but did she know it was walking around? No decent Mod supported death magic, but Donna's family was more extreme than most. What might they support?

As the Sun rose on November 1st, Tonya slipped out of the shed and hopped on the first bus she saw. There were only a few bus loops in Loon Lake and this one would take her close to campus. She had made it through Halloween, but it was unclear whether she or the other students were infected with the eating disease. She suspected Aunt Helen knew something, as well as the lady at City Hall who had spoken to Tonya in a trance.

Why spread a supernatural disease? There were simpler ways to kill. And who were the real targets? Tonya hoped she could figure it out before the police realized she'd run off.

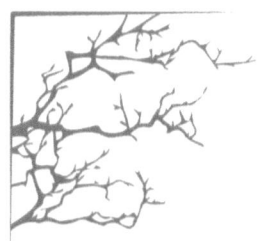

RIBS

Roberto pulled the comforter over his head to block the sun. He wasn't ready to get up yet. His head was full of strange images. As he lay in the twilight between sleeping and waking, the last thing he remembered was lying in the forest attacked by roots. What a nightmare! He rolled over, sending pain screaming through his ribs.

It hadn't been a dream.

He looked at his surroundings and saw Lynette, sitting at her study table.

"Morning," he said.

"Hi, Baby. That was some weird scenario I found you in last night. At first, I thought it was part of Priya's installation, until you tried to scream."

"How did you get me out?"

"One strand at a time." From the tabletop, she picked up a pair of heavy duty shears. The blades were stained green and black.

He sat up gingerly, trying not to move his ribs but each breath made him gasp.

She ran her fingers through his hair. "We should get that looked at."

"No hospitals, no doctors." Roberto remembered the hypodermic-wielding ambulance attendants.

He heard her stomach growl.

"Want to go for breakfast?" she asked.

"I am hungry, but it can wait." Lynette sat beside him and moved in for a hug but her weight shifting the mattress made him wince.

"Sorry. Does it hurt that much?

"I'm fine." He stood up and dusted himself off.

"Come into the bathroom. Let me look at that." Lynette pulled tensor bandages out of the medicine cabinet. "Hold still but don't hold your breath."

Roberto didn't cry out while she wound tape around his ribs, but he gritted his teeth.

She finished and frowned at him. "That won't hold. We should go to the medical center."

"No. I can manage." He loved the look of admiration she gave him, as if refusing treatment made him a tough guy. Truth was, even if he'd broken his neck, he was afraid of being sent to the hospital. "Just give me a minute."

Roberto stayed in the bathroom where Lynette had left the first aid kit. He had broken a rib playing soccer once and knew what to do. Looking at himself in the mirror, he carefully wound the tape tighter than Lynette had. He winced and swore, clamping his jaw with pain.

"Roberto, are you okay?"

That Lynette. What had started out like a fling felt so different now. The concern in her voice went right through him, pain and pleasure mixed. It hurt him to make her worry, but at the same time, her concern gave him a feeling of warmth. He burst into the bedroom anxious to reassure her he was fine.

"I must leave this town." He grabbed a shirt off the floor, trying not to let the pain show on his face. "Come with me?"

Lynette's jaw dropped, but then they kissed.

When they unclinched, Lynette said, "Let me drive. There's an all-day pancake house by the highway. We can plan the trip while we eat."

As they walked out of residence, Roberto sensed he might never feel this free again. There was something moving in the air, and it wasn't just the cold breeze. Whispering below the surface of things, a voice called him back to the cemetery.

"After the pancakes," he said, "I want to take you somewhere."

"I don't care where we go. I'm just happy you're okay."

ASLEEP AT THE WHEEL

Lynette settled into the vinyl booth, content to let morning sunshine warm her face through the window. She ate three stacks of pancakes with maple syrup, bacon, sausage, scrambled eggs, buttered toast, and a side order of home fries, all without saying a word to Roberto who was doing the same.

Lynette ate everything on her plate, then put a hand on her aching stomach and looked up at her boyfriend.

Roberto grinned. "I can't believe you ate all that."

"The server is staring at us." Lynette stifled a giggle. "I just ate my calories for a week."

"Is that all? How about another round?"

She beamed. "Sure." Pancakes were like drugs and she couldn't get enough.

Outside the restaurant, Lynette headed for the driver's side of her car, but Roberto insisted on taking the wheel.

"But your ribs. Aren't they too sore?"

"I want to take you on a drive through the country."

"Around here *every* drive is through the country. What are you up to?"

"Nothing. I'm taking my *Querida* to look at the fall colors. The leaves don't turn gold and red like this back in Lima."

"Oh, all right, you drive, but don't fall asleep behind the wheel. I see you yawning after all those pancakes."

"*No te preocupes.* I know what I'm doing."

Roberto drove them north of town, pointing out cows and horses as if he'd never seen them before. The repetitive scenery on top of a huge breakfast, made Lynette's eyelids heavy. She would just close them for a moment. Roberto would be okay, unless he fell asleep and went into a ditch. Maybe she should stay awake to watch over him. Maybe . . .

The next time she opened her eyes they had circled back south. They were on Kenny Road, crossing the bridge into Loon Lake Village. At the Herbal Healing Shop, Roberto slowed, and she expected him to turn into the parking lot. Instead, he drove across the field between Kenny Road and the cemetery. The grass was short, but the jarring movement and the food straining her stomach made her bilious. *How could he drive over rough ground with cracked ribs?* They were halfway to the cemetery fence when she could take no more.

"Stop! You're wrecking my car!"

"I know what I'm doing."

Lynette looked at Roberto, who stared straight ahead with unfocussed eyes. It was like he was possessed! The doors were locked. Stealthily, she undid her seatbelt and slipped her hand over to release the door.

Roberto was fast. He grabbed her wrist and twisted her arm to push her into her seat.

"Ow! Let go of me! Stop the car!"

"Go back to sleep." He let go her wrist and started patting her shoulder. "Everything will be okay."

"Not if you ruin my suspension."

Without slowing, he looked at her with glazed eyes. "Oh, *Querida*, your car no longer matters."

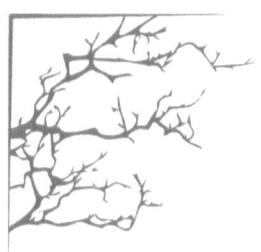

TOOTHY

Tonya looked out the window, relieved to see no police cars or ambulances driving in the next lane. The bus swayed as it moved, sending her head in dizzy circles. To avoid closing her eyes, she concentrated on the problem at hand. Tonya wanted to speak to her aunt. Aunt Helen could tell if the eating disease was a deliberate curse, and might know how to counteract it.

Tonya wished she had powerful Mod or Trad friends to help her. She feared a malevolent spell caster had used death magic on a gravedigger plant, and its telepathy was getting into people's heads and compelling them to gorge themselves. It wasn't too hard to see what would happen next. Gravediggers grew by absorbing dead bodies, and it was implanting hunger in people's minds, just as Professor Rudolph's voice had spoken in hers. The hunger, which she had also felt, would make them eat more and more so that when they died and were buried, it would have plenty of fat to absorb from their corpses. Tonya shivered. How could someone defile the Ash Tree to create such a monstrosity?

For hundreds of years, her ancestors had been burying their dead near the Ash because the recent dead were full of dark magic. Without the tree to purify the bodies of dead magic users, all sorts of evil could rise from the cemetery. It was the price of magic, but Mods didn't care since it didn't have to be paid in life. What did it matter to them if leftover power somehow infected the ground like pollution, causing unpredictable effects?

This dangerous power was something Mods and Trads quarreled over. It could be harnessed by death magic if it wasn't dispelled by the Ash. Somebody had used it to raise Professor Rudolph from the dead and set him walking, casting his voice right into her head. It was everything the Trads feared.

Tonya hadn't been invited to City Council meetings where Trads and Mods argued over the rules, but her mother and aunt had similar debates.

"I'm with Mayor Thornton," Mom had said. "What happens if Mundanes find out your cures work and declare Loon Lake a miracle town like Lourdes?"

"I could help more people," replied Aunt Helen.

"While we get trampled by outsiders, asking you to make the lame walk or cure their cancer."

"You're overreacting."

"Am I? What will we do when some Mundane offers your Mod friends so much money that they agree to bring back their dead loved ones?"

"They would never do that."

What made the uneasy Mod-Trad truce possible was the historical pattern of Mundanes who feared magic and burned or hung anyone who used it. Nobody in Loon Lake could ignore the Salem Witch Trials or the Spanish Inquisition, and nobody was naïve enough to think similar things couldn't happen again.

The bus stopped hard, sending a wave of pain through her head. The driver opened the door to pick up commuters and as they filed past her, Tonya caught a whiff of coffee and hash browns. Her stomach raged with hunger but that could be normal. By this time of day, she should have eaten breakfast. Maybe she wasn't one of the infected, just hungry. What she wouldn't give for a stack of her Mom's pancakes right now. She sighed. A lump rose in her throat.

Her phone pinged. It was a text from Aunt Helen:

Only trust family. Leave town. NOW. Love, Aunt Helen

Tonya tried to call back, but her rings went unanswered. She texted Aunt Helen:

Where are you? Where are my parents? I can't contact them. I need your help. But be careful. Somebody killed my professor then raised him from the dead.

She waited, staring at the screen but there was no answer. Aunt Helen just sent her a message so why didn't she reply? The bus lumbered on, but it would turn soon, leaving Tonya to walk the rest of the trip to campus. She rang for her stop and made her way to the back door.

No sooner had she stepped out and started walking when she heard limping steps behind her. When she sped up, she heard them keep pace. Tonya walked as fast as she could without running, but her pursuer was gaining. Despite her dizziness, she ran a block before she risked a peek back.

He was an old guy in a leather coat, almost on top of her! She needed a bike, a car, a rocket, to lose him.

Tonya kept running, searching for a house with an unfenced yard she could cut through. Loon Lake City was surrounded by farms and forest. One minute you were on a residential street near the north end of town, the next you cut north and found yourself toiling through a field of corn stalks.

She ran to the center and then took a sharp turn, gambling that her pursuer would not guess which way she went.

Out of breath, she emerged from the cornfield onto a familiar country road, hoping to flag down a ride. If a car didn't come soon, the white-haired man would figure out where she went and catch her. She eyed the top of the hill eagerly, willing any kind of vehicle to appear. She stepped into the road, ready to stop whatever came from either direction.

She didn't have long to wait. An ancient station wagon with fake wooden panels drove over the rise and slowed down. The sun-burned driver opened the passenger side door, releasing a chorus of slide guitars.

"What's wrong, Miss? You can't stand in the middle of the road." He wore a sweat-stained John Deere hat.

"It's an emergency. Are you going near campus?"

"Yup. Get in."

His face looked familiar. Tonya and her family attended the Cattlemen's Ball and similar fundraisers, but she didn't know many farmers by name. With luck, he wouldn't recognize her either. Tonya climbed in.

"Hope you don't mind sharing," he said, by which he meant his slobbery hound would sit across her lap and lean its head out the window.

"I'm just grateful for the lift." After watching the dog's long ears and tongue cast around in the wind for a while, she decided she liked this guy and his dog. They were a real pair. There was even a framed picture of the dog glued to the dashboard.

"What's his name?" She stroked his back.

"Fido."

"You're joking."

"Yeah."

Tonya was about to ask whether "yeah," meant he was kidding, when the dog pulled his head back into the car and gave Tonya a long, searching look before it opened its mouth, showing her every detail of its teeth and tonsils. She shivered.

Tonya had never been fond of toothy dogs. Too many owners let them roam free and it was always the bitey ones that ran after your bike. As a kid, she had been terrorized more than once by farmers' German Shepherds, keen to sink their teeth into her pedaling legs. At least, that's how it felt when she was a kid. It was kind of pathetic.

I know.

It took Tonya a moment to register that the driver's lips hadn't moved. He had answered with a voice in her head! Tonya shoved the dog aside, opened the door, and jumped out of the moving car, rolling into the ditch with none of the grace of an action hero. Maybe that was because of all the rocks she hit as she somersaulted along the ground. By the time she crashed to a stop, she was bruised like a banana and when she put her hand to her mouth, it came away bloody.

Struggling to her feet, she stood, teetering, as the car backed up to her. The door was still open, the hound fixing her with a steady stare. It wasn't a big dog, but when it leaped out of the car she screamed like a little girl and took off across the field as if pursued by wolves.

Tree. Tree. Climb a tree, she thought. Except she was in the middle of a corn field with nothing but stalks to slow her down and trip her.

The wicked thing caught her, growling and sinking its teeth into the cuff of her jeans. Tonya tried to shake free, but it wouldn't let go. What she wouldn't do to have some of her aunt's extra-persuasive talents right now. She was always good with animals.

She turned to face the beast. "Calm down Buddy. You don't want to hurt me, do you?"

The dog growled louder.

"That's it! I refuse to be intimidated by a mutt who, five minutes ago, was sitting on my lap with his floppy ears out the window." She circled her hands mysteriously and looked him in the eyes. "I am your new master," she intoned in her best lion taming voice. "Let go my pant leg."

"You gotta be kidding." The white-haired man emerged through the corn stalks. "*You* are the niece of the dreaded Witch of Loon Lake?"

How did he know her? And where had he come from? No one could have predicted she would jump out of the car into *this* cornfield. She continued to croon and move her hands mysteriously which seemed to calm the dog. At last, it released her leg and sat back on its haunches.

"Alright, fun's over. You're coming with me," said the man.

"You're welcome to him. What a strange dog."

"Don't try to be funny." He raised an eyebrow and held out his hand. Levitating above it appeared a tiny flaming orb, so bright it hurt to look at. "You must be wondering where your aunt has gone. Get in the car and we'll take you to her."

"Is Aunt Helen okay?" She didn't want to go anywhere with him. Nothing she had seen in her life prepared her for a man who could harness a ball of fire, and the telepathic farmer creeped her out. "Did you kill my professor?"

"Let's go." He talked like a man who had a gun on her, but he didn't. Over distance, she could outrun this limping old man.

"Make me."

Suddenly, the fireball levitated ten feet over his head, expanding to the size of a tennis ball. "Shall I burn up the cornfield along with you? How about the farmer's house with his family inside?" The man attempted a smile, which failed to turn up the corners of his mouth. It only sank his wrinkles deeper as his Grinch mouth stretched wide.

To think she'd been afraid of a dog bite a few minutes ago. For the first time in her life, Tonya wondered what her parents would do if she predeceased them.

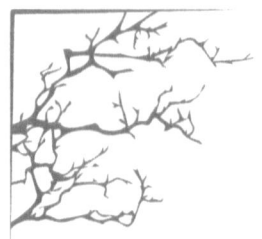

FOOD FIGHT

S un streaming into his dorm room awoke Drake. He sat up, shut the blinds, and lay back down. Halloween was over and, despite Tonya's dire warnings, he had survived. Too bad Priya's triumph had been spoiled by a bomb scare.

After they were ejected from the cemetery, the party had moved into a field just beyond campus where carousing had ensued until the cops dispersed them for trespassing.

"Are you up, Zain?" There was a lump in his roommate's bed, but that didn't guarantee anything. The guy was such a slob that Drake regularly spied lost props and camera equipment poking out of the bedding.

A quick check of the clock explained Zain's absence. It was 11:00 a.m. and Zain, unlike Drake, was a morning person. It was a good thing he was such a good sound editor, otherwise Drake might not forgive his cheerfulness about attending 8:00 a.m. lectures. By 11:00 on a Sunday, he could be any-where.

Drake's phone buzzed with a text from Zain: *Apocalypse now! Cafeteria. Bring cameras.*

Drake would rather go back to bed, but Zain's message sounded urgent. He threw on jeans and a t-shirt and went to the elevator, promising himself coffee. Oh, celestial elixir! The magical brew would open his eyes and restore his wits for whatever Zain was talking about.

THE SCENE IN THE CAFETERIA was beyond anything Drake had imagined in his wildest movie scenarios. Troupes of students brandished trays at the cafeteria ladies, who defended the food with ladles and long-handled pots. Young men and women were shrieking and stealing bananas, leaping up and down in triumph like it was Planet of the Apes.

A handful of campus police clustered together, but instead of stopping the thieves, they stuck their hands into heating trays and pulled out handfuls of bacon. The eating wasn't split exactly along student/employee lines. In some instances, cafeteria staff gorged themselves on sausages, while students walked out in open-mouthed disgust.

Drake pulled out his NEX-VG30H. He had to capture this carnage and stream it live, *now*!

Zain stood on a table, panning with his camera and tripod.

Drake yelled up to him, "It's the Super Bowl of food fights!"

"It's no food fight Duck, it's destiny. Cue the suspenseful music. Here comes the trailer." He put on a horror narrator voice: "In a world gone topsy-turvy, it's a showdown between the hungry, and the voracious. Cafeteria!"

Drake would have found it funnier if the fighting weren't so intense. Zain was standing back and recording while staff broke wooden spoons over students' heads. *Shouldn't somebody break up the fight?*

A skirmish between servers in hair nets and students waving plastic trays drew his attention when a muscle-bound guy stepped up waving a baseball bat. This looked bad, and the authorities were too busy stuffing their faces to notice.

"Hey!" said Drake, "Put the bat down!"

The guy's shoulders were so broad he'd be tall sideways. He stepped up to the cafeteria ladies and swung the bat like a gorilla. The cafeteria ladies stood between him and the bananas.

"Outta my way," said Gorilla Guy.

"Please. Talk this out. Tell the ladies what you want." Drake held his palms up in the universal sign for *please Gorilla Guy, don't split my skull with that baseball bat.*

"I want the food, *all* the food." Gorilla Guy smacked the bat into his hand and stepped up to Drake, squaring his impossibly broad shoulders.

"No, it's mine!" shrieked one cafeteria lady, launching a flying tackle at Gorilla Guy and knocking his legs from under him. A moment later, she was sitting astraddle him with the bat raised over her head, smirking. "Who's calling the shots now, you snotty rich kid! I'm sick of you, all of you!"

A handful of servers converged on Gorilla Guy to hold him down. They chanted "Hit the rich kid! Hit the rich kid!"

"Whoa, whoa," Drake said to her. "Think what you're doing. He looks like a killer but he's somebody's child. You can't just bash his brains in."

Drake stepped close and tried to get at the bat, but she took a swipe at him. Her prey tried to sit up and throw her off, but she laid the bat across his throat and pushed down with all her weight until he couldn't breathe.

"Stay still. *All* the food is mine!"

Gorilla Guy stopped struggling. She raised the bat up, ready to deliver the death blow. Her eyes were frosted blue.

The student lay there, eyes wide, hyperventilating.

"Do you have children?" Drake asked.

She blinked, and the frost cleared from her eyes. She looked around as if noticing the bizarre scene for the first time. Her mouth fell slack. She looked at the student beneath her and startled, then leaped off, coming toward Drake, bat in hand.

"You're up next." She handed him the bat and strode off, tossing her hairnet to the floor. "I quit!"

She ran out the emergency exit and Drake watched her flee past the statue of Sir William Mackenzie and out of the courtyard.

Opening the door had set off an alarm. Over the racket, nobody could hear what anyone shouted. With no chance of arguing for peace, Drake looked around for hotspots where he should intervene.

Zain never stopped filming, even as students threw themselves on the edibles from all sides and cafeteria ladies tried to beat them back with wooden spoons. The students outnumbered staff, so why were the servers risking injury to defend the university's food? The answer came when he saw them gorging themselves as well. That is, the ones who seemed crazed, with frosted eyes like Professor Rudolph.

Drake noticed a clear-eyed server taking advantage of the chaos by scooping cash from the till. Most of the campus police were too busy stuffing their faces to uphold the law but Drake found one lucid officer and pointed the server out.

The first bagel flew over the officer's head while he was crossing the floor, phone to his ear as he reported the situation. A second bagel hit him full in the face.

The cafeteria erupted into a blitzkrieg of flying dishes and utensils as students fought their way to the hot tables. The serving staff, like medieval defenders under siege, used long-handled spoons to catapult showers of hot oatmeal, scrambled eggs, and fried tomatoes at their enemies. This tactic, intended to repel students, instead attracted them. Platoons of students laid down their arms and started lapping porridge off the floor like puppies.

A pair of girls started to fight over the last bagel on the floor. The brunette yanked the blonde by her arm and spun her to the ground. Drake stepped in and snatched the brunette's bagel right out of her mouth. He tossed it away to end the fight, but similar skirmishes erupted all around. Kids were kicking, shoving, punching, and biting each other over the dregs of food.

Six police officers rushed in with Tasers, starting a stampede out the emergency exit.

"Zain! Zain! Get out before you get trampled!"

He could shout all he wanted but there was no way Zain could hear him over the alarm and the crazed mob. The unrelenting noise was making Drake's head throb, on top of the caffeine withdrawal. He needed coffee!

Between the din and the lack of morning caffeine, Drake's headache was an icepick to the temple. Knowing he shouldn't, but too tempted by the scent of java in the air, he made his way gingerly into the fray. What an addict. All he could think of was that first sip.

He advanced toward the hot drinks, but didn't like the frosty-eyed looks the servers were giving him. Especially that blonde hefting a big ladle. She shook it at him, guessing his desire.

Behind her, in a steamy row, awaited the coffee carafes. He had lost all desire for food. Who wouldn't, after watching students gulp it off the floor doggy style? What he desperately needed was to grab an extra-large java.

"Easy there. I just want a coffee," he told the blonde. He reached into his pocket, making no sudden moves, and pulled out a meal plan card. "I'll pay for it. See?"

She didn't look impressed but lowered her ladle a bit. "The coffee is mine."

"Let's do this nice and slow. Want to take my card?" He extended it, a peace offering amidst the melee.

She paused, and they locked eyes, gazes unwavering as laser beams as she pivoted 180 degrees around him with her ladle raised, looking for an opening. Now Drake stood with the coffee carafes behind him, she with her back to the cash register.

"I'm just going to take one cup." He took a step backwards. She didn't move so he turned around and filled a large cup.

The back of his head exploded with pain. He staggered around to face his attacker.

"Nice try." Her ladle was slightly dented where it had connected with his head.

"What was that for? I was paying for it."

"Sure kid, except this card is out of credits." She held it up like a trophy. "Put down the coffee or taste my ladle again!"

That did it. Drake picked up fistfuls of sugar cubes and pelted them at her. She held her hands up to fend them off. He snapped a lid on his coffee and ran.

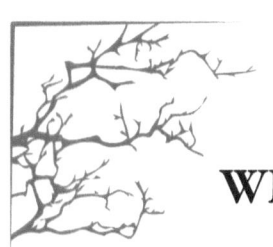

WHAT IS FOREVER?

His belly aching from so many pancakes, Roberto pulled up to the cemetery and parked.

"Come, *Querida*." Roberto opened the passenger door for Lynette. She looked up at him, her eyes unfocused, her face slack.

"I want to stay here. You go."

"Just let me kiss you then." He pressed his lips to her forehead. She tried to protest but he undid her seat belt, picked her up, and started carrying her across the field. There was a break in the fence big enough to lift her through.

"Where are we going?"

"Shhh. I've got you." He kept walking, being careful not to catch her dangling arms and legs on bushes as he went. He stopped at the foot of the Ash.

"We can lie here together."

Reverently, he set her body onto its ancient roots. She looked up at him through lidded eyes.

Well done, said a voice inside Roberto's head. *Now lie down beside her so we may all be united.*

Roberto did as he was told, cuddling up to Lynette and nuzzling her neck. Later, they would merge into the cold Entity, but for now why not enjoy her warmth?

She had been wrong to rescue him yesterday, but he didn't blame her. Even he had screamed and cried for help at first, but after the breaking of ribs and passing out he had eventually felt no pain. The voices in his head were not grieving or angry. They were a chorus, welcoming him to join something larger.

It reminded him of being a small boy inside the Cathedral of Lima, awestruck by the sheer height of the vaulted roof, the beauty of walls and carvings glowing with gold. To be one with something mighty, to be part of a community on Earth and beyond; such things had once inspired him. Joining the Entity reminded him of that childlike exhilaration, but this new being linked him to minds he had never met. Its commands were absolute. It was intoxicating, but it also trapped Roberto between life and death, for as long as the Entity wished to hold him there.

He ran a thumb over Lynette's cheek and gave her a smile of encouragement. The Entity's rootlets were nearly surfacing. He could hear them worming up with a high-pitched burble that echoed in his mind. She would try to fight when they first embraced her, but Roberto would calm her and hold her still. He smoothed her hair, then lay on the leaves, so close to her warmth, he felt almost alive.

Memories of Lynette dancing filled his mind in defiance of the Entity, but in vain. There was no resisting the thoughts and commands flooding into Roberto's head.

How different were his prospects now, compared to boyhood pleasures and college expectations. His parents had sent him to uncover the town's mystical secrets and his *abuela* had made him promise to stay true to his upbringing, no matter what happened.

Such promises belonged to another time. He had become part of the Entity, and now Lynette would join him in its power.

Hair-like roots poked up through the leaves, expanding and fattening as they wormed into the air. Roberto held her tight. "Don't be afraid. It'll be over soon."

And we shall be united forever.

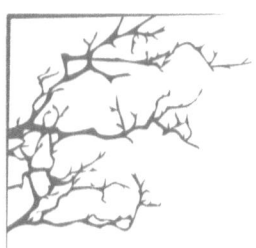

CLOSER

The Entity could feel a new stream of nutrients trickling, like the memory of chicken fat dripping down the Professor's chin. The root hairs grew faster now, attracted to new sustenance, bringing news and organization, expanding networks, and linking consciousnesses. It was almost time.

But life cannot crystallize when there are elements still missing. As Romeo-brain lay down beside Juliet-brain, the Professor's thoughts echoed through the collective. *Would this be enough vital essence, enough synapse and gray matter to reanimate the Entity for good?*

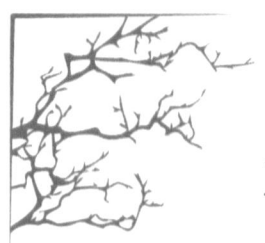

ENTITY RISING

L ynette awoke in another world.

It's so dark here, and so crowded.

Don't worry Querida, *I'm still here.*

The Professor's voice ran through her like thoughts in her own head. *Every wish and desire, every hope and memory, every fatty sheath and delicious neuron has become one with the* Entity.

It feels like snakes moving around me, Lynette thought, and the others thought it too. She heard their voices around her and inside her.

Who are these people? Are we dead?

I'm still holding your hand.

She heard Roberto's voice but could no longer feel him.

Where is my body? Why can't I move? She wanted to run away but couldn't. She felt herself spreading through the ground like the roots of a tree, her head buzzing with voices.

Querida, *don't panic. We will have a body again. We will move across the Earth more powerful than before.*

Roberto's promises didn't reassure her, especially when the Professor's voice exclaimed: *The Entity is rising!*

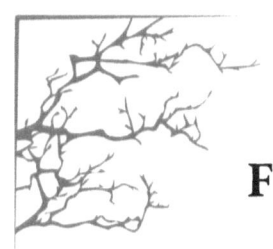

FREE THE NINJAS

D rake reached the residence. He flipped the lid and finished his java in eight gulps. Campus looked like an action director's psychedelic nightmare. He could almost hear the trailer voiceover in his head. *In a world gone insane . . .*

Tonya had tried to warn them. Unbidden, her image came into his mind. She had a face to entice the camera, flawless skin, prominent cheekbones, and angel lips; that is, if she wasn't staring and drooling like a zombie.

With a pang of guilt, he regretted not stopping her last night. She had made him promise to stay out of the cemetery, but he shouldn't have listened. He raced up to the room to get his car keys. Inside, he grabbed a coat and a blanket in case she was cold when he found her. He tried calling.

Tonya didn't answer. Maybe she was mad after last night. Priya didn't answer either. He texted them both to call and let him know they were okay. In the meantime, he would go out and look for them.

Drake looked out the residence window. The courtyard was filled with slow-shuffling students, their mouths and faces stained with food. Had they all been at the cemetery last night? It was hard to tell. Tonya went there last night to stop them. It looked like she hadn't been successful. He had to see her and reassure himself that now she wasn't shambling mindlessly like the rest. He headed to Tonya and Priya's residence.

He took the stairs two at a time to the third floor and banged on Tonya's door. No answer. Could she be passed out inside like Professor Rudolph? It felt weird breaking into someone's room, but this was an emergency. Drake pulled out his student card and slid it between the door and the frame to open it.

Inside, it wasn't hard to tell which stuff was Tonya's. Lynette's bedspread was red, spangled with pink and white hearts. Tonya's was simpler, striped in shades of gold and blue. Lynette had pop star posters and a hot firemen calendar on the wall above her bed. Tonya had one large print, Gustav Klimt's "The Kiss."

Drake shuffled the papers on the little desk and looked for a phone book or a scratch pad or a note on the corkboard, but whatever numbers and addresses Tonya had, were probably saved on her phone. He thought of trying her laptop but that would be creepy. Instead, he called Zain.

"Help me find Tonya and Priya?"

"Not now. I'll miss the apocalypse."

"They're not answering and Tonya's not in her room."

"Check Priya's room in case they're together," said Zain.

"After last night, I doubt they're on speaking terms."

"They're smart girls. They probably drove Priya's car out of town by now."

"Call me if you see them." Clearly Zain wasn't going to help.

Drake checked the common room, but avoided the cafeteria and courtyard which were overrun with food-obsessed students. He phoned the hospital, campus police, and the OPP, but got busy signals. Apparently, anarchy clogged up the phone lines.

That left the cemetery, the one place he didn't want to find her. If she was there, the sooner he got her out the better. From what he'd seen in the cafeteria, the campus police were no help, but he trusted his friends.

Drake admired the Ninjas' scrappy discipline. He also knew them. If any of them started acting funny, he would notice—a thought which filled him with dread. The Ninjas had helped mount cameras in the cemetery and attended Priya's opening. Could they still be clear-eyed and healthy? Zain's enthusiasm in the cafeteria was suspicious. Recording during a riot was something a journalist would do, but Zain was no journalist. Was his coolly detached attitude professional, or a sign of infection?

Drake sent the Ninjas a message to look for Tonya, Priya, and Zain, and report on how they seemed. *We have to stick together to survive.*

Responses came in almost immediately.

I'm on it.

Will report ASAP.

I'll send you a pic from out my window.

At his call, Drake imagined Ninjas springing out of bed, donning black pants and crew shirts as they grabbed smartphones or hoisted cameras to begin surveillance.

The feed of pics they sent Drake was not encouraging. All the residence cafeterias had erupted into food riots.

Get off campus, Drake texted back. *It's not safe.*

The Ninjas left by bike, bus, and car, sending Drake footage and pics of the chaos they passed on their way out of town. People pigged out in parks. Squabbles and fights erupted in doughnut shops. Altercations spilled into the parking lots of nice restaurants. Formerly genteel tea shops devolved into mobs of grannies wielding purses like clubs. As the feeding frenzy spread, bakeries became battlefields, with cream pie shells exploding overhead.

Drake tried to calculate the scale of the outbreak. Had all these townsfolk caught their affliction in the cemetery? Tonya seemed sure of her theory but whether it started in the cemetery or not, eating hysteria was sweeping through town. Worse yet, some Ninjas hadn't responded. Were they infected?

He sent a final text to the Ninjas*: Abort! Abort! Forget sending pics. Leave town as fast as you can and don't come back until I say it's safe.*

Enough surveillance. He had his answers. Tonya and Priya were nowhere to be seen and the disease had spread past campus into Loon Lake. He would search for the girls himself.

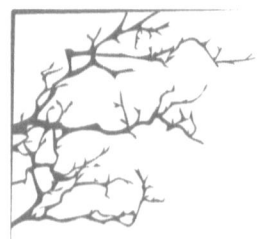

FLAMES

Tonya stood in the cornfield, trapped by the white-haired man. Over his shoulder, a fist-sized fireball floated and bobbed, reminding her of how the shop was wrecked. He didn't speak, apparently content to stare at her as if *she* was the freak.

"Do you know Donna?" She wanted to know how many enemies opposed her.

"Go." He pointed back across the field to where the strange farmer was waiting in his station wagon. Tonya's mind swam with questions. *Did this man know where her parents were? Were they still alive? What did he want from her?*

"Move." The fireball glowed a little brighter.

Tonya moved. She didn't believe he was bringing her to Aunt Helen, but she feared he would kill her if she didn't cooperate.

"Did *you* text me from Helen's phone?" she asked, not daring to look back.

"Head for the car. I'm right behind you."

He needn't remind her. As she went, the fireball warmed her neck and singed her if she slowed down. Compared to the flaming death ball above her head, getting into the car with the creepy farmer and his hound suddenly didn't seem so bad.

Walking back through the cornfield, her toes kept catching on furrows. She stumbled.

"Look where you're going!"

She scanned the field for an escape route. "What do you want me for?" *And who was he?*

"Hurry up. We're almost there."

They reached the road. "I can't believe you're letting that *thing* drive the car."

"Get in." He gestured for her to take the passenger's seat, with the dog.

She watched the ball of fire fly to him, shrinking to marble size as it hovered over his outstretched palm. She got in. He climbed in behind her. "Try anything and I'll send my fiery friend into your ear."

Tonya sat very upright, eyes on the road. "Where are you taking me?"

Her ear burned. She jerked her head away from the heat. Foul smoke caught in her throat and she coughed, clamping a hand over her blistered ear. Tendrils of hair fell away, leaving ashes on her fingers.

"Any more questions?"

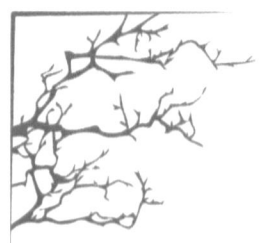

BRING A BAT

Since the cafeteria riot, Drake was wary of the other students. Zain wasn't responding to texts or calls so he decided to go back and retrieve his friend when an OPP cruiser pulled onto the grass in the courtyard, right in Drake's path. There were huge speakers mounted on the trailer it was towing. Fire trucks drove up next, parking on the drive that encircled the campus. Next, police vans pulled into the residence parking lot, disgorging police in riot gear.

They moved with athletic grace, wielding shields, batons, helmets. It was spooky. All those trained professionals rushing to encircle the campus, but making almost no sound, if you didn't count the static of their walkie-talkies.

Drake noticed firemen lifting hoses. They advanced in a line, edging toward the cafeteria doors. *Did Zain get out?* Drake had to check before his friend got arrested or worse—the water ruined his camera!

As he raced the firefighters to the cafeteria, Drake heard a shrill whining above. In the sky, flitting and hovering like a giant dragonfly came a police drone. *What footage!* If he survived, he must buy a drone for the Ninjas.

Near the doors, Drake strained to see Zain through the tinted glass. The firefighters at Drake's back forced him into the crowded part of the lawn. He elbowed his way through shambling students muttering "pancakes" under their breath. Would they attack him? At least they weren't saying "brains."

Drake pushed on until an accidental shove caused one shambler to turn around and aim icy eyes right at him. A couple grabbed his clothes while a third shoved chilly hands into his pockets and started rummaging.

"Food! Give! Food!"

He turned out his pockets, but they wouldn't let go. Breaking free, Drake ran, dodging quickly but careful not to touch them again, for fear of attracting more hungry attention.

"Food!" roared the crowd. Drake didn't slow down. He had to get Zain out. Riding a wave of students rushing the cafeteria, he was carried to the door. Their dead eyes and the drool coming from their mouths left no doubt. They were infected, and they were taking him with them.

The flash of sunlight off a camera lens helped him spot Zain, on the opposite side of campus near the Athletic Center. That put him well outside the ring of police and their riot shields on the west side of campus. Drake tried to resist as the authorities backed students into the cafeteria bit by bit.

"Zain!" He waved and shouted, but Zain was too far away to hear. As Drake reached for his cell to contact his friend, an impossibly loud sound flattened the crowd. He found himself on the ground, ears ringing. Who knew sound could knock you over? He looked for the source.

A uniformed officer stood on the back of the speaker truck wearing orange ear muffs. The unbearable sound had come from his enormous speakers.

"Test. Test. Test." The sound diminished but still sent people cowering, holding their ears as the officer lowered the volume. When he spoke again it was bearable:

"There is an epidemic in Loon Lake. Do not panic. Stay on campus. Food and supplies will be provided. Report directly to the health center at the first sign of unreasonable hunger. The medical staff will give you directions. Follow them exactly. The government is looking for a cure but, in the meantime, no one may leave. Loon Lake is under quarantine, and this quarantine will be maintained by force if necessary."

Drake felt his phone vibrate. Zain's picture popped up on the display. Drake answered but his ears were so affected he couldn't hear anything.

"Switch to text," he shouted.

Zain: *What is this, North Korea? They hit us with the sound cannon.*

Drake: *Are you okay?*

Zain: *Yeah, but students are passed out like it's New Year's Eve. Where are you?*

Drake: *I'm near Mackenzie Cafeteria, on the other side of campus. Are you still recording?*

Zain: *Hid camera, now using phone in case cops take it.*

The whole time they were texting, Drake was working his way through the crowd toward his friend. He reached the ring of police officers surrounding the residences and looked the nearest in the eye. "I'm not infected. Look at me." He held up his hands in surrender.

"We have orders to contain all students."

"Sure, sick students, but if I stay here, how do you know I won't get infected too?"

"Nobody gets past this point."

"What, forever?"

"Stop arguing."

"Or what?" Drake kept his voice very steady.

"I have my orders."

"I don't understand. Why quarantine the dorms on campus? What about the grad student building on the other side of the lake? What about the students renting rooms in town? Are you going to quarantine them too?"

"Maybe."

"Just let me cross the lawn. I promise not to leave town." Drake tried to get around him.

The officer moved to block his path. Shifting the club into his left hand, he pulled out a Taser.

"Okay, I'm staying," Drake retreated into the crowd. Mingling until he was lost to view, he headed for a different part of the line, in search of a friendlier cop.

The second officer pulled his Taser without even pausing to speak. There was no way to reason with these guys.

Speaking loudly, Drake gathered a group of slobbering students around him and edged toward a point where the line of cops was spread further apart.

Pointing dramatically, he shouted, "Hey, that cop has donuts!"

While the pastry-crazed students mobbed the cop, Drake used the diversion to slip through the line and run to Zain.

"I can't believe how fast they came." Zain spoke, phone in hand, still recording the commotion. "One minute there's a little food fight in the cafeteria, and the next . . ."

"It's like somebody tipped them off," said Drake. "In zombie movies, the cops never win."

"Right. They never get a quarantine in place before humanity starts turning into foot-dragging scavengers."

"I can't believe they got it right, in Loon Lake," said Drake.

"Why not? The Provincial Police might watch horror movies for training."

"What?"

"Disaster management, the singularity, alien invasion. Cops have to be ready for anything." Zain's eyes glowed with excitement.

"You do know horror movies aren't real, right?"

"Sure about that? This is the biggest zombie outbreak ever."

"Except nobody's trying to eat our brains," said Drake.

"I could kill a steak though, couldn't you?" Zain's mouth went slack and his eyes went dead. "Something landed on your shoulder. Turn around and let me look."

"No!" Drake held his hands in front of him.

"Just kidding. I'm not infected."

"Good, but if I see food in your hair, or cheeseburgers in your eyes, I'm cutting your head off."

Zain shrugged. "What are friends for?"

"I need to make sure Tonya and Priya are okay. Come for the drive?"

"I'll bring a baseball bat and the camera," said Zain. "If we make it out alive, we're gonna be famous."

COLLATERAL DAMAGE

Tonya watched the corn field shrinking through the back window of her kidnapper's car. Beside her, cows and telephone poles blurred past. She remembered the farmer reading her thoughts and speaking in her head. The white-haired man acted like he was in charge, but the farmer held power too. She sensed so much loose magic in the car, it was hard to tell where the energy was coming from.

"Well Len, how do we do this?" The farmer leaned on the steering wheel.

"Just get us there." Len sat behind Tonya. He must be the one responsible for the magical fire in her aunt's store. *How many fireballs could he conjure in a day?* Magic had its limits and needed to be recharged. Too bad her aunt hadn't taught her more about those limits.

They were driving back toward Loon Lake. The station wagon slowed down and turned in at her aunt's shop. Why had Aunt Helen texted Tonya and then gone dark again? It wasn't like her, but her aunt hadn't been acting like herself for months.

They parked away from the building, close to the road. Even before they told her to get out, she guessed they were taking her across the road to the Ash Tree.

"Time to meet the Boss." The farmer led her into the cemetery.

"Shut up." Len walked a few steps behind her right ear.

"I practically grew up in the Ash," said Tonya. "It won't infect me."

The farmer stopped and leered back at her. "The Entity already owns your mind. Now it wants your luscious curves." With rough hands, he cupped bosoms of air. "Heh, heh, heh."

Tonya gave him a hard shove, but his body was so solid, it didn't move.

"Get going," said Len.

It wasn't a long walk to the break in the cemetery fence. They didn't say another word until they reached the Ash, the trunk almost black in contrast to the few remaining yellow leaves. At its base, the grass was disturbed as if the earth had been turned over.

Len pointed to the dirt at its gnarled roots. "Lie down there."

"You don't want me. I can't even do magic."

He grabbed her by the necklace, hauled her towards him, then shoved her down, snapping the chain.

"Give that back!"

Her head lay near the tree, close to where white roots had grown into her professor's eyes, ears, and nose.

"Lie still." He held the leaf pendant aloft, examining his prize.

Shivers shook her, but it wasn't fear, it was magic. Her senses flooded with cut grass and herb scents too vivid for memory, but they weren't coming through her nose. It was the tree! Her scalp tickled and thrummed as green-flavored energy flowed irresistibly from the ground and through the tree roots into her. She tried to stop it. The speed of flow was frightening, but she had no control. As the tickling sensation intensified she started to giggle.

"Shut up!" said Len. The tiny fireball above his shoulder inflated to baseball size.

Tonya tried to stop laughing. She held her ribs in a crisscross hug, but snickers escaped. Tonya spluttered, "I can't help it." Power surged through her, strong and delicious.

The farmer frowned. "Better keep quiet, people will hear you."

"But not for long." Len smirked and went for her throat but an invisible force knocked him back. As he fell, Len dropped the necklace on Tonya's chest. She grabbed the pendant and slipped it into her pocket. What was this enchantment that repelled Waldock yet let her necklace fall through?

Power rolled around inside Tonya. Even with Len's fiery threat hanging hot and heavy above her, like a joke at a funeral, she exploded with laughter.

Len hurtled the fireball at her head. It filled her vision, but Tonya couldn't budge. At the moment of impact, she shut her eyes.

WHAT IMPACT? ENERGY flowed around her. The moment stretched on. She was alive, still. How was that possible? After a moment that felt like minutes, Tonya opened her eyes.

The fireball was frozen in the air, spinning above her face, brightness hurting her eyes, but nothing more.

"Helen *is* her aunt," said the farmer. "Maybe we should leave her."

"*You* are telling *me* what to do? Look at her. She's helpless."

"Sorry." The farmer scratched his stubble.

"Don't worry. We don't even need her nutrients. Jack just wanted us to use her for payback."

"The sins of the aunts . . ." The farmer showed tea-stained teeth.

Len leaned over and Tonya squirmed away from the fireball.

"So, why aren't you cooked?"

She leaped to her feet, blinded by the swirling orange and white flames. Hovering in the air, the fireball matched her movements so closely she should have ignited, but the air between it and her face remained cool.

"Fine, if I can't burn you, we'll feed you to *Him* the slow way."

Tonya tried to run but Len grabbed her legs, toppling her over. The farmer held her down while Len bound her legs with duct tape. Next, he held down her left hand, and the farmer held her right. They pressed her to the ground, the fireball directly over her face. Tonya should have felt terrified but the power surging inside gave her hope. *Was tree power keeping the fireball back?* It had taken such effort to draw even a little power out of that branch when she demonstrated magic for Priya, but now she felt like a bucket overflowing.

"I don't get it." The farmer scratched his chin. "Why aren't the roots coming?"

"Patience. She's inherited Helen's gift for channeling power. We can use that."

"How?"

"Jack will know."

"So, she's not worthless."

"Look, they come," said Len.

Worming up from the ground on either side of her, the white shoots stretched and snaked side-to-side as they grew, then curved over Tonya's legs, arms, and body, like woody fingers, digging into her flesh.

Len clapped his hands. The fireball shrank and floated back above his shoulder like a flaming pilot fish. "Once the roots have her, she won't be able to resist."

"Let me go or my aunt will curse you." Tonya tried to fight her way free. "If I don't check in with my best friend in fifteen minutes, she'll call the police."

The farmer held up the roll of duct tape and waved it at his accomplice. "Want her quiet?"

"Please."

The farmer ripped off a silver strip and hunkered down. He extended the tape between his hands.

Tonya tried to struggle but the woody shoots held her fast. She couldn't even turn her head.

"Now you'll shut up."

She could see the pepper sprinkle of blackheads on the farmer's nose. How could a man with so many wrinkles still be oily?

He suddenly fell forward, landing on top of her.

"Ugh!"

"Sorry, are you okay?"

Tonya recognized her warm alto, even muffled through an unconscious body. "Aunt Helen!"

In a flash of green light, the roots and tape binding her disappeared.

Tonya pushed free of the farmer and stood up woozily. Helen and Len were taking cover behind trees, hurling projectile curses at each other and leaving burn marks on the trees. The farmer fled the scene and Tonya hid to watch the magical exchange of fire.

With each shot, Len's fireballs got smaller and duller, as Aunt Helen's green lightning began to fade. Ten minutes into the duel, Aunt Helen's mouth looked thin and gray. Her knees buckled, and she fell forward, throwing an arm out to brace herself against the tree shielding her. Len looked equally exhausted.

When he'd first captured Tonya, Len was quick-moving and strong. Wounded by Helen, he propped his limp right arm across his chest with his left. His body trembled, and his fireball had fallen to the ground, flattened, like an ashy fried egg. Tonya thought it would have taken magic users hours to reduce each other to such feeble states but this had taken minutes.

Noting Len's weakness, Aunt Helen closed in for the final shot, but it fizzled.

"Taste this!" He came at her with a tree branch raised to strike.

Helen retreated, pursued by Len, slipping and sliding in the autumn leaves.

The sound of a hound dog barking announced the farmer's return. He was carrying a rifle.

The dog bounded after Helen while the farmer dropped to his knees to take a shot. Tonya dove at him, knocking his arm off target. In the scuffle, she tried to pry the rifle out of his hands, but he was too strong.

Nice try, little girl.

His words in her head, stung like a slap. He tossed her off with a laugh.

She fell on her back, her head just missing a rock. Angry, Tonya picked it up and ran at him, whacking him on the back of the head.

He dropped, senseless. Tonya picked up his rifle, being careful not to touch the trigger. Tonya didn't want to shoot anybody, not even in self-defense. She looked at the farmer's limp body and the bloody bump where she struck him. Her stomach lurched. *Had she killed him?*

Somewhere a crow cawed. Another answered, throaty and verbose. Tonya stood very still, listening for Len and the dog. The sound of rustling leaves drew her attention to flashes of color, moving between the trees. Someone was circling around behind her. She turned to follow their movements, but they were obscured by the branches.

Lightning hurtled toward her. Tonya sidestepped but too late—it was going to hit her. She closed her eyes and braced herself for the impact, but . . . nothing happened. She opened her eyes.

Suspended in front of her, the lightning sparked and crackled in midair, frozen by some invisible barrier.

Tonya was so fascinated by this phenomenon that she didn't notice movement behind her. Before she could react, strong hands grabbed her. She struggled. The man gripped her throat and squeezed until she couldn't breathe.

"Don't faint now, girl. I prefer a *walking* human shield."

It was Len. He pivoted behind her, keeping Tonya between himself and Aunt Helen, when she broke out of the bushes in front of her.

"This is more like it, eh? I can cast spells at you, but you can't retaliate."

"This is bigger than you or me, or Tonya." Aunt Helen coughed until she choked. Finally, she gasped enough breath to say, "If Jack Waldock rises, don't expect him to reward you."

"He will, and there's nothing you can do."

Aunt Helen shrugged at Tonya and sighed. "Sorry, Love." She raised her arm to cast a spell at Len, right through Tonya.

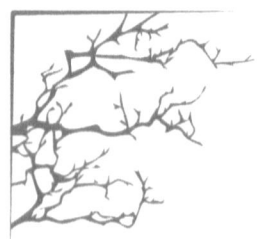

WORST FEARS

D rake's mind was usually more preoccupied with his next movie than his next meal, but it was late morning and his stomach growled. Too bad there was no time to eat. If he and Zain wanted to rescue their friends he'd have to be crafty and act fast.

Drake wove his car through the campus parking lot as wild-eyed students yelled and banged on their windows, desperate for a ride off campus. It sent shivers up Drake's spine when he noticed slower ones shambling their way. He drove at a crawl for fear of harming them.

Time passed slowly, until at last they reached the road through campus, where the foot-dragging crowd forced him to wait for a break in traffic. Handfuls of rocks pelted at his back window. He glanced at Zain in the passenger seat. "Are you scared?"

"Do zombies eat brains?"

"What's going to happen if we try to leave town by driving around the roadblocks? The police wouldn't shoot innocent students, would they?"

"Nah, but let's hope they don't redefine innocent. Let's go!"

"I don't want to leave without the girls."

Students ran into the road, banging on his windows, and blocking Drake's path. "Could you keep a watch out for them?" He kept his voice steady but didn't feel as confident as he sounded. Priya and Tonya had spent hours in the cemetery on Halloween. He and Zain had too.

"I'll keep my eyes peeled." Zain mimed ripping an eyelid off. "Pop!"

Drake was happy to let Zain do the looking. What if the next wandering sleepwalker was Tonya?

"I don't understand the police," said Drake. "If the cemetery is making people sick, they should be helping us leave town."

"Diseases spread person to person. Like, you know, if you get bitten by one of the walking dead out there . . ."

"This isn't the zombie apocalypse!"

"Potato, po-tat-oh. We still go splat-o."

Drake gripped the wheel as he drove west through campus. At first, he tried to leave via the main exit, but it soon became clear nobody ahead of them was getting through the police checkpoint onto Kenny Road. There had to be another way to get a car off campus, but every route out was barricaded. In desperation, Drake did a U-turn and pulled into the faculty parking lot which faced the lake.

"What are we doing here?" asked Zain.

"I want to think, away from the hordes."

"Literally. Alright Duck, let's watch those waves roll in."

The beach gave Drake an idea. Looking first to make sure he wasn't observed, Drake drove over the narrow strip of grass separating the parking lot from the beach. Loon Lake had a pebbly shore which allowed him to drive across it without sinking into the ground. He drove west along the shoreline, then cut up onto the boardwalk, continuing until they reached Kenny Road.

"Hold your breath they don't see us," said Zain.

Drake turned north, not daring to look back. From there he took small roads west and north in a zigzag pattern, looking to distance themselves from campus before they circled back south to the highway.

He looked for a route they could use to leave the area once they found the girls, but every time he tried to go south, the road was blocked by sawhorses and police vehicles. *Was there no way onto the main highway?*

Forced yet again to turn the wrong way, Drake slowed as they approached the northeast end of Loon Lake. He didn't see many other cars or people on the tree-lined road until they neared a complex with fast food joints, a grocery store, Canadian Tire store, and a gas station.

"I'm hungry," said Zain. "Let's eat here."

Drake slowed right down and cracked open his windows. An alarm shrilled through the air. Somebody had driven a car through the plate glass storefront of the grocery store and it sat, half-in, half-out. Safety glass glittered on the sidewalk where people scampered, arms full of packages.

"It's Christmas Eve for looters!" Zain rolled down his window and leaned out, adjusting his camera. "Park the car."

Unwilling to get closer, Drake pulled onto the gravel shoulder. Across the berm, people fled the store with boxes and bags of food, but few escaped peacefully. The whole adult population of Loon Lake seemed to be tussling in the parking lot. People fought tug-of-wars over cases of canned goods. Ladies in grocery store uniforms rammed shopping carts through the crowd. A middle-aged gang, armed with golf clubs and hockey sticks, intimidated people and commandeered their supplies. Drake couldn't tell the healthy from the infected. Everyone looked desperate.

A flash of color drew his eye to where the turquoise fringe of a leather jacket flapped by his window. It was a woman running past, cradling a turkey like a wide receiver. She was pursued by three young men.

One of the guys attempted a flying tackle.

"Get your head back in the car. I'm driving between those guys and that poor lady."

"Wait. She's getting away."

The woman dodged between parked cars and hopped on the back of a waiting motorcycle. A fat man in leathers roared away with her, flipping them the bird.

"We should go," said Drake. Dull-eyed shoppers had noticed their car and started shuffling toward them.

"First let's get supplies or we'll starve when the town runs out of food," said Zain.

"Open that door and you're not coming back."

Zain looked at him with a pained expression until a guy in a suit jumped onto the hood and started beating the windshield with his fists.

"The lineups were gruesome anyway." Zain did a zombie face. "Argh!"

"Not funny." Drake's empty belly ached. "Know what I'm gonna do when this is over?"

"Eat ten steaks?"

"Donate to the food bank. Nobody should live like that." He pointed to the guy beating on the windshield. "I'm so hungry, I can't think of anything else." Drake started the engine and took off, cranking the steering wheel hard to dislodge the man.

"Let's get outta town," said Zain

"One more stop first."

Drake texted their location and ETA to Tonya and Priya. Then he pulled back onto the road and circled back around the east end of the lake.

"Are you insane? You're headed back to campus."

"We can't leave without the girls." Drake hit the accelerator.

They were between campus and the hospital when he heard a siren. Red lights spun in his rear-view mirror. An OPP car flashed its high beams and Drake pulled over.

He got out his papers and rolled down the window, but the officer was in no rush, still sitting in the cruiser and talking on his radio.

"Trust the Ontario Party Poopers to nitpick us in the apocalypse!" said Zain. "You were hardly speeding."

"Exactly. Shouldn't the OPP be stopping that riot at the grocery store?"

"Like good little piggies."

"No matter what happens, don't get out of the car." In the wing mirror, Drake watched the officer amble up to the driver's side.

"Let's see your license and registration." The cop looked at his papers, as if this were another sleepy day in Loon Lake, when doing ten over the limit was the worst event conceivable.

He peered in the window. "Have either of you boys been eating? Uh . . . drinking?"

It was a small slip, but after that Drake knew. A glance confirmed the presence of drool at the corner of the cop's mouth. He fought the urge to jam his foot onto the accelerator.

"No sir. We're perfectly sober. It's barely lunchtime."

"Have you any food in the car?"

"No."

The cop flashed a broad smile and peered into the back seat. "Everybody has something."

"Not a crumb."

Drake waited. The officer's eyes were glassy, and he circled the car in a trance. Drake's instincts screamed at him to go, except the officer still held his license. He started counting down from ten in his head. If he got to zero, he would drive away, with or without papers. The cop moved like wading through tar.

He had counted down to one when the officer returned and said, "I have to warn you . . ."

Drake stuck his hand out and snatched back his papers. "Sorry! Gotta go. It's the end of the world!" He pulled onto the road with a screech of tires.

"Why'd you do that?" Zain asked. "Now he'll come after us."

"Don't worry. He's too slow to catch me."

Drake floored it and wove past a couple of cars and a tractor. They had a head start. Drake thought he'd lost him, until the cop turned on his siren and the other vehicles had to pull over. Drake slammed down the gas pedal.

"What are you doing?" Zain's voice went up an octave. "He's a cop. Stop or we'll go to jail."

"Relax. *I* might go to jail," said Drake, "but if I don't lose him, we might never find the girls." He risked a glance at Zain to see if his friend looked as panicky as he sounded.

Zain grabbed his arm. "Duck, slow down!"

Drake looked back at the road, which had veered left. He hit the brakes and steered left, but the car kept going straight. They crashed through a guardrail along a strip of grass and skimmed over a pond. For a moment, Drake thought they might clear it, but the back end caught water and dragged them down. The pond was deep, and they were in the middle, sinking.

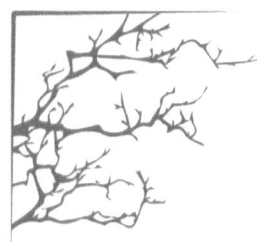

DEAD DUCK

Icy water climbed Drake's legs as it rushed into the car. The hungry officer had caught up and stood by his cruiser, watching them sink.

"They can make *me* go to the station, but no matter what happens," Drake pointed at the cop, "don't get into a car with Officer Hungry."

"Course not. What, you think I've never seen a horror movie?" The water was to his chest and Zain's teeth chattered.

"You should go now."

"I'm not leaving you, Duck."

They were crouching on the seats with a wisp of space between their heads and the roof. Sirens approached. Drake felt the tires settle gradually into the muck as the water rose to his neck. "He's slow. You could get away."

"I can't leave you to be hunted. He thinks it's Duck season."

"Go!"

"You mean act as a decoy?"

"I mean go."

"Not till I run out of Duck jokes."

"I've gone cold on comedy." Drake's teeth chattered.

"You're just jealous of my cool wit." Zain forced his door open and waded away, holding a damp camera bag over his head.

Drake climbed onto the roof of the car. Icy air cut through his jacket but at least he was out of the Polar water.

An ambulance arrived, lights flashing, followed by a second police cruiser. The driver got out and ordered Drake to put his hands up. "Wade out to shore, now!"

"The water's freezing. Are you trying to kill me?"

The newcomer and his partner stood beside Officer Hungry at the water's edge. "Come now, or I'll charge you with resisting arrest!"

"If I get hypothermia, my parents will sue."

This got the three officers talking until Officer Hungry returned to his car and spoke on the radio. From the middle of the pond, Drake couldn't hear him or read his lips. He hoped a crowd would congregate. He didn't want to think what Officer Hungry might do without civilian witnesses.

BY THE TIME POLICE picked him up in a rowboat, Drake's teeth were chattering uncontrollably, and he was shaking. Back on shore, paramedics wanted to take him to the hospital but Officer Hungry took them to one side and whispered something Drake couldn't hear.

They gave him a blanket and got back in the ambulance.

His head felt fuzzy and he wanted to lie down. As the paramedics drove away, Drake still hadn't been charged with anything. Was it possible they might let him go? He stumbled toward the highway but Officer Hungry grabbed his shoulders and marched him to the squad car.

As his brain started to thaw, Drake noticed the cop's movements were swift and sure. He had been in a daze like Professor Rudolph before, but now he seemed normal, except when he put Drake into handcuffs and their hands touched. The cop's fingers were cold as the pond. Drake shivered.

From the back of the police cruiser, Drake watched a tow truck operator and a man in a dry suit hook up the back end of his car. How many of these seemingly normal people, he wondered, were cold-blooded too? Were they dead? Sleepwalking like Professor Rudolph? Maybe the riot police who surrounded the campus were part of a conspiracy. They *had* arrived very quickly after the food fight. The question troubled him on the drive back to town.

At the police station, Drake shivered, handcuffed to a hard bench. They kept him waiting long enough that his hair dried out although his feet still squelched in his shoes as they led him to a solitary cell. Pangs in his stomach reminded him that he'd only had coffee for breakfast. They had offered no food, even though it felt long past lunchtime.

Processed, he sat on a narrow steel cot built into the wall of a holding cell. There was a stainless-steel toilet without a lid. On the floor beside it, a quarter roll of toilet paper had gotten wet and warped, hopefully with water. There was a solid door with a small window in it.

Drake wondered if the holding cell would make a good film location. It was authentically stark, colorless and depressing but, unfortunately, too cramped to fit a film crew. He'd need a much bigger room to recreate the claustrophobic feel of this narrow space. Drake paced. They said they were holding him for reckless driving but hadn't asked him to make a statement or offered him a phone call. From time to time, officers would pass his door and peek in the window. It didn't make him nervous until the last one looked Drake up and down slowly, a drop of drool escaping the corner of his mouth.

How long could they keep him without letting him contact a lawyer? Drake had surrendered his phone at the front desk, so he didn't know the time, but his stomach announced it was hours past lunchtime. He tried banging the door, but nobody came. To take his mind off his stomach, Drake decided to nap on the steel shelf. He was just lying back, wishing he had a blanket, when a tall, puffy-faced officer unlocked the door. He ordered him out, then walked him along the corridor to a cage-like cell housing three other men.

"Can't I go back where I was?"

"No. We're extra crispy, uh, busy, today." The officer held Drake's gaze a little too long, mouth agape. Drake feared whatever happened next might belong in a viral video, or the *Hannibal Lecter Cookbook*. It was a relief when the officer locked him into the cage with a bunch of criminals.

At the beginning, the other prisoners ignored him. He sat on a bench and watched them beg passing officers for food, which never came. They might as well have been starving POWs in a war movie. Nobody was concerned with their rights.

A cop walked down the corridor with a box of donuts. The prisoners started whistling and banging on the bars.

"Don't go, Sweet Things!" the fat one moaned. "Come closer."

"I could eat you all up," said the skinny one.

The big guy rolled his eyes and grabbed at his stomach, making obscene chewing sounds.

Their wolf whistles got no reaction, so they shouted abuse after the retreating guard.

THE REST OF THE AFTERNOON, prisoners retreated into their corners to chat or snooze. None turned their back on the others.

Dinner never came.

After lights out, the day's dark comedy morphed into a psychological thriller in which sinister inmates drooled and stared at Drake. The skinny guy had bulging eyes and long scraggly hair that hung past his shoulders, like the ears of a beagle. The fat one looked more like a couch potato than a criminal, but his hungry stare gave Drake the shivers. The big guy was a head taller than Drake and built like Zeus. Every time he moved, the others shifted to keep Drake between Zeus and themselves.

It was creepy but manageable until Skinny Dog took a bite of Mr. Potato. Screams, wails, fists and feet flew as Zeus joined in the fray. Drake would never be able to recreate this chaos with actors. How could they simulate the prisoners' grimaces and cruel laughter as they grabbed, mauled, and snapped at each other?

Zeus bared his teeth and turned his drooling attentions to Drake who fled into a corner, covering himself with his arms and legs until someone grabbed his neck and he realized he would have to fight. Sitting in a shark tank, it was best not to wait like a helpless piece of chum. Drake stood his ground and shoved Zeus hard, which failed to budge him.

Zeus laughed. "You look tender and I want sushi."

"Go find a fish."

"I'm looking at one."

Drake planned his counterattack based on extensive Kung Fu movie viewing. "Well, are you going to make a move or are we going to stand around, talking about it?" Drake squared his shoulders and puffed out his chest. He was fired up in a new way.

Laughter sounded out of the dark. It was hard to see much of Zeus, just a tower of pumped up flesh, a murderous eye glint, and a gaping mouth.

Drake put his fists up. "You want me? Come get me."

"You talk big for a little boy."

Drake stood to his full six-foot height. He curled his fingertips like an action hero, beckoning Zeus closer.

The big guy threw a punch and Drake bobbed left, balanced on the balls of his feet. The man came at him again but this time when Drake weaved away, Zeus kept coming past him, throwing a punch at his gut on the way, then stepping into the corner behind Drake. Drake turned to face Zeus, which put his undefended back too close to the slavering, biting inmates behind him.

Bad odds. One-on-one, he might have dodged blows like Jackie Chan, but now? As he tried to feint right, then left, Zeus flashed a smile. From behind, somebody grabbed Drake's shoulder and took a bite.

"What do you say, boys?" Zeus grinned. "He's scrawny, but there's enough to go 'round. Dig in!"

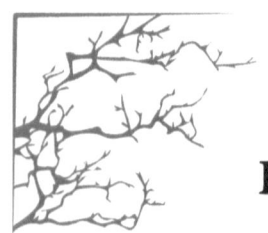

PRIYA SURPRISE

Hubbub on the campus lawn drew Priya to her top floor window. From that height, she discerned diving team jackets jostling among the student mob, as well as serving staff and security guard uniforms. Students streamed out of the cafeteria carrying boxes, bags, and trays of food.

Tonya had been right after all. The cemetery had infected at least a hundred students, and now they were penned in by riot police with gas masks and Plexiglas shields. Her guilt was confirmed when she opened the window and heard them chanting, "Feed us! Feed us!"

In the distance, she could see similar scenes repeated on the lawns around the other two residences visible from her window. At the same time, students who weren't penned in were getting into cars and driving away but they didn't get far. The roads around campus were backed up like rush hour as vehicles lined up for inspection at police roadblocks.

Police loudhailers declared the quarantine of Loon Lake would be humane. Priya believed their promises of food deliveries and medical treatment, until a wave of students tried to break through the barricade on the lawn around Mackenzie College and the police forced them back with dogs and tear gas.

Priya had participated in political demonstrations but they were nothing like this. Police pelted students with tear gas canisters and then, instead of letting them disperse, trapped them on the lawn with shields and clubs. Some students buried their burning eyes and faces in the grass. Others fell to their knees, swaddling their heads with their shirts, or clawing at their eyes.

She scanned the crowd for Tonya, Drake, or Zain but it was hard to make out faces in the crowd. Could her friends be okay? In the hallway outside her door, the sounds of showers and plumbing suggested a few people in the dorm were attempting their normal routines. For now.

Priya grabbed her phone and scrolled through last night's texts and messages from Tonya, warning her to stay out of the cemetery.

More promising was a text from Drake. He and Zain were headed back to campus to pick her up. All she had to do was find Tonya and the four of them could leave together. She called Drake.

"The customer requested cannot be reached."

Zain's was the same. *Why would they send her a message then switch off their phones?*

She texted the other Ninjas who, to her relief, had heard from Drake. At his urging, they had all left town.

Tonya didn't answer her phone, so Priya walked downstairs to knock on her door.

No answer.

Priya stood outside Tonya's door, hugging herself, hoping her friend wasn't infected. From the window in the hall, she looked down on a desperate scene. What would happen to the rioters on the lawn?

She looked down at the roadway through campus. Cars waited in a long line that wasn't moving. Officers on foot were turning back pedestrians. It didn't look like she could get anywhere fast, so she decided to wait for Drake and Zain.

On a whim, she called Shin. When he didn't answer right away, Priya let it ring six times.

"Who is this?" It was Marta's voice. Surprised, Priya almost didn't identify herself.

Despite previous fainting spells, Marta sounded alert. "Priya, where are you?"

"Stuck in my dorm room."

"Me too."

"Are you and Shin okay?"

"I knew it! You're still after Shin, well forget it. We're getting out of here. My Mom is picking us up in an hour."

"Can I come with?"

"That would be against protocol."

"How's she getting in anyway? Campus is under quarantine."

"Oh, you know. Friends in high places. Nice talking to you. Bye!"

Priya thought she was going to hang up but in the background, she heard a scuffle.

Shin came on. "Are you in your room?"

"Yeah."

"I'm coming to get you."

"Worry about Marta. She's the one who's sick."

"Her Mom's picking her up in an ambulance, but she won't take you."

"Nice."

"We're not sick," he said. "Let's walk out together."

Marta came back on the line. "If you care, tell him how risky that is. Mom can get us out if he doesn't do something stupid, like wait for you."

"The police will let us out if we're not sick, right?"

"Sure, but Shin's coming with me." She spoke in her usual, forceful tone.

"You sound healthier."

"What's that supposed to mean?"

There was a knock at her door so Priya disconnected.

"It's me, Shin."

Should she open the door? She doubted it was safe for Shin to go with Marta, but anywhere was safer than staying on campus. She turned the knob and, leaving the safety chain on, opened it a crack.

"Hey Priya."

She noticed he was panting and flushed, probably from running up the stairs.

"Aren't you going to open the door?"

Priya hesitated. Something in his manner was different. "You should go back to Marta."

"She'll be fine. I'm worried about you."

"Don't be."

"Are you sick?" Shin tilted his head to get a better look through the opening. "Let me help you."

She didn't deserve his concerned looks, not after ignoring Tonya's warnings last night. "I feel fine, now go."

"I'm not leaving."

"Why are you so stubborn?" She unlocked the chain, but only to properly convince him to go. There would be treatment in the outside world and Marta needed someone strong to watch over her. Priya convinced herself of these motivations even as she flung open the door to let him in.

Which is why it took her completely by surprise when she and Shin rushed into each other's arms.

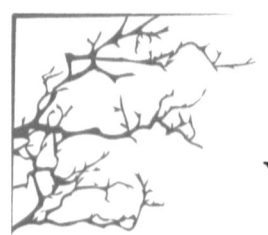

WHO ARE YOU?

What would a curse feel like? Tonya closed her eyes, bracing for the impact.

It wasn't like flames or a fist. It hurt like a full-body cramp. Muscles she didn't even recognize spasmed and throbbed as the energy passed through. The hands gripping her relaxed and she heard Len's body hit the ground behind her. She turned and saw his hands splayed, white against the autumn leaves. The rifle shattered.

A cold breeze ruffled her hair as she stood. Tonya flinched when Aunt Helen put an arm around her and steered her toward the cemetery gate. "We have to see a doctor," She leaned on Tonya so heavily they stumbled.

"I need to find my friends first." Tonya stepped away from her aunt and pulled out her phone. "Just a sec."

Aunt Helen snatched the phone and put it in her purse. "Sorry, Love. I don't think it's safe for you to see them, do you?"

Tonya didn't answer. *Could her aunt somehow know she was infected?*

Aunt Helen ordered her out the gate. Leaning on Tonya's arm, they walked to the parking lot of her shop where they stopped in front of her car.

"Get in, you're driving."

Tonya looked at her aunt's face, pale and tinged with gray. Dark circles under her eyes reminded Tonya of a skull. Unable to refuse a dying woman, she got in.

Aunt Helen waited for Tonya to adjust the mirrors then handed over the keys. "Head north. I'll let you know when to turn."

Tonya pulled onto the road. "When will I get back to my friends?"

"Just keep driving."

The woman on the seat beside her looked like Aunt Helen. She sounded like Aunt Helen, and she had fought against Len and the creepy farmer, but her aunt had never acted like this. This aunt slung spells like an assassin. Could Donna's people have somehow taken over her mind?

"So, how are my parents?" Tonya glanced at her aunt's face, hoping to detect a flicker of emotion.

No reaction.

The car slowed as traffic bunched up ahead. They were stopped at a roadblock. Helen got out of the car and went to talk to the officers in charge.

The next thing she knew, one officer walked back and directed Tonya to drive up the shoulder, passing cars to go around the roadblock.

Aunt Helen stumbled back into the car. "Turn right and then north at the next light."

"How did you do that?"

Tonya knew very well her aunt had charmed them, but she wanted to hear it from the source.

Aunt Helen coughed, which set off a fit of deep, retching coughs that left blood on her tissue. The fit passed, and she laid her head against the window and appeared to go to sleep.

Tonya continued north until the road became a country highway. Worry gnawed at her until she could take no more. She wasn't getting any farther away from town until she knew Drake and Priya were safe. Ahead, she spotted the perfect spot to pull a U-turn and started the maneuver.

Aunt Helen slammed her hand over Tonya's heart, causing her chest to vibrate. It felt like a hundred tiny hammers were trying to batter their way out from inside. She hit the brake.

"Are you with me, or Waldock?"

"Who are you? You're not my aunt. She would never kidnap me." Tonya shivered. *Or kill anyone.*

"I knew you'd be difficult." Helen laughed, until a fit of coughing cut her off. "Trust me, things will go a lot easier if you just do what I say."

TO SERVE AND
PROTECT, AND SERVE

D rake roared as inmates threatened to sink their teeth into his arms. He tried to spin away but they held him fast. He launched himself against the side of the cell, banging Zeus's head against the bars. He might be outnumbered but he was going down fighting.

Gunfire exploded in his ears.

Deafened by the shot, Drake located a cop who was shouting at them with such force it dislodged clouds of powdered sugar from his lips.

Gradually, Drake's ears adjusted, and he could understand what the officer was saying.

"No more biting! No tooth marks."

"There's a camera." Drake pointed out a wall-mounted surveillance cam.

"Faulty wiring." The cop tapped the side of his nose. "Don't worry."

"Worry? These men jumped me. They're trying to eat me." He held up an arm which was ringed with tooth marks. "What if I get an infection? I demand medical treatment."

The officer stared at Drake who refused to drop his gaze.

"You're a pain in the butt. Next thing you'll be asking for a lawyer."

"Yes, please."

"We *love* lawyers," Zeus smirked.

With hot sauce, thought Drake. "So, can I see a doctor?"

"We have a nurse."

Officer Icing Sugar couldn't open the cell door fast enough. Drake waited obediently, hands held out for cuffing. He wished he could call his parents and ask them to send him a lawyer too, but if he admitted he was in trouble, they'd drive straight to Loon Lake and put themselves in jeopardy. He'd rather settle for a local lawyer, preferably one without tooth marks.

"Can I make my phone call now?"

"See the nurse first." The Officer wiped his mouth on his sleeve, then made Drake walk in front of him until they reached the infirmary where he uncuffed him and sent him in.

It was a large room with a high ceiling and thick walls. The young nurse's immobile face could have been waxwork.

Once the door closed behind him, Drake clasped his hands together. "Please, you have to get me out of here. Those prisoners were trying to eat me!"

"You're delirious. Once you come down things will make sense." Her voice was flat.

"I'm not on drugs. Ask me to walk a straight line or say the alphabet backwards."

"Do both if you like. Some drugs are performance enhancing."

"This is a misunderstanding. I haven't committed a crime. I was being chased by a dangerous man when they brought me here."

She frowned into a tan folder. "The duty sergeant says you are AKA Duck."

"My name's Drake, you know, like a duck."

"Nice alias, tough guy." She told him to stand beside a tray of medical instruments.

"Aren't you afraid to work with these cops? First, they eat the prisoners' lunches, then they stand back and watch them bite each other."

"Cannibalism, in Canada?" She raised one eyebrow.

"You're looking at the wounds." He turned so she could see his back. "I must look like I survived the Franklin Expedition."

"The what?"

"Explorers trapped in the Arctic, starvation, madness?"

"Don't make a fuss. I barely see tooth marks."

"What about my wrist?" He turned and inverted his arm, so she could see the beads of blood.

"Don't be a baby." She sprayed cold liquid on his wrist and it went numb.

"Point is, why eat the prisoners' food?"

"Who says they did?" Licking her lips, she turned him around to treat his shoulder blade.

Drake craned his neck to look back at her. "Why do the prisoners act like they're starving?"

"Not my business."

She stung his wound with antiseptic spray.

Drake winced. "How long has this been going on?"

"What?"

"Attacks between prisoners, cops who pull cars over to search for food."

"Stop whining."

The nurse directed Drake into a plastic chair. "When the doctor comes, keep your mouth shut or I'll make sure you're committed for life."

"I won't lie."

"Think institution for the criminally insane." She stooped so close he could see the specks in her gray eyes, "Duck, there are *lots* of open cases a drugged-up suspect like you could help us close . . ." She unlocked a cabinet. "What shall it be? Cocaine? Oxy-Contin?"

"Help!"

"Nobody can hear through these walls." She laughed. "Too bad you didn't call someone to bail you out sooner."

"Would you drag your parents in here?"

"If they were still alive, I'd send them running for the hills." She looked up at the tiny window, a patch of blue in the thick wall.

An officer came and waved her into the corridor. Drake couldn't hear what they were whispering.

They returned together. "You made bail," she said.

"You'll be back." The officer licked drool from his lips. "Walk." He pointed down the hall.

Drake went ahead slowly, heart pounding. It seemed like the whole world wanted a chunk of him.

They emerged from the corridor into the light and Drake saw Zain, standing by the exit. He wanted to run out and join him, but first he had to return to the booking counter.

The desk sergeant took so long to locate the bag with Drake's belongings, that Zain came back to wait with him.

"I'm so glad you came to get me," said Drake.

"Good, because I sold your camera for bail money."

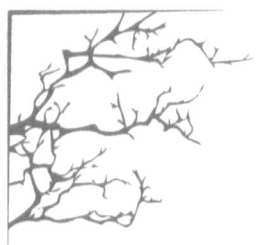

MUSHROOM

Under the earth's surface, Roberto allowed himself to sink deeper beneath the Ash Tree. Around them, root threads wormed, whiskering across his cheek and into his ears. Around his waist and limbs, the white roots grew thick as pythons, pinning him in place.

"How do you feel, *Querida*?" He strained against the roots to feel for Lynette lying beside him. She sighed, as if dreaming.

The pressure built in his ear canals as gathering threads crowded against his eardrums, pressing until they pushed through. He saw fireworks and a blinding white light, pain made visible. His arms and legs felt warm for the first time since the autumn leaves started turning. Struggling against his bonds was impossible but Roberto changed his mind. There were still things to do and see in the world above. Something wriggled up inside his spine. Ugh, it felt like a centipede climbing inside his back!

Wrong, I'm threading a hypha up into your brain, answered a voice in his head.

A brighter boy would have figured that out, responded another.

He's intelligent enough, an acceptable candidate.

A chorus of agreeing voices filled Roberto's mind.

Now I know Querida *means dear.*

Roberto recognized the voice of Professor Rudolph in his head. *Your girlfriend is no great addition, I'm afraid.*

Suddenly, Roberto became conscious of himself as he was, a cooling body in the cold ground. Snaky threads carried his thoughts below, conjoining his mind with something sinister and decayed, a dead thing that refused to join the wholesome earth around it. If he were still alive he would scream.

Who are you?

You're mine.

Was he really dead? Couldn't it be a dream?

In dreams, Roberto might be flying or kissing a girl or reliving the first time he water-skied. The problems of the day, his parents' insistence on Loon Lake University, and loneliness might rub against each other in the tumble dryer of his mind. Other times, he remembered colors, like the blue sky over Lima's beaches or the deep crimson of his parents' Persian carpets. But in dreams there was no odor like this.

Voices in his head crowded out his thoughts. He felt bound to an Entity of collapsing flesh. The roots which entrapped Roberto conjoined him with the collective, so he could no longer tell which senses were his own as the earth began to rumble and spread beneath him, tumbling Roberto into a reeking charnel pit.

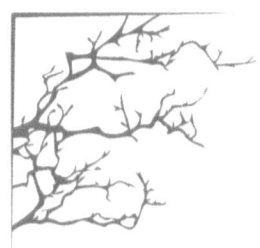

BLUE CHEESE SANDWHICH

"Are my parents in danger?" Tonya's hands blanched and trembled as she gripped the steering wheel.

"Turn this car around and I'll tell you." Aunt Helen cleared her throat noisily and opened the window. She held her face in the wind, letting stray hairs dip and dance.

Tonya glanced at the back of Aunt Helen's head. Her white ponytail was thinning, revealing scalp like the floor of a replanted forest. When had she lost so much hair?

Tonya made a three-point turn and continued north, waiting for her aunt to speak.

"Well?"

Aunt Helen sighed and stared straight ahead. "I found out Len was back in town, so I sent my sister on an eco-tour of Australia. Your parents will be camping for the next two months."

"Why haven't they phoned?"

"Every week I email them to say things are okay. Besides, they don't have much internet in the Outback."

"Is that why they won't answer my calls?"

"I made them forget they ever had you."

"You can *do* that? How could you!"

"I had to make them forget. I can't keep manipulating them at a distance."

"I can't believe you'd do that to your sister."

"She'll make me pay for it. Eventually, the charm will wear off. Is she ever going to be mad when she remembers selling the house."

"What?"

"I had to pay for their trip somehow."

"They told me you were in the hospital, that they were moving to Toronto to visit you. They wouldn't let me see you, said you didn't want me to. Mom was really clear about that."

"I'm not proud of any of this. When my sister finds out I impersonated her on the phone and manipulated her mind . . ."

"Let me talk to them."

"It's for their own good. The other side is watching, trying to get leverage on me. If your parents come back, or Waldock finds them, I can't protect them."

"I don't get it. If you knew it was so dangerous, why didn't you send me with them?"

Helen's head drooped. "I wish I could."

"Now I know why Mom hates you."

"I hate me too, but I need you. The whole town does. I should be in hospital and if I die . . ." She sniffed. "It won't come to that but you're my backup, in case I can't stop Waldock."

"Who?"

"You've met his helper, Len."

"And his friend the telepathic farmer and his dog."

"A telepathic farmer? That man never lets up."

Tonya kept one eye on oncoming traffic to watch for help. Maybe her aunt was fighting against this Waldock for the right reasons, but brainwashing her parents and keeping Tonya from her friends? She acted worse than her enemies. And an eco-tour? Her sporty father would be happy anywhere, but Tonya couldn't imagine her mother going on any trip without nice bathrooms and boutiques. No question about it, her aunt was evil.

They drove until Tonya's stomach growled out loud.

Her aunt gave her a funny look.

"What? I haven't eaten in hours."

"Are you sure that's all it is?"

"I can't promise I'm not infected. I was in the cemetery with the dead body of Professor Rudolph. I'm afraid I inhaled cursed spores."

"You have good instincts. Pull over here. Stop. Now!" She indicated a gravel lane so overhung with trees, Tonya would have driven past it. They turned off the highway and up the lane.

Her aunt ordered her to park beside a weathered Victorian farm house.

"I was hoping for a restaurant."

"First we visit a doctor."

They got out and Tonya looked around. The sagging porch and moss-covered shingles looked more like they should belong to a farmer than a doctor, and not a successful one.

Tonya stood waiting on a porch overrun by carpenter ants. "Can't we drive back to town?"

"Shhh. The walls have ears."

Once again, her aunt refused to discuss things. Working summers in the Herbal Healing Shop, her aunt had often demanded quiet, especially when her teenaged niece asked about magic. It was something she hid from her parents, but below the surface of things, Tonya felt energy moving through the shop. Before that summer she had been forbidden to study or even discuss magic. Her aunt embraced it but after today, Tonya wondered if using magic was what had made her aunt sick, and turned her nasty as well.

"Is this doctor of yours a friend?" Tonya wasn't sure her aunt's friends could be trusted.

A tiny lady opened the door. She was young, although it was hard to tell if she was closer to thirty or twenty. Her face hardly moved when she talked, even when she ordered them to "get in quick," and snicked the door shut behind them. Tonya wondered why this lady in her crumbling farmhouse was wearing a pink angora sweater and pearls. A pair of Italian leather pumps stood on the shoe rack, beside mud-caked rubber boots.

"You kept us waiting long enough," said Aunt Helen.

"The bad penny is back."

The women stared each other down, ignoring Tonya.

"Sorry about this." Aunt Helen shrugged. "What else could I do?"

"You'd better sit down." The lady brought them into the parlor and seated them on an antique sofa upholstered in hairy black hide. She left the room.

Tonya's stomach rumbled and ached. "Is she bringing us lunch?"

"How should I know?"

The lady returned with a towel over her arm and a bowl of something green and bubbly which she set on the coffee table. Definitely not appetizing, although if Tonya had to fast much longer, the grubby towel might start to look tasty.

Was she a witch too? Tonya expected the lady to chant over the basin or recite a spell, until she put her hands in and washed them. Her aunt and Tonya did the same.

"I'm Tonya."

The woman ignored Tonya's outstretched hand. Without taking her eyes off Aunt Helen she asked, "What do you want?"

Tonya burned to ask this doctor if she was infected like the others. Did *they* hear telepathic voices in their heads? Did *they* crave food all the time like her? Did *they* feel stressed out of their minds like her; or were they relaxed like Professor Rudolph, sleepwalking mindlessly into collapse? She hadn't enjoyed a peaceful moment for days. Well, unless you counted some of her moments with Drake.

"Let's go for a walk," announced Aunt Helen. "*This one* needs to eat something, and I can't stand the sight of food right now."

The image of Lynette's chocolate binge sprang into Tonya's head. *Lynette and the Professor were sleep-eating and sleepwalking. Was she? Would she know if she was? Did her aunt know about things Tonya was doing but couldn't remember?*

"You never call, you never write, and you only come see me when you want something." The lady attempted a kvetching voice, which didn't come off as funny.

Aunt Helen's expression was grim. "Is this a bad time?"

"I'll be right back." With a click of high heels on tile, the woman left. Tonya heard water running and her heart leapt. The lady was in the kitchen. Finally, some lunch!

When it was brought out on a tray, however, the bread had a sprinkling of white around the edges that looked like mold. She tilted her head to peek at the slices of cheese which seemed too blue. She lifted the lid. Inside the sandwich was part cheddar, part kid's science fair experiment. Who ever heard of blue cheddar? Rather than mention the burgeoning mold colony she just said "Thanks," as the women headed outside.

Tonya looked back at her revolting lunch. Even the glass of water looked cloudy. Was this fancy doctor trying to poison her? Forget that. They had a head start but from a side window she spied them going around the side of the barn. She zipped her coat up to go out, but there was one more thing to do first.

She found a phone in the kitchen and dialed zero. An automated response greeted her, but Tonya persevered, pressing buttons until a live voice answered.

"Operator."

"I'm lost at a farm house. Can you tell by my number where I am?"

It was an odd request and took some explaining but at last Tonya got the address, a rural route northeast of Loon Lake. Without letting the door slam behind her, Tonya slipped outside to find out what the women were doing. If her aunt had a dark secret, she didn't want to miss it.

She edged her way along the side of the barn until she came to a knot hole in the wood and peeked through. Hay blocked the view, so she crept a bit farther.

The cavalier way Aunt Helen had sent her parents away on holiday, if indeed that was what she had done, meant she was capable of anything. The only certainty was that her aunt was an active witch with powerful enemies. She had practically kidnapped Tonya and made her drive here against her will. Why?

Near the corner, a board had fallen away. Peeking through the gap she saw Aunt Helen arguing with the woman, who was red-faced and gesturing wildly. Her aunt lounged against a post, arms crossed in front of her chest. What Tonya wouldn't give to hear what they were saying, but no matter how loudly the woman appeared to be yelling, Tonya heard nothing.

Was this another magic spell or was the wind at Tonya's back carrying away the sound?

Without warning, Aunt Helen hefted a two-by-four and swung it at the young woman, knocking her to the ground.

She didn't move. Was she okay?

Tonya wanted to help but Aunt Helen was returning fast. Tonya dashed to reach the house before she was seen. Who knew what she would do to a witness?

Tonya skinned in with moments to spare and ran to the kitchen. She pulled a knife from the butcher's block, slid it into her purse, then ran back to the living room. She leaned on the sofa panting and watching the window for her aunt.

On the table, the sandwich sat untouched, staring up at her as if it had seen everything and was thinking of informing on her.

Her aunt breezed in and glanced at the sandwich.

"You didn't eat it, good. That means we can go."

Tonya didn't move.

"Now."

Tonya tried to think of some way to stall so she could figure out whether the woman was still alive.

"I have to make a call first." The moment Priya gave her Drake's number, Tonya had learned it by heart.

"Why didn't you call while I was outside?" Her Aunt glared.

"Can I have my phone back now?"

"Forget the phone. We're going back to civilization."

"Good. I'm worried about Priya."

"I mean Toronto."

Would driving Aunt Helen make her an accomplice? "I don't care where we go, as long as we stop for lunch soon." When they did, she planned to escape.

Her aunt made her drive for an hour before she finally relented and let her stop at a sandwich shop. At first, Tonya thought her aunt would stay in the car for fear of being recognized but then it dawned on her. On an isolated farm, the victim might not be discovered for days. Her aunt was safe as long as Tonya didn't blab.

She had to get a message to Drake.

It was oddly calm in the restaurant, where patrons smiled and chatted as they waited for counter staff to make their sandwiches. Tonya lined up with Aunt Helen until it was their turn to order.

"Choose something for me? I gotta go." She ran off to the washroom.

Once inside, she waved a twenty-dollar bill at a woman wearing blue eyeshadow. "Could I please borrow your phone? It's just one text, but it's gonna save my life."

"One moment." The lady was lathering her hands over and over. Next, she rinsed thoroughly and left the water running while she dried her hands and shut off the tap with the used paper towel.

"Please, it's urgent." Tonya looked over her shoulder, certain that Aunt Helen would come in any second.

The lady rummaged in her purse. "There we go. Nice and clean." She took the twenty and handed Tonya her phone.

Tonya ducked into a bathroom stall before the lady could protest. "This is top secret." She wasn't taking any chances her aunt would catch her texting.

Tonya sent Drake an SOS message with her last known address and the approximate location of the sandwich shop.

"Hey! The woman's voice rose. "You are *not* going to pee with my phone in your hand!"

"Don't get upset." Tonya finished quickly and passed it back under the stall door.

"You are *disgusting*!"

Tonya heard her stomp toward the door. "I'm sorry."

"Oh yes, and why is that?" It was her aunt's voice.

How long had she been in the bathroom? What had she seen?

"I'm having stomach problems."

"I got your lunch. We have to go."

"Coming." She flushed the toilet, twice for realism, and opened the door. Helen stood right outside the stall, arms crossed.

It was hard not to flinch. Tonya half expected her aunt to aim the next curse or two-by-four at *her* head.

Aunt Helen stepped aside to let Tonya wash her hands but hovered over her shoulder. "Quick like a bunny."

In the mirror, Tonya could see the snaky glitter in her aunt's eyes. She lathered and rinsed as slowly as she dared but who was she fooling? Tonya could pretend to be sick or she could try to refuse, but her aunt would still make her drive to Toronto.

BACCHIC LARD FEST

The Entity flexed its roots in delicious ecstasy, absorbing the fat of decomposing acolytes. At last it could see through their eyes—and what a glorious scene! There was an eating orgy in the graveyard. Teenagers scarfed down pizzas amid the tombstones while a group of ambulance drivers lay atop the autumn leaves, gorging themselves on tubs of lard. The pace of eating increased. Attendants threw away their spoons, cast off their shirts, and started licking lard off each other's hands, arms, and chests. It wouldn't be long now until they passed out in the leaves, sacrificing their adipose to the Entity.

Silent to the living ear, there rose a cacophony of subterranean thoughts, over which the Entity's voice rose exponentially. Soon when it spoke, none would disobey.

Excited at its rising powers, the Entity raised fruiting bodies into the air, allowing the crisp breeze to caress and tease them. When the fruiting bodies matured, they would scatter spores. In cemeteries downwind, new gravedigger fungi would blossom, seeking defunct flesh as in ancient times. Each new gravedigger a supernatural wonder, whispering telepathic warnings to the living.

It might reproduce in the usual way, but this was no ordinary gravedigger fungus. Dark forces had engineered it to do much more than spook the nervous. Brooding at its center lay something out of harmony with the power it had conglomerated. Pushing aside the playful thoughts of once-youths and once-adults, and overwhelming the intellect of the once-living Professor Rudolph, a new voice soared within.

Rising from his tomb, nestled inside the very tap root of the Entity, thrummed the First Voice. It was time for the originator of this supernatural entity to harness the growing collective consciousness into a more powerful incarnation. His years of waiting were almost over.

I am rising!

The voice resonated through the minds of the dead below and the still-living on the grass above. Fruiting bodies withered and withdrew underground, repelled by death magic. Even the ambulance attendants paused in their slippery frolic. All eyes turned inward. Every thought and desire snapped into sharp focus. The collective mind became one, and in that mind one thought resonated through the rooted ground, and the wind-whipped sky above:

I am Jack Waldock!

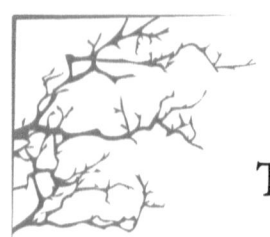

THEIR GOOSE IS COOKED

Zain drove Drake away from the police station in a rented Mazda Six. "I am *so* going to put all this into a movie." Zain pointed at the trees with one hand. "We should do a thriller, and a horror flick."

"Without a camera?"

"A minor setback. We could tell one scary-assed story with what's backed up in the cloud. Plus, Loon Lake is trending. People are posting clips of to-the-death food fights and graveyard eating binges everywhere!"

"What do we do for a star?" asked Drake.

"How about that crazy girl, wandering around in a yellow Hazmat suit, shouting into a megaphone?"

"Tonya?"

"I've seen how you two look at each other. Pucker those lips and she'd give you a close-up." Zain smirked.

"Tonya!" Drake rummaged through his bag of personal possessions and pulled out his phone. "She sent me a really long text message."

"Something scandalous?" Zain wiggled his eyebrows.

"Tonya's been taken by her aunt and forced to drive to Toronto."

"Lucky her," said Zain. "If they get around the quarantine they'll be safe."

"Tonya says Helen brainwashed her parents and sent them to Australia. She saw her aunt murder a woman with a plank. We have to find her!"

"We should tell the police like responsible citizens."

"After what I just lived through, I don't think the police will help."

"Phone the Army?"

"Stop being a chicken."

"All right, Duck. It's a wild goose chase but I'm game till the feathers hit the fan. Let's get the girls and fly the coop."

HARD TO STOMACH

Tonya didn't send Drake a message expecting rescue but who else could she trust? When she warned everyone to stay out of the cemetery Halloween night, only he had believed her. For all she knew, he was the one person on campus who wasn't infected. She didn't put it in the text, but if she disappeared, she was counting on Drake to be a witness who could tell her parents and the authorities about Aunt Helen.

Drake wouldn't give up. She knew he would search for her, but how could he find a moving target? Once they got in the car, Tonya would be miles from the sandwich shop. She had to escape her aunt, but the powerful witch would not be easy to cross. Would Aunt Helen see her hands trembling? Would she look into her mind and see her niece's intentions before she could act?

Tonya went to the driver's side of the car and pulled the knife out of her purse. She stooped, punctured the tire, and got in quickly, hoping her aunt didn't notice.

Aunt Helen got in beside her. "Drive."

They barely made it out of the parking lot.

Hours later, standing beside the desolate road shivering, Tonya wondered if it had been a mistake. The sandwich shop behind them was closed. While all traces of warmth leeched out of Tonya's toes and fingers, they stood staring at the crippled car. *If they stayed outside all night, would they get hypothermia?*

"Nonsense. You are perfectly dry and wearing a heavy coat," said Aunt Helen.

"You can read my thoughts?"

"Only when you move your lips."

Tonya looked at her aunt to see if she was joking. "What am I thinking now? Have I stopped moving my lips?"

"Barely, but it doesn't take a mind reader to know you slashed my tire."

"I don't want to go to Toronto."

Her aunt tsk-tsked. "You could have just said something."

"Would you have listened?"

It was late afternoon, but night was falling early. Long shadows obscured her aunt's features. "You're afraid of me."

"Should I be?" Tonya hoped her suspicions were wrong.

"You must have seen something at the farm."

"So, you admit it."

"What?"

"You killed that woman."

"Is that what you think?"

They stood facing the road, saying nothing. Not one vehicle passed.

Eventually, Tonya broke the silence. "I'm trying to understand why you need me in Toronto."

"For your own protection. On campus, you'll get infected."

"How do you know I'm not sick already?"

"You didn't eat the sandwich."

"Sure I did."

"The sandwich at the farm house."

"Why did you attack that woman?"

"I have enemies."

"You brought me into that lady's house and killed her while I was sitting in her living room!"

"Clearly not, if you were watching me."

"What if I *do* trust you had your reasons and agree to go with you?" Tonya watched her aunt's face, but there was no reaction. "Use your magic to fix the tire and we can leave. It's freezing out here."

"You're not hungry anymore?"

"We ate lunch at 4:30."

"I'll call the Auto Club."

"Tire rubber is natural. It's made from trees. Can't you cure it with a charm?"

Her aunt shook her head.

"I thought healing was your specialty."

"I'm too sick, thanks to my enemies."

Apparently, she couldn't influence people over the phone either. Tonya overhead her aunt reluctantly agree to an Auto Club membership before they would send a tow truck.

Tonya and her aunt sat inside the car with the seats tilted back. Tonya stared through the windshield at the sky. The cold clear day had transformed into a frigid, starry night. Tonya searched for something to say.

"I'm really sorry about this." She was still waiting for a response when, by the light of the rising moon, she noticed her aunt had fallen asleep.

To the south, the bright lights of a yellow sports car crested the road. The hard top was down, and she recognized a familiar bass line booming. She cracked open the car window, to be sure. It was Edgar Winter's *Frankenstein*, theme song of the Digital Ninjas.

Tonya smiled to herself. Drake had come for her.

The Mazda blurred by, screeched the brakes, then reversed back. Zain was in the driver's seat. He squeaked to a stop beside Tonya who rolled down her window.

Drake opened his door. "Get in!"

"I can't. My aunt's sick and alone out here." She got out of the car and Drake came to meet her.

"I thought you were afraid of her."

"It's cold and she's sick. What if she gets hypothermia?"

"I don't understand you."

"The tow truck should have arrived by now. I think the driver's lost."

Behind Drake, Zain revved the engine. "Hurry up. We've got zombies to flee and bagels to go!"

"Just give me a sec." Tonya touched her aunt's shoulder. "Wake up."

She was slow to rouse. "Tonya?"

"I'm leaving with Zain and Drake. Come with us."

"What?" Drake raised an eyebrow.

"I can't leave until the tow truck arrives," said Aunt Helen. "Why don't you kids wait with me? I love to meet my niece's friends."

Drake shot Tonya an incredulous look.

Tonya couldn't tell if Aunt Helen used her powers of persuasion, but Zain got out of the car and whispered something in Drake's ear.

Drake stood, visibly more relaxed. He poked his head in Tonya's window and spoke to Aunt Helen. "It's good to finally meet you. My condolences about your shop."

It was awkward. While Tonya and Aunt Helen sat in the front seat chatting, Drake sat in the back. He kept shooting Tonya glances in the rear-view mirror, as if to reassure himself she was okay. Eventually it got so blatant her aunt whispered, "I know that boy's sweet on you but are you sure he's right in the head?"

"At least he cares about me."

That earned her a grin from Drake, but Zain remained outside, preferring to speak to them through Tonya's window.

"Have you heard from Priya?" Tonya asked.

The guys described how their escape from the food riot had led to a high-speed chase with Officer Hungry which landed them in a pond.

"The inmates nibbled on him in jail," said Zain, "like getting a fish pedicure, but with less nail polish and more screaming."

"Are you hurt?" Tonya reached for Drake's arm.

"I'm fine."

"You must be traumatized."

"Not after watching three hundred zombie movies." Zain struck a heroic pose. "We're desensitized and ready for anything!"

Drake smiled grimly.

"It seems like everybody in uniform is against us," said Tonya.

"Which is why we should leave," said Aunt Helen.

"How do we know things won't be worse in Toronto?" Tonya laced and unlaced her fingers.

"Jack's getting close to critical mass."

"Jack?" Zain stroked his chin.

"Local history." Aunt Helen sighed.

"Tell us." Drake smoothed his hand over his bandaged wrist.

Aunt Helen looked away. "I can't."

"It's too late to keep secrets. Priya's already seen a demonstration of my powers and Drake believes."

"We want to help," said Drake.

"Do you know what happens to outsiders who know about magic?"

Drake nodded.

Helen sighed. "There used to be rules. In my day, you'd never see cursed Mundanes wandering the streets. Waldock's supporters will do anything."

"You're powerful enough to stop them," said Tonya.

"Don't flatter me."

"I've heard the stories. At seventeen, you could make your parents do anything."

"Hardly. I made them scrap curfew, write a few school notes."

"You made them buy you a prom dress they couldn't afford."

"Big mistake. We wound up living on baloney and beans for months while they paid in installments."

"Why didn't you use magic to earn the money?" asked Drake.

"The Trads were running Loon Lake then, too."

"Nobody can use magic for profit, or in front of Mundanes," said Tonya.

"I bet you learned your lesson," said Drake.

Tonya scoffed. "My first day of high school, the Phys. Ed. teacher tried to have me removed from her class. Said she'd never teach anyone from our family again."

"I may have influenced a few A's."

"You never went to class."

"My parents turned on me. They took me to see Bartholomew Waldock, then mayor, who insisted I be expelled."

"Waldock? Isn't that . . ."

"A month later, Waldock's son Jack came and paid me a visit. I was crazy bored from being kept home, and he was strong and handsome. Together, we discovered all sorts of interesting ways to spend my time."

"You dated Jack Waldock?" Tonya's jaw dropped.

"If I saw him tomorrow, I'd bury him."

Zain asked, "Why?"

"The first time didn't take, which is why I might need your help."

"I can't." said Tonya. This is a problem for City Hall, not us."

"The mayor is a hardcore Trad. He won't use magic to stop the Entity, which is Jack's way back from the dead."

Drake gasped.

Zain cocked his head. "How do you know he can come back?"

"He has help. Tonya, you've met his crony, Len? When they were young, Jack's powers grew with every corpse Len snatched for him, until they became too dangerous to criticize. Waldock specialized in mind control and Len used dark magic to conjure fire. I tried to help people fight back with fire charms but Waldock could get into people's heads and make them forget to use them. By the time I put him down, I had no choice. Loon Lake was living in fear."

"What does he want?" Tonya held up her hands.

"He wants to run Loon Lake like his father never did, and get back at me for killing him. How was I supposed to know he wouldn't stay dead?" She put her hand on Tonya's shoulder. "Or that he had already planted the seeds of revenge inside me."

The tow truck arrived, and Aunt Helen went to speak to the driver.

"We should run before it's a wizard war," said Zain. "I've seen *Harry Potter*. Waldock sounds worse than Lord Voldemort."

Tonya hesitated. Aunt Helen had never shared her past like this before. She was talking about burying a man like it was nothing.

Tonya went up to the tow truck where Aunt Helen was negotiating with the driver. She accosted her aunt and whispered, "Can you promise me no more violence?"

"There'll be plenty of violence but I'm not strong enough to hurt him anymore."

Drake approached. "You seem pretty strong to me," he said.

Aunt Helen turned to face them. "I really *have* been in and out of the hospital, and I must go back."

"What's wrong?" Tonya asked.

"There's a growth in my belly. I've had chemo and I need an operation that I've been putting off."

"Why would you put it off?" Tonya clasped her hands together.

"I wanted to stop him first, in case I didn't survive, but now my time's run out." The tow truck headlights deepened dark circles under her eyes. "I thought I could do it, but you'll have to fight in my place."

"What?"

"Fighting Len drained me more than I realized. I can feel the cancer taking hold."

"Heal yourself." Tonya shrugged.

"The stronger Waldock gets, the weaker I get. This thing he planted inside me all those years ago, links us. The stronger he gets the faster it grows."

Tonya stepped forward and gave her aunt a hug. "You have to get better."

"Save Loon Lake." She stepped away and regarded Tonya at arm's length. "Use your talents."

"I've never practiced. All I know how to do is drain energy."

"Perfect."

"But I can't control it."

"Only draw from living things."

"I can draw energy from a branch, but it kills it."

"Then you can kill a person."

"No!"

"Or you can control yourself and just take a little."

"What good is that?"

"It will come to you in a fight, trust me."

"And if I can't control it?" asked Tonya.

"Use the Ash. When you're close to it, you'll be stronger."

"You can't leave me alone to fight Waldock."

"The Trads are afraid to oppose him, and half the Mods are on his side. It's up to you."

"Stay and teach me what to do."

"He'll be weak at first. Act now, and you'll be ready enough."

"Your generation started this feud."

"Kill him while you still can," said Aunt Helen.

"I'm not murdering anybody."

"Sorry Tonya. If I put off treatment again . . ." She looked away. "You'll be on your own either way."

POUTINE NOT RIOTS

On the ride down to Loon Lake, Zain drove their Mazda past clusters of the shambling infected. It was all the more terrible when they had to slow down because foot-draggers crowded into the road. From the back seat, behind Drake, Tonya looked into their eyes.

Hungry! Feed me! Tonya caught snatches of their ravenous thoughts. Those who had already eaten themselves into a stupor were dreamy and full of yearning. *Must lie down in graveyard to decompose.*

"Can you hear that?"

"What?" Zain drove carefully past yet another clutch of wanderers.

"What's wrong?" asked Drake.

"It's nothing. I'm just tired." She hated lying but was afraid to admit she could hear their thoughts. It was like when she heard Professor Rudolph's voice in her head but ten times worse. There were so many of them.

As they neared Loon Lake, another voice resonated in her head.

Feel me rise!

The voice was accompanied by a strange sensation. She could feel herself tunneling up through gravel and clay. Tonya gasped. She was linked to the Entity! She could feel what It felt and hear Its voice cutting through the cacophony in her head. She covered her ears and closed her eyes, desperate to keep It out.

"Stop!"

A kaleidoscopic jumble of images overlaid her vision. It was the view from a hundred sets of eyes, compressed. Among the multiplicity of images, she saw headstones, hospital rooms, moonlit trees, and food. Loaded spoons and forks and fingers simultaneously stuffed a hundred frantic mouths as if they all belonged to her.

"Are you okay?" She could hear Drake's voice but couldn't see the inside of the car anymore.

To banish this nauseating sensation, she blinked hard and tried to look out the window. She felt her body seated in a moving car, but the shadowy view of passing trees faded into a more vibrant image. Her sight was overwhelmed by the compound vision of the Entity. Multiple images moved in conflicting directions, like the view from 100 computer screens packed together. Why?

And then it came to her. She was seeing through the eyes of the shambling victims that filled the town. They must all be linked by the Entity and, somehow, she was linked to them too. They saw collectively, like an insect's compound eye.

As if her belly contained a hundred aching stomachs, she felt the hunger of multitudes. Her mouth filled with conflicting flavors: liver and ice cream, cold French fries and hot Brussels sprouts, cupcakes and curry. She swallowed, hoping to clear her mouth but the sensations increased. Somewhere in Loon Lake, someone took a deep whiff of Limburger cheese. Ugh! Tonya's mouth filled with bile. She opened her window and heaved, scattering sour fluid into the rushing air.

"Hey, watch the car!" Zain shouted. "It's a rental."

"Sorry. It's the kaleidoscope vision."

"What?"

"Nothing. I'm better now." She couldn't admit what was happening in her head. Her friends would think the Entity controlled her and ditch her at the side of the road. Maybe they should.

She sat back in her seat. "Sorry to put you boys through this."

"It's okay." Drake leaned forward between the seats. "If people had listened to you, none of this would be happening."

"It's not all bad," said Zain, "This morning students were rioting in the cafeteria."

"That's good?"

"He recorded everything."

"I wish I could have recorded your adventures at the police station."

"Seeing you is the most fun I've had all day," said Drake.

"Plus rescuing you from your aunt was probably the least risky thing we've done in hours," said Zain.

"So be straight with me Tonya." Drake put a hand on her shoulder. "What's really wrong with you?"

"Did my aunt seem weird to you?"

"Yeah," said Drake. "She makes the hair stand on the back of my neck."

"Me too!" said Zain.

"She has that effect on a lot of people," said Tonya. "So, where are we going?"

Wherever I like.

Just as she had heard the farmer's voice, the voice in her head was Zain's. He was controlled by the Entity!

Tonya leaned forward between the door and Drake's seat and whispered in his ear, "We're in trouble."

"Why?"

"Zain's infected," she whispered.

"Then why isn't he a foot dragger?"

"He's controlled by the Entity. When I say go . . ."

"Now, kids, it's not polite to whisper." Zain's voice was cold.

"Jump!" Tonya yelled. She grabbed the lock button before Zain could engage it. The car sped up as she leaped into the ditch.

Tonya tucked and rolled over the pebbly shoulder and into the long grass. She came to a hard stop against a bush, gaining new bruises on top of the old. For a moment, she lay still, her brain confused by the tumble. With trembling fingers, she felt her skull, testing for soft spots, or blood, but her head was intact. It only felt like it had been split open.

Then she remembered Drake. Had he followed her, or did Zain have him?

"Drake?"

There were streetlights along the highway this close to campus, but the ditch was crammed with shadowy weeds. She couldn't see him anywhere. "Drake!"

She stood on the frosty grass trying to isolate Waldock's sinister voice in her head. The Entity looked through hundreds of eyes. If it could see Drake now, would It be gloating because It had him, or would there be regret because he got away? The cacophony faded to a murmur, as if It knew she was trying to listen in. At least she could think and see clearly again.

Where was Drake? She worried he hadn't made the jump.

"Hey!" Drake limped up to her, grimacing with every step. "You're wrong about Zain. He's my best friend. I'd know if he was turning zombie."

"Then why did you jump?"

"Couldn't leave you alone out here."

"Are you hurt?"

He shot her a crooked smile. "I'm fine."

"Except you're with me. Zain's the frying pan but I'm the fire."

"Huh?"

"Could you tell if I was under the Entity's control?"

"How do you know I'm not slavishly following the Master myself?"

"Master?" Tonya smiled with relief. "For starters, he's not called the Master."

"How would you know?"

Tonya hesitated. She wanted to trust Drake. "I hear the Entity's voice in my head."

"Entity? Is that the plant thing your aunt was talking about?"

"Fat-absorbing telepathic fungus. Nobody's safe. Anybody could fall under its control, even me. Get out of town. Steal a car, anything! And don't talk to anyone until you're gone. Zain is infected, Lynette and Roberto, the diving team, students, professors."

"I'm not leaving you here by yourself."

"Waldock hates my family. Anyone with me is a target."

"You expect me to save myself and let some mushroom thing get you?"

"I'll be fine. What about Priya? She has a car and she needs your protection more than I do."

"I'm calling."

"Good." Tonya had no intention of staying with her friends, but Priya and Drake could save each other. Tonya had a plan, a terrible plan.

Drake's phone buzzed. "Hello, Priya?"

"What's she doing?" asked Tonya.

"Says she's looking for a way around the roadblocks, or a place to pull over for the night."

After Drake explained where they were, Tonya asked for the phone.

"Do you have money?" she asked.

"It's the freakin' apocalypse out there. You bet I went to the bank machine."

"Good. Fill a bunch of gasoline cans, as many as you can fit in the trunk."

"Why?"

"I can't talk about it over the phone."

"Do we need water and food? Is this a road trip?"

"I'll text you a list but get the gas, fast, and don't talk about it. Anybody might be a spy."

"What?" asked Priya.

Drake grabbed the phone. "She sounds crazy but she's not. I'll text you the coordinates."

They hid in the bushes to wait. Tonya figured her plan to save the town could work as long as nobody saw them, *and* Priya brought enough gas, *and* the Entity couldn't read her mind, *and* she could convince Drake and Priya to leave her alone near the cemetery.

Tonya took a deep breath and tried to think of something calm, like sunrise over Loon Lake. She inhaled through her nose and exhaled slowly, picturing the mist rising over still water.

When she was a kid, she once spotted a loon, so large that perspective made it seem closer. Around it dove tiny chicks who traveled under water, instead of dunking and bobbing like ducklings. She was fascinated by the babies' jittery movements until they disappeared. The mother was still there, but the water around her was suddenly empty.

Tonya ran to get binoculars to see what had happened. Had they been swallowed by a muskellunge? Muskies were known to eat chicks. Tonya held her breath until she could bring the mother into focus with the binoculars and she understood. The babies had climbed onto their mother's back. Tonya had seen loons many times since, but no mothers ferrying their chicks. How privileged she felt to have witnessed it.

Tonya closed her eyes. All was quiet in her head again. Her heart had stopped pounding and her mouth tasted clean. She loved Loon Lake with its jumping fish and hardscrabble seagulls. The beauty of moonlight rising over black water at night, and the way sunset turned the trees on the island gold. The flat-out perfection of nature here made her feel even guiltier about what she had to do.

Her guilt trip was interrupted by the rumble of a familiar clunker. Priya! She stepped onto the side of the road, blinded by oncoming headlights.

"Wait," said Drake. "What if it's Zain?"

"I'd know that knock, ping, and rumble anywhere."

Priya pulled up and leaned over the passenger seat to crank open the window.

"Get a muffler!" Tonya got in beside her.

"Get ear plugs!" Priya smirked. "What have you two been up to in the bushes?"

"Nothing you can't play in prime time." Drake got in the backseat.

"Too bad. Next time, I'll drive slower."

"Did you get everything I needed?" Tonya asked.

"Right down to the wheelbarrow. Now tell me what this is about."

"You don't want to know. Drop me near the shop then get yourself and Drake out of here."

"We're coming with you," they chorused.

Tonya decided to argue after they got to the shop.

When they arrived, Drake helped her unload the wheelbarrow and pile it up with water containers and gas cans.

"This plan of yours doesn't involve torching the store again, does it?" Priya's eyes narrowed.

"Of course not, but it does involve you guys leaving."

"No way," said Priya.

"Thanks. Really, I'm all set. You two should drive as far from Loon Lake as you can."

"Not without you," said Drake.

"Montreal is nice," said Tonya. "Lots of culture and nightlife, and you can eat poutine without food riots."

"You, me, nightlife? I thought you'd never ask." Drake stepped closer. "I get why you're trying to spare Priya but we're in this together. I'm not leaving you in danger."

"There's nothing you can do."

"Just because I'm a Muggle or whatever? I'm not walking away."

"You can and should."

"Once I know about magic they can hurt me, isn't that what you said?"

"I think the mayor has more to worry about right now than one Mundane."

"What are you two conspiring about?" Priya came over.

"Promise me you and Drake will get out of Loon Lake." Tonya willed Priya's obedience, but she lacked her aunt's talent to enthrall.

BARBEQUE FLUID

"**C**ome into the shop with me. You can help me look for fire charms." Tonya had grown up hearing stories of her aunt's charms protecting houses from chimney fires and lightning. She had tried to convince her aunt to place an anti-fire charm on the whole county, but Helen refused to give up barbeque.

If her aunt weren't such a sparerib fan, Tonya grumbled to herself, they wouldn't be searching for charms in a scorched cupboard full of broken jars. It was such a jumble after the fire, she might as well search with a shovel and a sieve. She checked all the logical places, and then the less logical, until she gave up on the ground floor.

Upstairs was intact but barren. In her aunt's bedroom drawers, she found only herbs, lotions, and drawstring bags. The little sachets conjured up happy summer memories of when they minded the store together. That's when her aunt should have trained her to use magic. Then Tonya would be able to fight Waldock like a witch, instead of depending on her wits and gasoline. She raised her fist and addressed the charred ceiling.

"Hello, Old Families! Time to step in! Where are you when we need you?"

Of course, they didn't hear. She picked up the phone and dialed City Hall, but the phone rang and rang.

"C'mon Old Families. Pick up. I don't have a hero complex. We can share the glory." She hung up with a sigh.

"You have us," said Drake.

Don't remind me, thought Tonya. Once outsiders like Drake and Priya knew about magic, soon everyone would. She could imagine the Mods, rubbing their hands in glee as the epidemic exposed the existence of magic to the world. Once everyone knew about Loon Lake magic, the Mods would have won. Tonya sighed. Revelation Day was her Mom's great fear. Mundanes would pour into Loon Lake looking for miracles. Mom had warned her sister, "They'll have us casting spells at gunpoint."

Tonya signaled the others to follow her into her aunt's bedroom. "Can you guys help me search the attic?"

She climbed a step ladder and lowered a trap door. "Go on up. You're looking for little sachets of herbs."

The moment Drake and Priya stepped into the attic, she shut the door behind them and bolted it in place.

"Hey, let us out!" yelled Priya.

Tonya removed the ladder. "I'll come back for you later."

The ceiling muffled Drake's voice. "Let me help you!"

"Sorry. I have to do this alone."

Remembering the hand in a jar, she went to the kitchen to look in the fridge. Tonya's plan required strong protective charms.

As she cracked open the Frigidaire, the reek of rotten food hit her. She stepped back, nostrils prickling as her eyes adjusted. Through the glass shelves, she could see foul liquid in the bottom of the vegetable drawers. She closed the fridge and checked the cupboards.

Nothing.

She gave up on finding fire charms but decided to stick to the plan anyway. Tonya groped around under the sink, grabbed the kitchen fire extinguisher, and ran. When she added it to the gas cans, the wheelbarrow got so heavy she could barely lift it.

Bending from the knees, she took a deep breath and lifted the handles. She started across the field but every time she hit a bump, gas cans threatened to bounce out. Tonya took off her coat and bundled the cans inside it to keep them together, then headed north to the western gate, staying on the edge of the road.

Through the gates she didn't see one jogger or cyclist. The only signs of life were cawing crows until she reached the old section. Approaching the Three-Century Ash, Tonya spied a snoring pileup of shirtless men and women, apparently comfortable on the leaf-strewn ground. In contrast, Tonya's teeth were chattering. Nearer the Ash, teens lay scattered like cast off laundry.

A mound of disturbed earth ringed the tree. Tonya considered how to scatter the gravedigger fungus's sprawling would-be victims. They were sleeping peacefully, hands resting on distended bellies. Did that mean they would have to eat more before the Entity would absorb them? She kicked one snoring student with her foot.

"Hey!" He got up and started coming after her, slowly.

"Sorry." Tonya held up her hands.

Before he could reach her, he dropped back to his knees and started scooping leaves into his mouth.

Tonya put a hand on his shoulder. "Wake up. Go home."

The man shrugged her off then lay face down in the leaves. He was asleep before she could explain the danger.

At least he'd woken up able to move. When things started to heat up, these passed-out victims would be able to get up and flee to safety.

To be sure, she would make sure everything was ready to light before she woke them and sent them running, in case the Entity took control of them and made them try to stop her. Could It do that? Or could It make them grab her and bite her like the prisoners who attacked Drake? She would have to take that chance. Tonya unloaded the wheelbarrow and cleared away leaves with her foot, looking for the right spot to pour gasoline . . .

Was that white thing a bird's egg? She put her face closer. A big opal caught the light, attached to a not-quite buried . . . finger. Ugh!

The finger seemed familiar. Where else had she seen metallic purple nail polish?

Lynnette! Tonya cleared loose soil away with her hands. Poor Lynette. Tears welled in Tonya's eyes.

She was panting with effort by the time she unearthed the head. She touched the cheek which felt warm. Lynette was alive! Tonya dug like a dog after a rabbit. She uncovered the torso and put her head to Lynette's chest. Her heart was beating! Tonya tried to pull her roommate out of the hole, but white roots grew around Lynette's arms and legs, as well as into her mouth and ears. On closer examination, not all the roots were white. Some were pink, like veins draining fluid from her body.

Tonya gagged. She fought down the urge to vomit, but this was Lynette, not some faceless monster. She had to free her, but how, without a saw to cut the roots? Tonya rummaged through her bag until she found a metal nail file. It was dull and small, but she put all her weight behind it and pulled, breaking through roots one by one. Lynette didn't move or make a sound during this painstaking process. Was she unconscious or in a coma? Either way, when Tonya snapped the last root, the body was limp.

Your efforts are touching, but in vain. Give up.

"No!"

How fast do you think you can carry her?

His consciousness felt so close. In moments, He would be free.

Tonya dug the body out of the earth, then slid her hands under Lynette's armpits and dragged her onto the wheelbarrow. At least Lynette was light. Tonya rolled her up the path as far as she dared then ran back to the Ash. She wished she could move Lynette to a safer place but there was no time. All around her, frosty-eyed denizens of Loon Lake were stirring and getting off the ground, their unfocused eyes directed at her.

Without a charm to help, Tonya would have to control the fire with the extinguisher, no matter what Waldock's frosty-eyed minions did to her. The Entity had almost surfaced and Waldock was growing in power every moment. She could feel it in the growing strength of his voice in her head. Tonya had no choice but to attack now, then retreat with Lynette in the wheelbarrow as best she could. Losing control of the fire would be a disaster, but if she didn't act, they were dead anyway.

First, Tonya soaked a wide ring of grass around the tree with water, to form a protective barrier. Next, she soaked the ring of earth beneath the tree with gasoline. She chose a stout stick from the ground and wet the end with gas, then hurried up the path as far toward the gate as she dared. She lit the end then turned and took aim, but the sight of the majestic Ash brought her up short. How could she do this? To burn down that tree, to even harm it, was a crime.

The gas on the stick flared. The ember glowed and then dimmed, but that wasn't her biggest problem. The shamblers were closing in. Once Waldock guessed her plan, he would send the horde to rip her apart. There was no time to lose, yet still she couldn't do it.

The Ash Tree had protected her ancestors for centuries against the death magic which collected in this cemetery. To burn it down would be a sacrilege the Old Families could never forgive. She hoped destroying the gravedigger fungus would stop the Entity before it could rise. She hoped doing so would not harm the tree, which sheltered the fungus among its roots. If she killed the fungus and it didn't stop the Entity from rising, burning down the tree would leave them even more vulnerable to Waldock's death magic. It was a bitter dilemma, but somebody had to stop the Entity before it could bring Waldock back.

Hard as she could, she threw the stick. Flames leaped as gasoline ignited with a *whoof*!

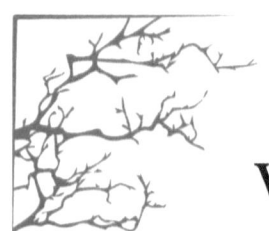

VOLCANO CAKE

Tonya had soaked the earth in a broad ring around the Ash Tree, so she could safely burn the gravedigger fungus without setting the cemetery alight. Cold wet fall weather would help stop the flames from spreading across the grass. That was her theory, anyway.

It seemed to hold until sparks started leaping over the ring of wet grass onto the litter of fallen leaves beyond. Tonya stomped out little fires as they multiplied, quickly switching from her feet to the extinguisher. Flames flared in a widening circle so fast she couldn't get to them all. Leaves caught fire and rose into the air, igniting bushes in fountains of red and gold.

The passed-out infected, awoken by primordial fear, fled the woods in all directions. Tonya stayed to fight the fire, sweating rivulets as flames grew. She would die if she failed to contain the blaze, and so might Priya and Drake, locked up in the nearby shop. She sprayed and sprayed until the extinguisher fizzled out.

"No!"

Trees crackled like overhead campfires and squirrels of flame leaped from branch to branch. Tonya squinted through smoke. The fire roared unstoppable, howling like a beast as it devoured more and more fuel. Her face was burning, and smoke stung her eyes. She had no choice. Tonya ran for the wheelbarrow.

As she ran for the gate she shouted, "Wake up! Lynette, you have to run."

Lynette didn't stir so she lifted the heavy wheelbarrow and retreated.

The fire was all around. Her shoes were smoking. Each wheezing breath ended in a cough. Tonya considered the awkward cargo she was pushing. Was Lynette even alive? The harder it became to push her, the more tempting it was to assume she was dead. Without Lynette, Tonya could run fast enough to save herself.

The shop felt farther away with every step as flames licked at her face. She would never make it to the Western Gate. She turned the wheelbarrow and headed through the long grass, toward the break in the cemetery fence.

It was uneven ground and the weeds were denser than she thought. The wheelbarrow's tire stuck in a clump of cedars. Frantically, she tried to pull it back or wriggle it out, but it wouldn't budge.

"Wake up!" Tonya shook her gently, but Lynette remained limp. There was no way but to abandon the wheelbarrow and carry Lynnette on her back. She crouched and pulled her friend's arms over her shoulders, gripping the wrists across her chest. Tonya stood. She saw stars. On the verge of blacking out, she bent lower and breathed through her nose until the light-headedness passed. As soon as she could see again, Tonya strode around the cedars dragging Lynette like a hundred-pound backpack, her dangling legs snagging on the undergrowth.

Now Lynette *really* owed her a favor. If they ever got out of this, Lynette would have to make her visiting friends acknowledge her. Heck, she should probably insist they swap beds too. Tonya had always wanted the one under the window!

Tonya scoffed at her crazy, oxygen-deprived thoughts. She moved between trees and tombstones until the billowing smoke choked her. She was doomed, fighting her way out of temperatures that belonged in a kiln, or Pompeii . . .

Panicked citizens in togas and sandals stampeded through her mind.

Where did that come from?

They were being buried alive in volcanic ash. She felt their terror as they asphyxiated or roasted alive.

What was happening to her? Tonya had never been to Italy. She had never even seen a movie about Pompeii. She only knew of its famous volcano. Why was she seeing the cranial sutures on a dead baby's skull? Why was that man in a toga staring at her as he lay down to die?

A wave of darkness clamped her chest. Her body kept struggling through the woods to escape the fire, but her mind faced a larger danger. Even if she reached the gap in the cemetery fence and climbed through, all was hopeless. There was no escaping the force suffocating her mind. Tears caused by smoke and frustration streamed down her face. Tonya blinked and closed her eyes to clear her vision but when she opened them, she saw neither smoke nor forest nor fire. Kaleidoscope vision forced itself upon her again. This was the view Waldock saw, through the eyes of all his victims. He was forcing it upon her, superimposing supernatural vision over natural.

Functionally blind, she dropped to her knees and groped her way to the road. Lynette's body was too heavy. She could try to save them both and potentially die in the fire, or crawl out fast and save herself. She still had time if she was quick. She could preserve her worthless, infected life, but for what? The Entity had won.

Tonya clenched her fists until her nails drew blood. She had tried so much and fought so hard, meanwhile Aunt Helen abandoned them. *Her* generation started this war. What right did they have to impose their vendetta on mundane citizens and innocent college kids? What right did they have to kill Lynette in their crossfire?

She forced herself back to her feet and pushed through flaming branches. She might be lost. She might be bombarded with hallucinations, but Tonya refused to let Waldock beat her. Lifting Lynette and draping her onto her shoulders like a cape, Tonya used one hand to anchor Lynette's arms in front of her while she used the other to feel her way through the trees.

She was moving blind when the crunch of gravel underfoot signaled she had reached the edge of the cemetery. She opened her eyes not far from the break in the fence.

"Tonya!" Priya and Drake's voices chorused from the other side of the fence.

She could see again! Tonya rushed to the opening. "How did you get out?"

"No thanks to you. We knocked a hole through the roof," said Priya.

With Tonya's help, Drake lifted Lynette into his sinewy arms. "What happened to her?"

Tonya gasped to get her breath back. "Call the Fire Department."

"Already did." Priya looked into the sky where smoke and flames rose high into the air. She pointed at Tonya. "You trapped us in the attic, then lit the cemetery on fire. Are you trying to kill us?"

THE SCENE OF HER CRIME

Tonya pressed her palms together. "You were supposed to leave when I asked you."

"Is Lynette okay?" Priya's voice trembled.

"She's breathing but I can't wake her." Tonya tried to cross the road but stumbled on a rock.

"Can't you see the ground where you're walking?" asked Drake.

She felt him pass a hand in front of her face. Tonya could make out his tall form amidst a blur of colored light. She still had kaleidoscope vision intermittently, although now her eyes were starting to come clear. It was as if the presence of her friends could draw her back to reality.

"I'm fine. Lynette needs a doctor." Tonya felt her knees buckle, her adrenaline spent.

"So do you." Priya pulled Tonya's arm around her shoulder. "I can't believe you set a forest fire."

"The car's this way." Drake took the lead with Lynette in his arms. Tonya crossed the field, supported by Priya. Tonya heard Lynette cough. As she let Priya direct her steps, Tonya's black thoughts returned. Her mind swam with visions—hundreds of Pompeii's dead. She saw stacks of ancient bodies, now with familiar faces: her parents, Aunt Helen, girls from the dorm, boys from her classes, plus Zain, Drake, and the other Ninjas. It felt like a premonition. Would Waldock kill everyone she cared for?

Tonya forced one foot in front of the other, supported by Priya.

Sirens approached but the fire truck was obscured by smoke billowing out of the cemetery behind her. She fervently wished they would save the Ash Tree but not the Entity buried under it. Faint hope. The volunteer firefighters would be lucky to save the Village as fire spread through the grass around the cemetery.

She suppressed a giggle rising inside her, the terrible guffaw of one who found everything incredibly funny. *Who did these little people think they were? Who were they to thwart His victory? They were mice. Less than mice. They were insects, and He was chief exterminator!*

Despite her blistered face, Tonya chuckled, then burst into a coughing fit of laughter.

Drake stopped walking. "Laugh, it beats crying. Not many women could have carried Lynette to safety like that." He smiled at her.

Tonya returned his gaze, wishing she deserved his admiration. *How to explain she heard Waldock in her head? That she felt their minds melding?* "You should get away from me fast as you can."

"Not a chance." He smiled. "We're almost there."

With a tire screech, an ambulance pulled up and a pair of attendants came out. The first attendant held up a loaded needle. "She looks like she needs attention."

Drake and Priya carried Lynette forward. The male attendant shot a crooked smile at a woman who looked like his sister.

They were the same attendants that Marta sent away, Tonya realized. "Don't get in the ambulance."

"Why?" asked Priya.

A third uniformed attendant came out of the woods and went for Tonya. "You seem delirious. Let me give you some oxygen." It was the farmer, wearing a first responder's uniform.

She dodged away.

"Waldock has allies in the hospital," she called to Priya and Drake. "Run for the bridge!"

Tonya ran up the road, but police stood on the bridge, milling in front of a squad car blocking the way. She slowed down when she noticed how their sunglasses glinted in the sun. No more kaleidoscope vision. Why would Waldock allow her to see clearly now?

Oh no. She could see because he was using her eyes to see. Waldock was focused on looking through *her* now, right at her friends.

"You have to get away," said Tonya. "Get away from me."

The three attendants caught up. Two knocked Drake down and the third scooped up Lynette. Priya ran after them, shrieking and yelling.

Noticing the commotion, a police officer came over, but instead of rescuing them, he handed the farmer a firefighter's axe.

"Come with us," ordered the farmer.

They could no longer refuse. As the farmer led them away, Drake gave Tonya a sideways look. "What do they want us for?"

"Arson." The farmer brandished his axe. "Keep walking."

"Waldock can kill me discreetly in the fire," said Tonya. "When they dig me out of the ashes, Waldock can call me a criminal."

"Why did you set the trees on fire?" Drake asked.

"To stop the Entity from rising. I had to burn Him while he was still underground, but I failed. The Entity will rise and Waldock with It."

"So? We can take him." Drake pretended to throw a punch.

"I'm so sorry to get you mixed in this."

At the Western Gate she told the farmer, "You aren't going to be able to breathe in there. I barely got out alive."

"The firefighters are putting it out," he said.

Tonya watched jets of water spray into the inferno but if it was making a difference she couldn't see it. The water turned into steam on contact. All the trees and grass were aflame. If they couldn't extinguish it before the wind changed, it could spread northeast across campus or west into Loon Lake Village.

"Shouldn't you be rescuing people?" Tonya stopped and faced the farmer, hands on hips. The skin on the palms of her hands smarted with blisters.

"Time to pay for your crimes."

Tonya's will to fight drained away. What had she done? She thought the fire would burn the Entity in the ground and prevent him from taking physical form. Instead, *she* destroyed the Ash. Who knew what terrible energies would fester in the cemetery without the Ash to draw them out?

"Len was right about you." The farmer glowered, stained teeth against a berry brown face. "Your death in the fire today will be justice."

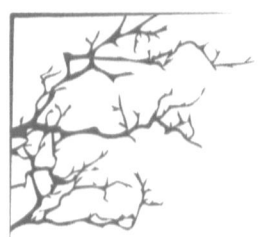

COOKING PIT

The farmer forced Tonya and her friends to trudge through gray ash speckled with embers. Making their way over and around fallen trees smudged their faces and blackened Tonya's tender hands.

They marched to the cinder-covered mound where the Ash Tree once stood for three hundred years. Green shoots poked up through the still-glowing leaf litter, burning on the surface. Underneath, the grass grew unharmed, right where she had poured the most gasoline. Someone had cast a powerful ward here.

From deeper in the blackened cemetery, a pair of firefighters arrived with shovels.

"Start digging," the farmer told Tonya.

"Digging?"

"Or else I start chopping." He swung his axe toward Lynette's limp body which was slung over an ambulance attendant's shoulder.

Tonya exchanged glances with Drake as they started digging a pit. Everything was her fault. She should have guessed her friends would break out of the shop and come for her. She decided to obey her captors, at least until she could find an escape.

Using her weight to stand on the shovel, Tonya wasn't moving much dirt, and featherweight Priya practically bounced off the hard clay. After fifteen minutes of minimal progress, the farmer kicked Priya with his boot. "Dig faster. Next time I hit you, it'll be with the axe."

It took time, but they chipped through surface clay to the softer dirt below. It hurt Tonya to watch Priya scan the blackened trees, fruitlessly searching for a sign of rescue.

"It's not your fault," said Drake.

"It is." His kindness stung.

236

"Hey, lovebirds. Back to work!" The farmer held his axe over Lynette who lay limp on the ground.

"How do we know she isn't dead?" Priya stood tall, hands on hips.

"I can cut her, to see if she still bleeds." The farmer flashed his teeth. "She's not helping dig anyway."

"When they find us buried in a pit," said Tonya, "the police will know we didn't die accidentally."

"Back to work or I whack Blondie."

The pit grew slowly. Tonya guessed it took about half an hour to dig down to knee depth. How much deeper would they have to go?

"Enough digging. Everybody into the pool!" He laughed.

He picked up Lynette and threw her into the hole like a sack of cement.

"In you go. Chop, chop!" He waved his axe at Priya who jumped away from the hole and ran for it. One of the attendants caught her and carried her back, kicking and screaming. Meanwhile, Drake stepped into the pit. He picked up Lynette's unconscious body and stood facing the farmer.

Tonya took her shovel and ran at the farmer, aiming a blow at the side of his head. In midflight, he caught it by the shaft and wrenched it out of Tonya's hands.

"Do you see what I have to put up with?" the farmer addressed the sky. "A little help please."

Tonya's stomach dropped. Interior commotion drowned out her thoughts. Here was fear, grief, lust. Images of Pompeii welled up inside her, this time revealing their source in Professor Rudolph's memories. Were the thoughts of these firefighters and ambulance attendants crowding into her head too? Maybe. All were controlled by the Entity, or was that Waldock?

Confusion overwhelmed her. She lost her balance on the lip of the pit and the farmer pushed her in.

Waldock was winning, again. His onslaught confused her mind and kaleidoscope vision blinded her. Outnumbered, blind, and soon to be buried alive, she still refused to give in.

Tonya reached out with her thoughts, frantically searching for a way to escape, or expel the Entity. Energy thrummed through the earth. The Three-Century Ash had not been the source of power, but its conduit. Hurting from her burns and full of need, she drew strength through the untouched roots of the Ash and other trees. Along woody pathways, twisting and turning under the forest floor, reaching ever outward, she gathered strength from the ancient forces in the ground. Hundreds of her ancestors had fed this earth, as if waiting for the day she would claim her heritage. Already she felt better for tapping into their energies. Better, but also guilty. Mixed in with the life magic of plants, the soil harbored death magic. Forbidden magic had turned her aunt's hair white and driven a wedge between her and Mom. Would her parents reject Tonya too?

She stopped, switching to drawing life magic from the rare plants remaining in the area. It was weaker, but it would have to suffice.

With power trickling in, Tonya took a deep breath and focused her thoughts. Priya, Tonya, and Lynette lay in the pit as the farmer and ambulance attendants forced Drake to shovel dirt over them. Tonya rolled closer to Lynette. As long as she was unconscious, they couldn't fight or run. She took Lynette's hands into hers. Using all her concentration, she channeled the life magic she had gathered into Lynette.

With a start, Lynette opened her eyes and sat up. "What time?"

"Shhh. Lie back down and pretend you're still asleep. These guys are trying to bury us. If we attack, do you think you can run?"

"I feel great." She smiled.

"Don't move till I say, then run with us."

Tonya whispered to Priya. "Lynette's ready to run. Time to fight."

"Or run." Priya cut her eyes over to the side of the pit where enough dirt had caved in to make it shallow.

Tonya whispered, "Go!"

They ran for the shallow end and leaped out of the pit.

The farmer and his minions came after them, the farmer brandishing an axe and a shovel. Tonya and the others scattered so each hid behind a different tree, Drake with a shovel.

The farmer advanced carefully, axe in hand. "Come here Blondie. You can't have run very far."

To Tonya's right, Lynette trembled behind a burnt tree. The farmer was coming straight for her. Tonya readied herself.

As the farmer closed in, Tonya stepped out and grabbed his axe. The farmer shrugged her off and kept going after Lynette.

Drake stepped from behind another tree and clocked him from behind. "Here!" He tossed the fallen farmer's shovel to Priya who caught it, then guided Lynette toward the road.

Only one firefighter still had a shovel. Another stooped down to a gravestone which had been split by the heat of the fire. He picked up a baseball-sized hunk of granite and pitched it at Tonya's head. The others joined in, pelting them with stones, while the farmer came after them with his axe.

"Run!" said Tonya.

They raced away, zigzagging to avoid chunks of flying granite.

She might have gotten away, if it weren't for sudden fatigue. Despite the adrenaline and the shovel-wielding firefighter, her legs simply wouldn't move. She leaned against a tree hyperventilating, as if she had run for hours.

"Ow!" Smoke rose from the pocket of her jeans where the leaf pendant was heating up. She pulled it out, scorching her blistered hand, so she flung it in her coat pocket. What was going on?

Tonya watched her friends rain down shovel blows on the ambulance attendants. She yearned to help them, but when she took a step, her leg turned to rubber.

"No!" Full of energy only minutes before, she felt her eyes closing as she fell sideways.

TONYA AWOKE. HAD MINUTES passed or hours? The woods around her were quiet, except for the crackling of fire in the distance. Passed-out firefighters littered the ground, but she couldn't hear voices. Had her friends left her for dead?

Feel me rise!

The exclamation thundered in her head.

She gagged as if something coiled deep inside her were expanding up and out of her throat. Her breath came fast and shallow and she swallowed acid reflux. The Entity was here.

A crack split the Earth beside Tonya, tumbling dirt and trees deep into the ground. She backed away as the widening crack tilted charred trees and tombstones left and right, like a comb parting hair. The rift shook the cemetery as the fire went out with a *whoosh*.

Tonya had no time to wonder at this miracle because a giant head and hands emerged from the crack in the earth, followed by shoulders, and a massive back.

"What the hell is that?"

Tonya turned at the sound of Drake's voice. She could see him looking out the window of a mausoleum with the girls crowding in behind him. Tonya strode over to join them.

From inside the mausoleum, Tonya could examine the Entity from behind. It was composed of dirty bones and flesh, entangled with roots from the gravedigger fungus. Its shoulders were broad, its arms, massive, each ending in a giant hand with too many fingers.

It stepped out of the hole, rising to fifteen feet, more than tall enough to see down into the mausoleum where they were hiding. It turned as if it sensed her presence and shot Tonya a grin that made its hundreds of teeth look baby-sized. The effect was comical until she realized they were human teeth. Waldock had raised a colossus made of rotting bodies, intelligent fungus, and dirt.

Her friends peeped out the mausoleum door, unaware they had been spotted.

"Run!" said Tonya, but Drake picked up a shovel and ran out to meet the creature. He started hacking at the giant's shins, dislodging clods of dirt. The giant stood arms akimbo, grinning at Drake as each clod of earth he chipped off, immediately flew back into place.

Blowing Tonya a kiss, and obscenely waggling his tongue made of many tongues, the giant picked Drake up with both hands, shook him until he let go the shovel, then dropped him to the dust. He lifted a reeking foot to crush him.

"Wait!" Tonya cried.

The giant turned to face Tonya. Priya, who had been edging around him, ran up the giant's leg from behind, launching her shovel at his butt. She dug a foothold to clamber higher, then started taking mighty shovel swings at his back.

The colossus turned to see who was attacking him but Priya clung on, swinging around with him.

Drake dashed free as the giant turned on Priya, picking her off his back and throwing her against a tree.

Priya landed with a crunch that made Tonya shudder.

Well, aren't you going to attack too? The voice was in Tonya's head.

"Why? You'd probably make me kill myself with an axe."

"Good idea." The colossus left Priya and Drake and advanced on Tonya who tried to reach out to it with her mind as she had reached underground to the roots, but she was completely exhausted, barely able to move her own body. She closed her eyes and reached out, seeking green life energy with her mind. The giant was almost on top of the mausoleum when her mind connected with the Entity. The reverse polarity knocked her back like a lightning strike

Its energy was negative. It felt dead, cold, a black hole that sucked the warmth and light out of her. She sank toward unconsciousness on the cold, stone floor.

With all her strength she whispered, "Get me out of here."

"What's wrong?" Priya's voice from outside echoed, like it was underwater.

"There's something else in here, something worse than that creature. Help me out?"

Priya grabbed Tonya by the shoulders and hauled her out of the mausoleum. Tonya stumbled, unable to see anything but the gaping black pit in her mind's eye, sucking her down like quicksand.

Priya slowed. "Shouldn't we stand and fight?"

Outside again, Tonya's vision cleared. "You can't kill something that's already dead."

"Oh yeah?" Drake and Lynette came beside her, wielding shovels. "Haven't you seen a zombie movie?"

With a yell, Drake ran forward, attacking the creature's gut with his shovel. Priya pitched rocks at its head.

Lynette looked at Tonya, sitting on the ground. "Aren't you going to do something?"

Tonya tried to stand but her head was woozy. "I wish I could. You?"

Lynette took a shovel in hand. "I'll stay here and guard you."

Over her shoulder, Tonya saw the colossus stamp his feet, shaking the ground and sending Priya and Drake stumbling. He lifted a foot over Priya. At the last moment, before he could crush her, Priya put her shovel up.

The creature split its own foot open on the shovel. Roaring, it stood on the other foot, scowling a Priya. Next, it bent over to tear a tombstone from the ground and fling it at her.

Priya dodged and ran.

Drake circled back to the mausoleum. "We can't outrun it and we can't kill it with our shovels."

Lynette backed deeper into the building.

Priya was running but she wasn't fast enough. The creature grabbed her shirttail, laughing as she struggled to get away.

Tonya's anger flamed. She ran out and pitched a rock at the Entity.

It didn't even notice, so intent was it on toying with Priya. Was there no way to save her friend?

She hung her head, which was when she spotted the sewer grate. At the low point of the cemetery, in the middle of the road, lay the entrance to the storm drains. If they could get inside, the colossus would be too large to follow.

"Drake, Lynette," she whispered, "give me a hand." She picked up another rock, pretending she wanted to throw it at the creature. She edged up until she was standing behind the sewer grate and pointed to it with her foot.

"C'mon Priya! We've almost got you." Tonya's rock missed the Entity, but Drake pegged the creature in the eye, startling it long enough for Priya to wriggle free.

As Priya ran toward them, Tonya, Drake, and Lynette heaved up on the sewer lid. The rusted metal disk didn't budge.

"Is it screwed down?" asked Tonya.

"Give it a twist," said Drake. "It's probably rusted shut."

They jiggled it, rocked it, then finally turned it. With a screech, it lifted off, sending them stumbling back. It clattered to the ground.

"Ladies first." Lynette raced down the hole, and slid the lid closed behind her.

"Hey!" Tonya tried to lift it, but it was too heavy.

Priya was almost on top of them now, with the Entity right behind. Together, Tonya and Drake pried at the lid. It started to lift until Lynette grabbed on from underneath and hung off it by her hands.

The Entity got down on its knees. Was It getting tired, or could he see they were trapped and wanted to draw out the moment like a cat playing with a mouse?

"What's wrong with you, Lynette?" Priya strained to lift the cover.

"Don't be scared," said Drake. "You have to let go. There should be a ladder for you to stand on."

"Sorry. Not sorry!" Lynette started to giggle.

"Please!" Priya tugged at the lid. "Let go so we can get in the drain, otherwise that thing will get us."

That's the idea. Lynette's voice reverberated in Tonya's head.

Not Lynette too! Was there any mind the Entity couldn't infiltrate? When Tonya couldn't protect her own roommate, how did Aunt Helen expect her to save the town?

Instinctively, she looked up into the trees to regain her calm. Their great size and cheerful foliage usually made her problems feel smaller, but the nearby trees were burned, including the majestic oak overhanging the road.

What a way to go. The last sight she would ever see would be those heavy branches, dying and sure to come down in the next storm.

The Entity reached to snatch Priya which gave Tonya an idea. Just as she had killed a branch to demonstrate magic, she drew what life remained out of the oak branch overhanging the Entity's head. Tonya grabbed Drake and pushed him a bit closer.

"Hey! What are you doing?"

The Entity pinned Priya down with one multi-handed hand then reached forward to grab Drake.

Bingo!

In a burst, Tonya drew the dregs of life from the crook of the tree, sending the enormous branch crashing onto the creature's head. The creature collapsed and didn't get up. Drake ran over to lift its hand off Priya who stumbled free. "Is it dead?"

"I'll make sure." Drake took a shovel and brought it down on the fallen giant's neck, over and over, sundering the bones holding it together.

When the Entity's head rolled down the road, Tonya lay on the grass and closed her eyes. Draining life energy from the branch had exhausted her.

"What about Lynette?" asked Priya.

Tonya opened her eyes. "Don't go after her."

"But . . ."

"Waldock controls her mind. If you see her again, be careful."

"We can't just abandon her." Drake eyed the sewer cover.

"Until we stop Waldock, we can't restore Lynette's mind." Or mine, thought Tonya. "Let's find the car."

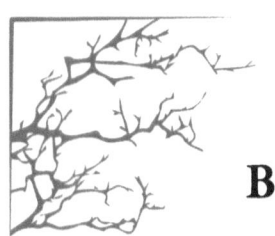

BEST FRENEMIES

Relieved the Entity was dead, Priya drove away from the cemetery and headed north until she saw a fire truck parked across the road ahead.

"What now?" Tonya asked, from the passenger seat.

"Hold on guys." Priya screeched the tires in a fast U-turn and set off in the opposite direction, but soon spied a second roadblock. To their left, the cemetery fire had left the area littered with charred stumps, fallen trees, and ash. To the right, corn fields and pastureland beckoned to the west. Priya wanted to reach the southbound highway west of town, the fastest route to Toronto from Loon Lake.

The little road west Priya found only took them a few miles until it too ended in a roadblock. There was literally nowhere else to go but back to the shop outside the cemetery, or east to the quarantined campus.

Priya turned south into a farmer's gravel laneway.

"What are you doing?" asked Drake.

"Trust me."

The laneway ran out, but instead of stopping, she took a bumpy overland route east that would pass below campus.

"This thing's pretty good off-roading." Drake was in the backseat.

"Yeah, it loves the bang, bang, thump on its undercarriage." Priya caressed the dashboard. "Sorry Baby."

"The important thing is, we're still alive," said Tonya.

"Where did that thing come from? Why did it want to kill people?" Priya kept her eyes on the field, alert to any hazard. It wouldn't take much to stop her little car.

"It's because of my aunt, and we're not out of danger yet."

"Can't anyone help us?" asked Drake. "What about your aunt's friends?"

Suddenly, Tonya grabbed the steering wheel and aimed them at an old stone fence.

"What are you doing?" Priya gripped the wheel in her left hand and tried to shove Tonya away with her right.

Tonya grabbed the wheel with both hands. Priya resisted, jerking the wheel left and right but the fence kept growing larger in the windshield. Priya braked but Tonya stomped on the gas. The tires spun, and the car smelled of burning oil. Priya stood on the brakes and wouldn't budge.

"Let go!" Priya punched Tonya in the head.

Tonya fell back, until she gripped Priya's neck and started choking her.

Priya saw stars. Her hands loosened on the wheel. Before she could pass out, Priya heaved on the parking brake, sending everyone flying against their seat belts.

Drake grabbed Tonya from behind and wrestled her off Priya.

"I'm so sorry!" Tonya sobbed.

"Out of my car! I'm not driving another inch until she's outta here."

"It wasn't me. I wasn't in control." Tonya's face was red.

"You tried to kill us."

"Let me hold her in the back seat."

"No."

"Could I ride in the trunk?" Tonya beseeched with clasped hands. "If Waldock's men find me, they'll kill me."

"Why? You seem to be working for them."

"Please."

Priya scowled. "Lock her in the trunk, but if she tries anything . . ."

She waited while Drake helped Tonya into the trunk. "Make sure it's locked," she called out the window. When he was finished, Drake came to sit in the passenger seat.

"I'm going to keep trying till we find open road. If I have to explore every side street and cut across every farmer's field, I'm getting us out of this place."

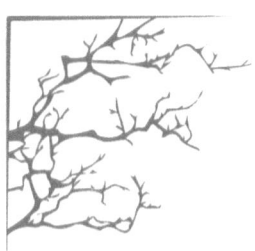

TRUNK

Inside the trunk, Tonya's head hit the roof every time they hit a bump. That pain was nothing compared to the emotional bruising. Who could she trust after her own brain betrayed her? Waldock had weaponized her against her friends. He'd done it by invading her mind.

Could she force herself into his consciousness along the same pathway? She remembered the sensations just before Waldock seized control of her body. There had been a tingling, and then a rush of his power flowing into her, first a trickle and then a torrent, obliterating her ability to resist. Reaching out with her mind, she tried to force her will back along the same energy path.

Nothing. She sensed no trace of the route he used to get into her head. This energy transfer stuff was too new to her.

Aunt Helen had never taught her how to use her powers and now she expected her to fight Waldock? And how was it Waldock had prevented his Entity from burning underground, even after Tonya soaked the earth in gasoline?

Protective wards were her aunt's specialty. Could she be conspiring with Waldock? Maybe she had lied about needing help to fix her tire. Wasn't a tire made of rubber, a natural substance that she could heal? Did Aunt Helen separate Tonya from her friends and delay their reunion so the Entity could rise unopposed? She could have lied about the cancer too. It seemed very convenient that her aunt reappeared just long enough to tell her to fight Waldock, alone.

Yet Helen had killed Len. Either she was on Tonya's side or there were more than two sides.

Her phone buzzed with a text from Aunt Helen. She braced herself to read it in the rattling trunk.

Aunt Helen had spotted the pearls-and-heels doctor from the farm working on her hospital floor. Despite being hit with a two-by-four, the lady didn't have a scratch on her. Not only that, the growth in Aunt Helen's stomach was expanding daily. What the hell, Tonya wondered, was really growing in there?

Aunt Helen's message instructed Tonya to collect a hand from the fridge in her apartment and bring it to Toronto. Tonya banged on the trunk, but the car kept moving. She texted Drake.

Tonya: *My aunt made an unusual request. Let me back into the car and I'll show you.*

Drake: *Nice try [Priya made me write that]*

Tonya: *I don't blame you if you don't believe me. Call my aunt yourself at this number . . .*

Eventually, the car slowed, and Tonya felt the gravel crackle under the tires as they pulled onto the shoulder.

The trunk opened, but she was so stiff and bruised, Drake had to help her out.

She stood behind the car and Drake stared at her. Under normal circumstances she would have welcomed the attention, but he didn't smile.

"It's safe to come out," he called to Priya.

"Let me put her on speaker phone." Tonya punched in Aunt Helen's number as Priya joined them.

"Hello?" her aunt wheezed.

"Priya and Drake will to come to Toronto, but we can't bring the hand."

"You must."

"Why?"

"Without it, I can't stop Waldock." Aunt Helen coughed weakly.

"I left it in my dorm, but there's a police cordon around campus. It's under quarantine."

"You have to get it."

"Think of something else."

"Bring it, or Waldock wins."

"Why didn't you say something before?"

Priya nodded and crossed her arms.

"Is that how you talk to a dying woman?"

"Campus is too close to the cemetery. If I go near it, Waldock will get in my head again."

Priya took the phone. "She says he made her grab the wheel and try to drive us into a wall."

"She has more power than she realizes."

Tonya took back the phone. "I didn't even know I was doing it. One minute I blacked out, the next I had my foot on the accelerator. Drake had to pull me off Priya before I strangled her."

"To overcome a mind like yours takes a lot of power. Jack won't be able to control you and a crowd of people, especially if you can lure him out of Loon Lake. Your friends can help."

"All these years you never trained me in magic, never warned me about the dangers. Why?"

"Your mother would have got a restraining order."

"When I worked in your shop, you could have at least taught me some self-defense. Now you're too sick to fight and I don't know what to do."

"This was never supposed to happen. I took care of Jack," said Aunt Helen.

"Is that why he's picking on me and my friends?"

"It's a long story."

Drake stepped close to the phone. "Tell us everything, or Tonya goes nowhere."

There was a long pause. Helen's voice went softer. "Jack and I . . . used to be close. He promised never to touch my family, but I was a fool to trust him. When I was in high school he seemed so daring, channeling life energy through me at first, and then we experimented in the cemetery."

"Death energy?" Tonya raised an eyebrow.

"I didn't know what we were doing. When my hair turned white it scared me and I quit, but not before I learned what he was. Any piece of Jack's original body will remain linked to him. I buried him, but I kept his hand just in case. Promise you'll bring it."

"We'll try." She disconnected and turned to her friends. "You can't go with me. It's too dangerous."

Drake put a hand on her shoulder and moved in close. "You heard your aunt, you need me."

"And you need my car," said Priya.

"Waldock could make me attack you again."

"Maybe," said Drake, "but I'm not letting you out of my sight."

"Me neither." Priya crossed her arms.

Tonya threw her arms wide. "I could kiss you both!"

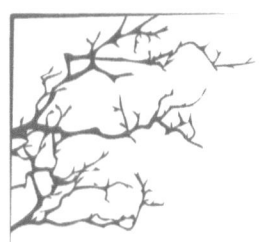

BAR FRIDGE

They drove onto campus. The police were gone, and students were sparse. Perhaps they had run out of food and shambled to the grocery store. Perhaps they were quarantined at the health center. Perhaps the risen Entity no longer needed them.

Priya parked in a tow-away zone right in front of Mackenzie College. "Let's be quick."

As they waited for the elevator, the routine action gave Tonya a sense of normalcy, as if when they got to her floor, the common room would be full of students.

Instead, the corridor was empty except for Roberto, waiting outside her door. "Thank God you're here. Everybody's gone, and I can't find Lynette."

"Neither can we." Drake looked away

"Help me look?"

"We have to go to Toronto," said Tonya.

"I'm coming with you." He followed them into the room.

"There's no space in the car," said Priya.

"Be careful if you find Lynette," said Drake. "She's acting strange."

"She'll be fine." Roberto's mouth was impassive, but his eyes darted around the room, scanning shelves and corners.

His odd response made Tonya wary. She took off her bandanna and grabbed the jar from the bar fridge. As she took it out, she wrapped it in cloth and held it to her chest.

Roberto dashed to her side, his hand reaching for the jar. "Let me carry that for you."

"Don't bother."

"I insist." Roberto lunged for the jar.

"It's quite alright." She yanked it out of range.

Roberto grabbed for it, trying to wrest it from her hands.

"Here!" Tonya threw it to Drake who caught it and ran out.

"Don't let him get it!" Priya yelled.

They ran out the door after Drake and down the fire exit stairs.

Tonya couldn't believe it. There was a guy with a tow truck preparing to hook up Priya's car. Armageddon had come, but they still worried about illegal parking. The driver turned to face them.

"Hey, that's Zain!" Drake pointed at the driver.

"Give me the hand back before you talk to him."

Drake tossed the jar to Tonya before he followed after Priya.

"Get away from Baby!" Priya shoved Zain who stumbled back.

The three friends dashed into the car and slammed the doors, but Tonya was too slow. Roberto caught her door and pushed himself into the back seat with her.

"Get out!" She kicked him in the chest but instead of falling back, he grabbed her by the ankles and dragged her out of the car. The back of her head connected with cement and she saw stars.

"Give me the hand or I'll kill her!" said Roberto.

"They can't," said Tonya. Roberto had to be under Waldock's control.

Certainly, but you are missing the obvious. Did you really think a man powerful enough to resurrect himself would choose to inhabit a body of dirt and bone? It took a long time to find a body worthy of me, from a suitably magical family.

"Roberto is Waldock!" she shouted. Tonya curled her body around the jar while Roberto/Waldock tried to pry her open like a starfish. Priya and Drake leaped out of the car and tried to haul Roberto off her just as Zain joined the fray. Roberto lifted her over his head like a barbell.

"Stand back. I'll drop her!"

Holding her body rigid, Tonya carefully unscrewed the jar and slipped the wet hand into her jacket pocket. Noiselessly, she resealed it and tied it back into her bandana to obscure its emptiness. She braced herself to hit the ground.

Drake and Priya grabbed her arms and legs and tried to wrestle her away from Roberto but Zain grabbed her around the middle and hauled her away from the others. When Roberto pried her hands open, she shouted: "No!"

Roberto and Zain took the jar and, laughing, jumped into the tow truck and sped away.

Tonya hurried her friends into their car and told Priya to head for Toronto.

"Shouldn't we get the hand back?"

"Let's just go," said Tonya.

Priya shook her head. She drove them on a circuitous route out of town then headed east, circling back down to the highway west. When they had been driving for ten minutes, without a roadblock in sight, Tonya held her jacket open to let Drake peek at the hand.

"Ugh!" Priya wrinkled her nose. "What's that smell?"

"The hand. We have to get it to Aunt Helen before Waldock realizes I still have it."

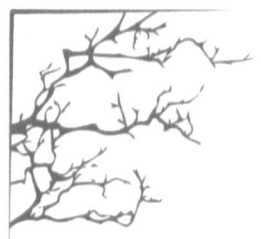

TORONTO

It would take over two hours to drive to Toronto, more in traffic. Tonya kept an eye out for Waldock's police minions while Priya sped as fast as she dared.

Tonya's stomach fluttered. While they wasted time fighting Waldock's giant decoy, their true opponent had taken permanent form.

"Can your aunt stop Waldock without hurting Roberto?" asked Priya.

"Oh my god, Lynette!" said Tonya. "She'll be devastated when she finds out Roberto isn't Roberto."

"We might not get a chance to tell her," said Drake. "We shouldn't have left her behind."

"What choice did we have?" asked Priya.

It occurred to Tonya that if Waldock controlled Lynette's mind, she and Roberto could live happily ever after, hunting down innocent people like Tonya and her friends. "I hope she's okay."

The car decelerated to stop-and-go as the two-lane highway backed up with cars.

"This better just be a tractor or something," muttered Priya.

It took five minutes of crawl before Tonya could see the cause of the slowdown. Police had parked a pair of vehicles across the road and were forcing cars to U-turn.

"Hold on people, I'm going around!"

"How?" asked Drake.

Tonya felt the roar as Priya hit the gas. With a sudden swerve, they crossed the oncoming lane and turned onto the gravel on the far side of the road. Tonya clenched her teeth.

Through the rear window, Tonya watched two officers rush into their car to give chase. Priya drove back onto the road and gunned it.

"Where'd you learn to drive?" said Drake.

"From a cousin who loves NASCAR racing. Never underestimate the power of big family."

Tonya saw police lights flashing in the back window. "They're gaining on us."

"Don't stress." Priya handled the wheel like a stock car racer, all concentration and grace. Seated beside her, Drake chattered about the "cool" ways they were going to rain down fire on Waldock, like the final battle in *King Kong*. It seemed both he and Priya trusted her again.

She shared a smile with Drake and the butterflies in Tonya's stomach gave way to a strange elation. She had her friends back and with Priya driving, she felt like they could outrun anybody.

To lose their pursuers, Priya executed a series of quick turns in a complex of big box stores, industrial units, and farmers' co-ops, then pulled in behind a parked tractor trailer to wait.

"Score!" cheered Drake as they watched the cops drive past, sirens blaring.

"Finally, we're free of them. Where to?"

"Let's head northwest for a bit before we head south again," said Tonya. "They won't expect it."

On open roads, Priya's heavy pedal foot helped eat up the miles but an hour and a half later, traffic bunched up as she approached the city. Drake offered to navigate using his phone's GPS but all routes into Toronto were congested.

"Uh, guys. I got a text from my aunt. They're prepping her for surgery."

"Tell her to wait." Priya goosed the accelerator.

Tonya texted back: *Don't sign the waiver.*

Aunt Helen: *Sorry love, no choice.*

"Once she's anaesthetized, she can't help us fight. She can't even tell us what we need the hand for."

Priya pulled out and passed a row of cars caught behind a dawdling van but even the fast lane was slow.

"Can't it wait?" Drake's voice was soft.

"The oncologist says it would be fatal."

"We're almost there. Maybe we'll be in time to speak to her." Priya exited the highway onto a westbound artery.

Tonya was relieved to reach the city. Priya seemed to know her way around. She pulled up in front of the hospital amidst an explosion of car horns.

"You two get out and go ahead. I'll park and meet you in the room."

TAR AND BUBBLES

Slipping past the nursing station, Tonya and Drake went to Aunt Helen's room. A woman in a white lab coat brushed by Tonya on her way out the door.

"Sorry," said Tonya, although the woman had pushed *her* out of the way. The lady didn't stop either, averting her face as she rushed off. Something about her angora sweater felt familiar . . . The farm house doctor with the pearls!

"Stop!" Tonya was about to run after her when her aunt's feeble voice came from the room. "Let her go."

Tonya entered a semi-private room with a high ceiling. There was a curtain pulled around the far bed, partially blocking the window. Her aunt lay in the bed closest to the door. Drawn back in a messy ponytail, her hair was greasy and pale, to match the skin stretched over her cheekbones.

"Promise you'll stay with me, until I wake up again."

"Of course." Tonya swallowed hard.

Firm and round, her aunt's stomach stood like a camel hump on her thin body,

"We're not going anywhere." Drake shot her aunt a shy smile.

"Is campus still overrun with students gorging themselves?"

"Worse," said Drake. "Waldock has taken over Roberto's body."

"Can we save him?" Tonya asked. "And what about my roommate Lynette?"

"Tonya found her," said Drake.

"Under the Ash Tree. We couldn't wake her until I channeled some life energy into her."

"Did you now?" Her aunt rose an eyebrow. "Show me the hand?"

Tonya opened her coat to reveal it. "What will you do?"

"I have one chance to end this before my surgery." She reached for Tonya who approached her bedside, expecting a hug.

"Give it to me."

Tonya felt a burden lift as she passed it over. She had been trying to save the whole town with only Mundanes to help her. Aunt Helen knew Waldock, and she had a lifetime of experience with magic. She would take care of it now and Tonya, who hated fighting and who found magic exhausting, could leave everything to her aunt.

Holding it to her chest, Aunt Helen began to chant Jack Waldock's name.

Priya arrived and Tonya waved her in. She and Drake stared slack-jawed at the emaciated woman in the bed, clutching the hand and mumbling to it. *Was she summoning Waldock?*

Aunt Helen answered her thought. "I'm drawing him back into his own body."

The gray outline of a man flickered in and out of existence on top of the covers. It looked like a hologram of Waldock, as he must have been just before he died—middle-aged but muscular, with a self-satisfied smile.

And then she felt It start to materialize; the Entity in her head; the being who had blinded her and controlled her and poisoned her mind with visions of death.

"Stop! You can't bring him back."

"I am back."

Tonya recognized Roberto's voice. She turned her head to see Roberto/Waldock blocking the doorway, shoulder to shoulder with the pearl-wearing Doctor.

Aunt Helen gasped. "Jack!"

Tonya could feel her aunt's energy spiking into the hand, the phantom Jack flickering a bit more into existence each time the energy peaked. If she kept going, would they end up fighting against two Waldocks?

One that we can kill, her aunt replied in Tonya's head.

Roberto/ Waldock strode into the room and tried to snatch the hand from her but Aunt Helen rolled away from him and slipped it under the covers.

"It's mine." Waldock shook his head. "Poor Helen, I thought you'd turned your back on necromancy."

"You'd be surprised what a desperate woman will do."

"My associate tells me you're about to have surgery." He clasped his hands and bowed his head in mock concern.

"You implanted this cancer seed." Aunt Helen tried to sit up.

"It was merely insurance. *You* made me use it."

"Oh Jack. Since we were kids, every nasty thing you ever did was always somebody else's fault."

"You aren't blameless." He put an arm around the Pearl Doctor's waist. "You tried to kill this lovely lady."

"My friend was already dead before you raised her. She deserved to rest in peace."

"She hurt me." The Pearl Doctor pouted at Waldock and hung off his arm.

Waldock kissed the top of her head. "Never again, I promise."

"What about Roberto?" Drake pointed at Waldock. "You killed him and took his body."

"Don't worry," Waldock touched the side of his head. "Your friend is still in here, along with all the others absorbed into the Entity."

"Let them free!" Tonya cried.

"I need their knowledge. When your aunt put me in the ground, she stole years of my life that can never be regained. It's not my fault I require many lesser minds to return me to the cutting edge, where I belong."

"And when you're done using them, will you toss them away? I presume you've fed their bodies to that Entity of yours." Aunt Helen sighed, her voice fading to a whisper. "All those innocent lives, just to reanimate one devil."

"But what a handsome devil." Roberto/ Waldock flexed his muscles.

Tonya had heard enough. She picked up a chair and smashed it over Waldock's head, but it bounced off a protection ward.

"Careful. Don't hurt yourself." Roberto/Waldock and the Doctor beamed at each other. "Besides, you can't kill me. I own you." He edged toward her.

Tonya stood her ground, fists clenched. Drake and Priya stepped up to join her on either side. "Release Roberto or we will kill you."

"Really, is that wise? Did Helen mention I can cure her cancer? Jack giveth and Jack taketh away." He laughed. "Hurt me, and you lose the only chance to save your auntie."

"Don't listen," said Aunt Helen. "Kill him."

"Your noble sacrifice is misplaced." Waldock sneered down at Aunt Helen. "It isn't just Helen who will die if I am murdered," said Waldock. "Do you think the Old Families will choose to age and wither when I can heal them?"

"My miracle worker." The Pearl Doctor gave Waldock a squeeze.

"You raised a monster of dirt and bone," said Tonya, "not a miracle."

"That was when I was still trapped underground. Now that I'm back I can restore bodies. You've met Donna. As a youth, she had such bad arthritis she could barely walk. I made her whole again."

Tonya objected, "To make her a slave who does what you say!"

"She *chooses* to support me because I'm right. Her mother died of Alzheimer's, but I can promise she never will.

Waldock closed his eyes and Tonya felt his voice in her head, ordering her to punch Aunt Helen. Fighting the urge to obey, she walked toward the bed.

Waldock laughed. "Your mother would cheer if you hit her. Helen made her sell her house and leave town."

"In jail, I spent a few hours with some of the people you've helped," said Drake. "They were animals."

Tonya was released from compulsion when Waldock responded. "Criminals are violent. You can't hold me responsible for how they deal with frustration."

"Like rabid animals!" said Drake.

"But better now. Now that I am embodied, I no longer need people's energy. My gravedigger fungus will settle back into its natural state.

Drake looked puzzled. "What about its victims?"

"Lynette's mind is gone," said Tonya.

"Unless I absorbed her into here," he tapped his temple, "she's free to go. I'm not the villain your aunt says I am. She's just old and bitter, a woman scorned. "He stepped around the bed to the wall side and caressed Aunt Helen's head. "Isn't that right, my Love?"

Helen flinched but when Tonya moved to intervene, she raised a trembling hand to stay her.

"You once had hair like a raven's wing." Waldock gently propped her head on a pillow.

"Is that why you've cursed me?"

"Oh Darling, it feels like you buried me only yesterday."

"How nostalgic," her aunt scoffed.

"I'm more interested in the future. Roberto's *madre* and *padre* will be so proud!"

"Jack is legendary." The Pearl Doctor nodded.

"What about the firefighters?" said Priya. "When they come to, they'll be so ashamed of what they did to us."

"They'll have a memory blackout, that's all. You burned down the cemetery, not me."

"You were making people eat themselves to death," said Tonya.

Waldock dismissed her with a flick of the wrist. "You destroyed the Three-Century Ash. Both sides will oppose you when my acolytes take charge."

"The only sides are good and evil, and you are evil." Tonya raised a finger.

"Wrong." He turned his attention to Aunt Helen. "I offer power and knowledge and adventure, good things," he crooned to Aunt Helen. "Why else would you have come so willingly?"

Helen looked to Tonya. "It was a mistake."

"You enjoyed every minute until you betrayed me."

Aunt Helen turned away.

A wave of melancholy washed through Tonya, except it wasn't Waldock's manipulations or visions of Pompeii. He was right. Aunt Helen had betrayed her family, but she didn't deserve to die. "Cure her cancer and I'll help you."

"No!" said Priya.

Drake caught her eye. "Are you sure?"

"You won't regret this." Waldock leaned on the bed. "I can perform miracles. The Trads want us to stand idle, waiting for death." He reached for the hand unerringly, as if he could sense it beneath the bedsheets.

"Don't do this." Aunt Helen gave Tonya the hand. "Keep it for me. Now go!"

"With the hand, he can come back in his own body. Isn't that what you wanted?"

Her aunt didn't deny it.

"If he's in his body, it will free Roberto."

"Yes, give me the hand. We want the same thing." Waldock edged toward her.

Her friends tried to hold her back, but Tonya closed the gap, holding the hand out to him. Waldock clamped a Roberto-sized hand around hers, so she couldn't let go of the slimy member, at the same time pulling her to him and wrapping his free arm around her. She was trapped, looking up at Roberto's square chin as the stench of chemicals gave way to rancid meat burning as he drained her power through the dead limb into himself. Tonya struggled to get away, but Roberto's athletic arms wouldn't budge.

"You have even more ability than your aunt." Waldock crushed her to him with one arm and used the other hand to fling the necklace out of her pocket. "Time to let loose."

Power rushed through her. Tonya wanted to resist, wanted to stop him from draining her but didn't know how.

"Feel that!" He laughed.

"Let go!" Aunt Helen reached for Tonya. "He isn't trying to save me. He wants revenge and he'll kill you just to hurt me."

"How can you say that?" Waldock's jaw dropped in mock dismay. Tonya felt him extract a big rush of energy. He started to giggle. Tonya remembered the same pleasure reaction as life force rushed into her under the Ash Tree.

Something expanded between them, pushing her back. His body was re-growing from wrist to arm, to shoulder and beyond until Waldock was complete, a blonde, smooth-faced version of the Waldock her aunt had tried to conjure. This young Waldock grabbed hold of her and Tonya saw stars as the energy drain increased two-fold. She felt herself blacking out. Roberto's body fell to the floor. She was helpless to resist or even slow him down. If she didn't break the connection soon, it would kill her.

Or she could replenish her energy. Closing her eyes, she sought out plant sources of life energy, but she was in a cement tower, stories above a concrete city. In her craving, the visible world disappeared, and Tonya saw only dark space around her, populated by points of light pulsing with energy. People, each a glowing point in her mind's eye.

The hospital around her transformed into a three-dimensional map in her head, a space composed of energy, and darkness. She reached out to these light points, drawing power from glowing sources in every room on every floor of the hospital. *Go gentle*, she told herself; these weren't trees.

She forced herself to sense the busy rush of doctors and nurses in the halls, the straining of orderlies lifting patients, the impatience of coffee drinkers lined up in the basement cafeteria. All that pulsing energy belonged to human beings. Take too much, and she would kill them.

As their power rushed through her into Waldock, his voice grew deeper and stronger. "You have the gift. No going back now. Take what you need."

Through gritted teeth, unable to hold back the energy he drew through her, Tonya said, "You're back in your body. Let me go."

"Sure kid, in a little while."

Tonya knew he didn't need to keep draining her. He shone brightest among all the points in her mental array. Some of the people were starting to fade. They would blink out soon but the harder he drained her, the more she was forced to drain them.

"Stop!"

"Whatever you say." He started draining her twice as fast.

Tonya saw fireworks. Unless she replaced the energy he was taking, she would die in seconds. Could she reach out even farther, to people in the streets, to trees planted in the nearby park? How far could she extend her reach and just how far would he force her to go?

She opened her eyes and caught Waldock smiling. He didn't care how far she could reach. He would keep draining until it killed her, or she killed every person in this hospital to stay alive. She had to end it, but how? He'd brought himself back from the dead. Even if she had a gun and she shot him, it wouldn't stop him. She had to use magic.

Waldock's example had taught Tonya to draw life force from people. She decided to let go the fading sparks of life around her and concentrate on the biggest source.

At first, Waldock was so ebullient he didn't notice Tonya drawing energy back out of him. Once he did, he tried to let go but she held him in a supernatural bond physical struggles couldn't break.

Now that she focused on a single source, the energy passed into her faster than before. She could sense she had enough to survive now, more than enough, more than she'd ever felt. She became lightheaded and giggly, and powerful and fierce. She really should stop!

She let the excess float her and Waldock off the ground until their heads grazed the ceiling like balloons. She made them turn a somersault in the air, laughing at Waldock's threats and curses. The universe was buoyant, ebullient—ecstatic. Her chest expanded until it felt about to burst.

Waldock felt heavy again, dragging her down until they settled to the floor. The chill of hospital tiles under her feet shocked her back to reality. Waldock had passed out.

"Is he dead?" her aunt asked.

"Not quite," said Tonya.

"Bring him here."

"No." Her newly awakened senses told her she would soon reach the dregs of Jack Waldock's life force, and a greedy new part of her wanted it all.

Drake and Priya carried Waldock's limp body and she came with them. Automatically she started drawing energy from Drake too. He jumped back as if stung.

"You must let go now," said Aunt Helen. "Leave Waldock to me."

Tonya tried—she really tried—but it wasn't just the pleasure of energy rushing in that made it impossible to stop. She had turned into a collapsing star and all life force sought her center of gravity. She wasn't Tonya anymore, she was a creature of energy.

"Stop now!" her aunt ordered.

It was dreamy, swimming in this excited sea, roiling with power. It bubbled in her brain and made her toes tingle. She floated up and turned a cartwheel in the air as little lightning bolts escaped her fingers and toes, lighting the room in pinks and blues.

The lights went out. Tonya dropped as something about Waldock's energy changed. It started to hurt going in, as if she were drawing tar into her veins and sand into her lungs. As she reached the bottom of Waldock's reserves, her head exploded with pain. This tarry force was not from life. Quite the opposite. This must be what Waldock gleaned from the dead.

Tonya reeled back, throwing her hands out as she fell, blind. She didn't want his wretched power anymore, but she couldn't break the connection. From across the room death force rushed from Waldock's body into hers until she was brimming with it.

"Bring her to me!" Aunt Helen's voice was strong again.

Drake picked her up and set her onto her aunt's bed. She opened her eyes and found herself eyeball-to-eyeball with Jack Waldock's desiccated face. Ugh!

Her energy draining had mummified him. Yet she still couldn't stop. She was Hunger, existing only to fill a never-ending void.

Aunt Helen took a deep breath and gathered Tonya's and the corpse's hands together. Tonya struggled to break free, but her aunt held firm and started to chant. As Tonya felt the black tar energy start to flow out of her, Aunt Helen began screaming, so loud and so long that screaming was the last thing Tonya remembered.

A NEW KIND OF MAGIC

Tonya awoke in a strange room. Through faded curtains, early morning light revealed a cheap white dresser. She was lying in an iron bed, layered with chipped paint. She slipped her legs over the side of the bed and sat up. On the floor sat a backpack, overflowing with her clothes. Where was she?

Tonya went to the tiny window and slid it open. Cool, pine-scented air filled her lungs and chickadees trilled in the trees. Could she be living in a forest?

"Give me a few more days!" An angry voice penetrated the flimsy wall.

Tonya opened her door and peeked out. The modest bedroom opened into a narrow kitchen-living room where Aunt Helen was arguing into the phone.

"I couldn't do it without her." Her aunt sighed. "Let me worry about blame."

"Hello?" Tonya's voice came out soft and phlegmy.

"I'll call you back." Helen hung up. "You're awake!" Helen came and embraced her. "Are you hungry?"

"Not really."

Her Aunt beamed. "I knew you'd pull through. You're a powerful young woman." She cupped Tonya's face in her hands. "There's color in your cheeks again."

"Your face is smooth again and your hair . . ." Platinum white, her aunt's hair looked thick and shiny, tied up in its usual ponytail. "Did you have the operation?"

"No need. When we overcame Waldock, I sent all his poison back into him."

"Where are Priya and Drake? Where are my parents?"

"Everybody's fine but we have something to discuss."

"Where are we?"

"Eat something first. You've been lying in bed for three weeks. All you've had is soup."

"Why?"

"Channeling energy is hard on you. Don't worry, recovery time gets shorter with training."

"Why aren't my parents taking care of me?"

"Your parents are fine. I can break the enchantment and bring them back any time, but first I wanted to talk to you."

"How can you use magic against your own sister, to suit your schedule? You're a . . ." Tonya felt her face flush. Her heart pounded. "You're a psychopath!"

"No, I feel plenty of guilt. Let me come clean?"

"What else have you done?"

"We're both guilty of using death magic."

"So, keep it a secret. We had no choice."

It leaves an indelible trace." She held out her white ponytail to illustrate the point. "Have you seen yourself in a mirror?"

Tonya let her hair fall forward over her face. It was silver blonde.

"What did you do to my hair!" She leapt to her feet.

"I tried to spare you. You must know that."

Helen tried to take Tonya's hands.

"Don't touch me!"

"The leaf necklace was supposed to stop you."

"I thought you were helping me!"

"I tried to."

"You should have taught me how to use magic safely, years ago." Tonya felt like slapping her.

"Your parents wouldn't let me. How was I to know I couldn't keep you safe?"

"You used me."

"There's going to be a trial. We should show a united front."

"Don't try to change the subject."

Helen sighed. "I got too sick. It couldn't be helped."

"Really? I get the impression this was a long time coming." Tonya stood, arms akimbo.

"You weren't supposed to drain Waldock so fast.

"Like I had a choice."

"A lot of Mods won't see it that way. A trial will split the town."

"Waldock was controlling people's minds. I think that's pretty clear-cut." Tonya gave her aunt a hard look. "Mind control is evil."

"Mayor Thornton and the Trads have been suppressing magic for so long, the Mods are desperate for anyone, even someone like Waldock, to bring change."

"The Trads will support us."

"After using death magic in a public hospital? Not a chance. The Ashton Clan set us a trap in Toronto. We beat their ally Waldock but now no side will support us. We'll be lucky if they don't wipe our memories and strip our abilities."

"They wouldn't!"

"Or, I can wipe your memory and take the blame for using death magic. You can go back to living a magic-free life. All you have to do is sacrifice your powers."

"Why?"

"To erase the traces of death magic on you, I have to absorb your powers and erase your memories since September."

"They'll see my hair."

"Dye it. You can walk away from this untouched."

"We did the right thing. I'm not ashamed."

"And if they put you in jail?"

"I won't let you face trial alone."

"I knew convincing you would be a problem."

"Your problems are my problems."

"In more ways than you know. Things are going to come out in the trial that I'd rather you heard from me." She covered her mouth and turned away.

"Tell me."

"You've earned the right to know." She unfolded a second chair and placed it at the table. "But first, food." Aunt Helen put on the kettle and started making sandwiches.

As her aunt worked, Tonya stared at the rickety card table. "Why are you living in a trailer?"

Aunt Helen set out sandwiches and mugs of tea. She put a cookie tin at Tonya's elbow and lifted the lid. The heavenly scent of spice cookies made her ravenous. She took a bite of sandwich.

"You must have suspected something," said Aunt Helen as she sat down. "We're so alike, and Barbara married a Mundane so young and so suddenly."

"It was a shotgun wedding, so what? My parents love each other."

"Tonya, listen to me. You . . . you're my natural daughter, and Jack Waldock . . ."

Tonya crossed her arms. "I don't believe you." She got up and started pacing. "Jack Waldock is not my father."

Her ability to channel energy like her aunt, Waldock's telepathic link with her, his delight at her inborn ability. It all made (horrible) sense. Blood rushed to her cheeks, but Tonya kept her voice level and her expression calm. "I can't imagine you falling for him."

"I wasn't even twenty and he was handsome, powerful. I didn't understand the consequences of his magic. When things went bad he shielded himself from blame."

"You're saying he seduced you and set you up?"

"I was foolish but not innocent. City Council banished me to Toronto where they could keep me out of sight but under surveillance. I had no job, no prospects, and no friends. I was at my lowest point when Barbara adopted you and took you back to Loon Lake. It was where you belonged."

"Bring Mom back right now. You owe her an apology for keeping us apart."

"I owe her a million apologies."

"So, make up."

"I'll try," Aunt Helen gave her a little smile, "but it takes two."

All these secrets, plus the upcoming trial—it was a lot to process.

"I'm going for a walk."

Helen didn't try to stop her.

Outside, Tonya realized where she was. Aunt Helen had set up a trailer in the woods behind her fire-damaged shop. She walked around the chain link fence enclosing the building and headed toward campus. As she passed the cemetery, the sight of trees reduced to ashes made the pit of her stomach drop. Maybe she deserved punishment.

A rumbling engine slowed and pulled up behind her. Out the window a female voice called: "Hey Blondie, looking good."

Priya! Tonya got in the car. "How'd you know I'd be here?"

"Your Aunt texted me. How do you feel?"

"Okay." The short walk had made Tonya's legs ache like it had been miles. On the drive to the dorm, Tonya stared out the window. "Where are the road-blocks?"

"Everything's back the way it was."

"As if that could ever happen. I'll be surprised if anybody's left on campus."

"Nobody left, and nobody's talking about what happened."

"How?"

"They all have the same blackout in their memories. It happened while you were recovering."

"But you remember?"

"Thanks to your aunt. She shielded everyone in the hospital room who saw what you did. She says you might need us as witnesses."

"What about the prisoners who attacked Drake at the station? The police must have reported that."

"Nope. The epidemic is forgotten."

"What about the grocery store riots? Somebody must have recorded them on a security camera or a phone."

"Your aunt brought in the Geek Coven. I think that's what she called them. Whatever they did, it made all digital evidence disappear. The locals act like nothing happened and the students don't remember. There's no hint of riots or epidemics in the media or on the internet. You can stop worrying."

"But Drake and his movie, are those pictures gone too?"

"Yup, and it gets worse. Nobody remembers my art installation." Priya sighed. "At least you know how shatteringly brilliant it was."

"Oh Priya, I'm so sorry."

"At least we survived. And as long as I'm living, there's next Halloween." Priya pulled up in front of their residence. "I skipped class to get you, but I have to write a test now. Call me later?"

Tonya went in to wait for the elevator. She caught a whiff of gym bags, men's cologne, and textbooks. She was home. At the sound of her key in the lock, the door flew open. Lynette was dressed for clubbing.

She stared at Tonya. "Your hair!"

"I feel like a new woman." Tonya smiled.

"I love it." Lynette threw her arms around Tonya and gave her a squeeze. "Priya told me you caught some awful virus. I've been worried about you."

"Likewise," said Tonya. "How long have you been up and around?"

"All day." Lynette didn't remember being unconscious at all, and when Tonya mentioned her trip down the storm drain, she looked at her quizzically.

"How's Roberto?"

"I'm trying not to care. He dumped me and went back to Peru but he's fine, I guess. You're the one who's sick. Shouldn't you lie down?"

It took a while for Tonya to convince her roommate she felt fine, but as soon as Lynette went out, she lay down on top of her bed and closed her eyes for a moment . . .

When she woke up again, it was dark outside. Lynette sat on the other bed, thumbing her phone. "Finished napping? I have a surprise for you. Wear something cute."

Tonya looked down at the t-shirt and track pants she'd worn from the trailer. It still surprised her to look in the bathroom mirror and see her platinum blonde hair, but Lynette was right. It suited her. As she brushed it out, Tonya imagined the look on her parents face when they saw her hair and guessed what she'd done. *Don't worry*, she would tell them. *I'm a real witch now but I'll never use death magic again. It's too exhausting!*

Tonya showered and put on her favorite tunic and leggings before she allowed herself to be led to the elevator. Lynette hit the up button. "Let's go see your BFF."

"You're coming with me, to Priya's?"

"She's not so bad, once you get to know her." Lynette led the way.

Priya met them in the corridor, which throbbed with music from inside her room. "You girls look nice." She flung the door wide.

"Surprise!" everybody shouted.

Tonya stepped into an applauding crowd.

"What's this for?" *Had somebody told them what she did?*

"I did." Helen stepped out of the shadows. "I told them some of it, anyway."

"When are you going to stop reading my mind?"

"As soon as I can teach you to think in whispers." Her birth mother laughed.

"About time you started teaching me." Tonya's temper flared, but she took a deep breath. "I don't understand. I thought City Council wiped the Mundanes' memories."

"I shielded Priya and Drake."

"And these others?"

"I cast a charm on the room. Everyone but Drake and Priya will forget you saved this town by morning, but for now you can bask in their admiration. Have fun!"

She winked at Tonya, then went to join a cluster of professors.

Tonya was happy to let her go. Priya's room was crammed with chatting, smiling students. Tonya recognized two cafeteria ladies out of uniform. Marta wasn't there, but Tonya smiled at some divers. There were even police officers and ambulance attendants in civilian dress. Whatever Waldock had done to them, they seemed back to normal.

Shin strode toward Tonya.

Lynette joined them, grinning. "I'm asking for a friend. Are you still with Marta?"

"No."

Priya joined them.

"So, you're with Priya?"

"No," Shin and Priya answered in unison.

Shin sighed in her direction. "She wants me."

Priya laughed. "In your dreams. We're just friends."

"How about a hug for your friend?"

Priya gave him a quick cuddle. When they unclinched, Shin had a big goofy smile. "What did I do to deserve you?"

"You don't—yet." They laughed.

Priya and Shin getting together? Tonya imagined Priya explaining feminist theory to Shin and smiled. They'd either kill each other or get married.

Tonya wanted to tell Drake about it, except, she guessed, he would already know. Had he visited her when she was sick? Of course, he had. Drake had been there when she came into her powers and eliminated Waldock. He knew all her secrets, but would he still like who she'd become? Her mouth felt dry, so she headed for the punch bowl.

Out of nowhere, Professor Rudolph shambled toward her, knees straight and arms outstretched. She backpedaled, trying to find a clear escape route.

Couldn't the others see him? Was he a ghost? She turned to flee but strong arms grabbed her from behind and held her in place.

She broke free and turned to see who it was.

Zain's dark eyes glittered. "Don't go now. We're just getting started." He pushed Tonya into the Professor's open arms. Before she could scream, he crushed her face into his flabby chest, smothering the sound.

He released her with a smile. "Thanks for everything! Your Aunt told me how you fought Waldock and brought us all back,"

"But your walk . . . I thought you were still . . ."

"Still what?"

Zain drew her aside and whispered, "Lying on the cold ground in the cemetery set off his arthritis, so now he moves like this." Arms outstretched, he did a Frankenstein walk. "Grrr! Grrr!"

Tonya grinned but not because of his antics. Beyond Zain, she spied a tall, blue-eyed youth approaching, silent as a ninja.

Drake wasn't the type to make a high school girl's heart flutter. Tonya had never heard him mention football or hockey, or any team sport. He was tall with broad shoulders, but it wasn't his body that attracted Tonya. She loved his artsy friends, his passion for movies, and the quiet way he'd stood by her in a crisis.

"Punch?" Drake offered her a cup.

"To us." They clinked plastic glasses.

"That didn't sound right," he smiled. "Now that you're feeling better, I'd like to take you somewhere with glasses that go ting."

"Are you asking me on a date?"

"Are you saying yes? Because . . ."

Before Drake could finish, she kissed him.

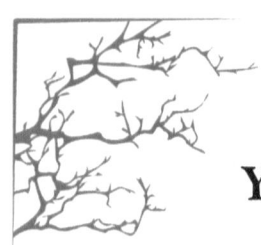

YOU CAN MAKE A DIFFERENCE

Thank you so much for reading *Feeding Frenzy*. This is my first novel and I hope you enjoyed reading it as much as I enjoyed writing it.

Books are ranked popularity which makes it hard for new authors to get noticed. If you enjoyed the story, why not help spread the word? Recommend it to a friend or leave a short review on Amazon or elsewhere. Your help is much appreciated.

Happy reading!

Maaja

LOON LAKE MAGIC SERIES

C OMING SOON...

LOON LAKE MONSTER

You never swim alone...

Stripped of magic and surrounded by friends spelled to forget her, Tonya defies City Council to investigate a rash of missing swimmers. Meanwhile, an occult conspiracy is secretly raising a brood of monstrous reptiles in the sands of Grand Island. When the Digital Ninjas decide to shoot a horror movie in the same location, Tonya must protect her friends from supernatural parasites, and the murderous cabal behind them. Can she save the town and force her enemies to restore her friends' memories?

DRAGON TOWN

Will the hero become the monster?

Feisty university sophomore, Tonya, finds a woman's body on the beach with its stomach ravaged. Missing persons return, impregnated with dragon's eggs. When medicine and magic fail to cure her, to survive Tonya makes a deal with her inner dragon. As the beast helps crush her enemies, can she outwit this new dragon self, or will a good girl start breaking bad?

ACKNOWLEDGEMENTS

This story started as an artistic dare with myself to write a novel in public, posting one chapter a week to Wattpad. This challenge forced me to write a novel I couldn't abandon in a drawer. About time too. My drawer was getting full.

Thanks to Sandra Kasturi for editing the novel, and for her support and encouragement.

I'm grateful to Richard Scrimger for his early manuscript advice.

I'd like to thank my Wattpad readers and followers, without whom I might not have considered publication. Similarly, I would like to thank the anonymous employees at Wattpad HQ who chose to feature the original version of *Feeding Frenzy*, and later voted for it to win a Watty Award.

I'm grateful to Carolyn, Rebecca, and Gunnar who read the entire manuscript and gave insightful feedback. Thanks to my friends from Bloor West Writers in Toronto, and the Anticipation Workshop online. I am grateful for their invaluable advice, encouragement, and critiques. Friends and organizers from Writers' Circle of Durham Region, Can-Con, Ad Astra, SFContario, Sisters in Crime, the Sunburst Award Society, Worldcon, and World Fantasy Convention, gave me chances to read and speak in public, educate myself about writing craft, and develop new relationships. I am also grateful for the 20 Books to 50K group and its positive philosophy.

Some of the production costs of this book were offset by a grant from the Writers' Circle of Durham Region.

Writing this novel would not have been possible without the support of my husband, Gunnar, our son, Thomas, and our extended family. I feel so fortunate to have friends and family who support my mad, artistic schemes. Thank you for all your assistance and encouragement.

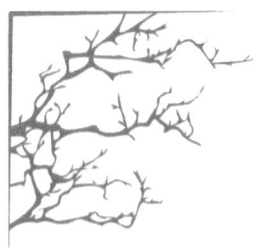

Dedication

For my parents, Ross and Heather.

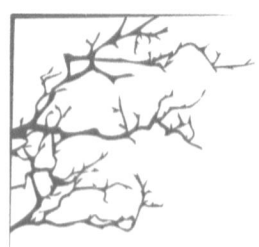

Loon Lake

Editing by: Sandra Kasturi

Cover design: Heather Hamilton-Senter

Feeding Frenzy/ Maaja Wentz, 1st ed.

ISBN 978-0-9940283-2-7 (Paperback)

ISBN 978-0-9940283-1-0 (Electronic book)

About the Author

Maaja Wentz is an award-winning writer of fantasy and mystery/thriller stories. Her latest short story, "Inside of a Dog," is upcoming in *Ellery Queen Mystery Magazine*.

The next two books in the *Loon Lake Magic* series are coming soon. **Join the Loon Lake reading club** to get free stories, exclusive deals, and news of upcoming publications. Don't miss out on special launch prices. Join the club at maajawentz.com.